# The Sky
# After the Rain

Lindsay Bergstrom

*For Keenan*

# 1

"No. Mom. You can't see Wichita."

Ava Schaffer's solid voice spoke in harmony with the moan of the Kansas wind. Her shapely body stood rigid, arms folded across the front of a green military-style canvas jacket she found in a deserted box of her father's western shirts, and bell bottoms, and eight track tapes. The wardrobe flashback and its companions had been banished by her mother to a hidden corner in the basement of the farmhouse before Ava was born. Ava's strong legs pressed against each other, stuffed into worn Levi's broken in with authentic oil paint stains and knee rips and wash fading. Polished black boots covered her feet, a gift from her grandmother the Christmas before the mean old woman with the crumpled face died. They were the only pair of shoes Ava owned. Her mother once voiced criticism about a woman from town who she only ever saw wear the same pair of shoes. She said it was the easiest way to tell the woman was poor.

Two short blocks of red brick street lined with the wooden storefronts of downtown Flynn stretched out below the sharply pointed toes of Ava's boots. The buildings' obnoxious Victorian colors contrasted like a page out of a storybook. Fawn trimmed with cerulean. Eggplant trimmed with coffee. Sage trimmed with salmon. Matching homemade wooden signs hung above doorways and plastic decals with curly fonts decoratively notated windows. *Flynn Post Office 66934. Flynn County Courthouse. Callahan's Auto Body & Repair. Lois's Cut 'n' Color.*

Ava's brown eyes tinged with gold refused to focus on the street. She looked further. Beyond the Main Street businesses concentrated in the center of town. Beyond the simple wood frame houses standing in rows on perfect north-south, east-west streets. Beyond the thick trees lining the river and verdantly dividing manmade structure from nature made emptiness. Beyond the tarnished iron of the elaborately framed, long defunct, Union Pacific Bridge. Beyond fields of overturned land owned by family and friends with new wheat seed incubating under ancient soil. Beyond the point where the yellow dashes down the center of Highway 94 blurred into the gray asphalt of the narrow twisting road and the infinite line of telephone poles alongside it became matchsticks. The distance she could see was miles. Ten. Maybe fifteen. Miles of earth tone landscape and matte blue sky.

Tears brimmed at the corners of her eyes, and Ava told herself they were a result of the cold blowing air, not the thoughts her mind was wrapped around. Thoughts of the land and the town, of her friends and her family and despite constant attempts to never think of the woman again, of her mother. Every thought, no matter where it started, wandered its way back to the tall, domineering woman in the endless pantsuits. Not only the direct ones, the emotionally linked ones, but every single thought. The cheese on the cheeseburger Ava ate for lunch at Martha's was cheddar by request, not the default American Martha threw on everything. Cheddar had been her mother's preference, too. The heather gray t-shirt she wore under her jacket, Ava bought while taking a break from the bright lights and the antiseptic smell of the hospital as her mother slept off the exhaustion created by a round of chemo. The teeth, the crooked incisors in the front, Ava saw in her own reflection every time she smiled into a mirror, were identical to her mother's.

She sealed these thoughts behind other thinking, wiped her tears with the rough sleeve of her adopted jacket, and cleared her throat. Down the wide street full of new trucks and old cars parked at 45-degree angles, the front door of the office of the *Flynn Tribune* opened with a creak and slammed shut with the resonance of shivering panes of lead glass. Corinne Yeards, crimson bob, wide midsection, shielded her eyes against the sun as she looked up three stories to the roof of Kettle's Feed & Seed. Her face squished into a smirk as she strained to see who was standing at the edge of the tallest building in town. Then the odd woman darted back inside the office of the only newspaper still printed in the county.

Ava continued to stare at the horizon, idly curious how long it would take before the whole town knew. Probably not long at all. Corrine fell into hysterics over the wellbeing of stray cats and the potential of slick winter sidewalks. It was her job to make news out of the nothing that occurred in Flynn, Kansas. Population 718. And outside of words on newsprint, rumors traveled though the countryside like dandelion fuzz on a breeze. Everyone talked about each other, because they had nothing else to talk about. Ava didn't care for the first time in her life, though, and she wanted to stay in this place a while longer. The warmth of the sun mixed with the chill of the breeze refreshed the bare skin of her face and hands. An occasional glance at the sizeable distance to the ground below sped up her heartbeats. Sensations that made her feel better than she had for a long, sad time.

Sun glinted off the polished red fenders of the 1961 eighteen-foot International Grain Truck, full to the brim with one of the final loads of corn for the year. Pode Wagner, soft gray eyes squinting into the glare, hand scratching two days' worth of dark whiskers on his face, stared the machine down as if it had done him wrong. He wanted to haul off and kick it, but he was a reasonable man and knew the action would do nothing other than maybe break a couple of his toes. More than kick the machine, he wanted to kick himself for using electrical tape on the cracked radiator hose instead of taking the time to buy a new one and properly replace it. It seemed liked the whole truck was held together with duct tape and bailing wire. One more harvest, his father said each of the past five years, and they could trade it in on a newer model. Newer meaning something maybe only five years older than Pode himself. Driven only three weeks out of the year, it was hard to justify the money spent when plenty of other things were further up the repair list. And there were always the emergencies. A caved-in irrigation well. A combine auger that refused to rotate. A machine shed door damaged in a tornado. So for lack of funding, the grain truck stuck around another season.

Steam rolled out of every crevice around the hood. The engine whirred and screamed as if the truck were in real physical pain. Heat blasting his deeply tanned face beneath the brim of his cap, Pode used the doorframe and the wheel well and the strength in his thick, practically muscular arms to hoist his 200 pounds up. Just before the skin of his fingers touched, he pulled his hand away from the still flesh burningly hot metal. He managed to break down right where the road out of town west was its narrowest and flanked with deep ditches and no shoulders. And he had lied to his father earlier in the afternoon when the man asked his son if he had fixed the truck, the younger Wagner resentful of being check up on.

Pode jumped to the ground, watched as a gold Cadillac crept up behind him at the speed of an elderly snail. Cautiously continuing around the truck in the wrong lane, the car stopped beside Pode, and the automatic window in the passenger side slid down smoothly.

Herman "Spud" Cox, who had been an old man for as long as Pode could remember, leaned over the cherry wood console, "You look like you might could use a ride, Wagner."

Pode bent in half, his left forearm across the edge of the window, and smiled a courteous if crooked smile that revealed only a single dimple on the right side of his face. He met the dark beads of eyes below Spud's thickly wrinkled forehead and tarantula eyebrows, "Thanks, Spud. Appreciate the offer, but I think I'll give Cort a call. Have him bring me a new hose. I don't want to leave it out here in the middle of the road steaming hot and overloaded a hundred bushels. Callahan ought to have something that'll work for it. If he don't, I'm sure NAPA will."

"Alrighty," The man sat up, then remembered something else, "Hey, we're about out of beef in the deep freeze. Y'all doing any steers anytime soon? I'd be interested in a quarter. Maybe a half. If I talk to the kids and they want some."

"Yeah, we probably will. I think Mom and Dad could use some more, too. Haven't taken any over to Clay since last spring. It'll probably be a couple of weeks. Once we're done with the corn."

Spud nodded his head once, firmly, "Sure, let me know."

"Will do. Have a good evening, sir," Pode stood up and waved. The immaculate 15-year-old car, in as comparatively good shape as the man driving it, crawled on down the road. A mile later it turned onto a dirt road off the black top and disappeared over a hill in a cloud of dust. It seemed people either lived forever or not nearly long enough in Flynn. There was no in-between.

The boiling under the hood of the grain truck had subsided. Gurgling and screeching turning into inconsistent popping. Pode searched the cab of the truck and found a couple of ragged red grease rags under the cracked vinyl bench seat. Wrapping one around his hand and folding the other, he used them like an oven mitt to push the hood up.

"Oww . . . ow . . . dammit!" Pode said under his breath as he fished the metal prod for the hood out of its home and quickly aligned it with the hole. Rolling clouds of steam billowed out, and Pode backed away a few feet, shaking the burn out of his fingers as he waited for the condensed heat to dissipate.

Before he saw it materialize over the hill at the edge of town, Pode heard it. The ridiculous performance muffler growling of the brand new Silverado preceded the monstrosity everywhere it went. Rounding the corner, coming right for Pode at a speed well above the limit, it swerved into the wrong lane far too soon and squealed to a stop in line with the nose of the grain truck. Still rocking, the driver's side door of the hopped-up pickup swung open and Doug Baker, always too tall and too skinny, even in his face, stood up over the top of his truck.

"Pode! Fuck! Am I glad I found you!" The intonation in his friend's voice was higher than usual. Panicked. "Ava's gonna fucking jump off the fucking roof of the fucking feed and seed!"

"What?" Pode frowned. The meaning of the words took a few moments to sink in.

"Get in! We gotta fucking get to town!" Baker's head full of longish, dirty blonde hair disappeared as he dove back into his truck. This was some sort of joke, Pode told himself. There was no way Ava, his Ava, was about to throw herself off a roof and splatter on the brick main street of their hometown. The engine of the ebony beast roared with urgency. Pode reached for the shiny aftermarket chrome door handle and hoisted himself up with the equally shiny chrome Nerf bar, wondering why on earth somebody would ruin a perfectly good truck.

At last, she was sleeping. The dose of children's cherry cold medicine was winning. Shannon Troskey sat at the edge of the twin bed and pulled a pink and yellow butterfly patterned quilt up around her daughter. Julia Troskey's little round face glowed vivid pink with fever, but she was in a cold flash, or the fever had broken, because she was no longer covered with drops of sweat. Kissing her forehead gently, careful not to wake her, Shannon stood up and drew the curtains on the single window in the corner of the room, shut off the bedside lamp shaped like a butterfly, and left the door wide open so she could hear if her dark haired beauty stirred.

Exhausted after a 12-hour shift and several hours of comforting her sick, achy child, Shannon trudged down the single hallway of the midcentury ranch home to the oblong kitchen. The butcher block table, a hand-me-down from her parents, was littered with gray-hued pages torn out of a coloring book. And crayons. Crayons were everywhere. The table, the floor. The seats of the chairs. Sticking out from underneath the refrigerator. Like brightly colored wax shrapnel from a Crayola bomb.

"Maaaooohhhm!" a voice rang out, singsongy and clear. At the mess at the table, standing up on her knees on a chair, Kate Troskey's dark curls worked up into a frizzy brunette chaos. On the other side of the table, a well-loved oak high chair was sidled up to it, filled with a chubby six-month-old Grace Troskey. Dark curls were starting to form on the baby's perfectly round head.

Between the girls, Kale Troskey helped Kate color the picture in front of her with one hand as he pried a soggy crayon from Grace's tiny fist before it went into her mouth again with his other.

"Whhhaaaat?" Shannon sang back to her daughter, stopping to gently smooth her hand over Grace's soft head.

Kate was the wild child of the three so far, the truly misunderstood middle child. The toddler looked up, a grape juice stain on the front of her white t-shirt hemmed with rainbow bric-a-brac. She shrugged her shoulders and tilted her head to the side and giggled. Attention. That was all she desired from her mother, after watching her sick older sister occupy it all afternoon. Kale, dark hair messy, matching purple stain on his shirt, smiled as he glanced from Kate to Shannon. The husband and wife shared a look that made Shannon blush.

Somehow, after 10 years together, the attraction only grew. It grew every time one of their children yelled "Daddy." It grew every time she watched him fold laundry, big hands trying to make sense of little shirts and little dresses and little socks. It grew every time she pretended she was sleeping and he turned on the corner lamp in their bedroom and she watched his shadow clumsily strip off his jeans, hopping off balance on one foot, before climbing into bed beside her and wrapping his strong, warm arms around her and kissing the bare skin of her shoulder.

Shannon's phone, abandoned on the kitchen counter with her bag and sunglasses, lit up and trembled a few inches across the tile, making a rough rattling sound as it moved. She didn't want to look. It wasn't the hospital. She wasn't on call, and they knew she had a sick child. If it was her mother, she'd call her back later. If it was Ava— if it was Ava she should answer. If her friend was finally calling her, finally breaking, she should answer.

"Nooooo!" Kale dramatically shook his head in slow motion as she crossed the kitchen to retrieve the vibrating phone. "Don't do it!"

Shannon sighed as she picked it up. Then frowned, reading her Aunt Lois's name and number on the screen. "It's Aunt Lois. Huh." Holding the phone in front of her for one more round of vibrations, she reluctantly decided to answer, a million terrible imaginings in her head. Lois had never called her. Ever. Shannon only had the number saved by familial default. "Hello? This is Shannon."

"Oh, Shannon," the middle-aged woman's husky voice gasped.

"Is everything OK?"

"I don't know. Shannon, dear, your friend Ava is standing on the roof of the feed and seed across the street. We're all afraid she's gonna jump right off."

"What?" Shannon's voice was hollow. Kale, Kate, even Grace's birdlike coos were silenced, as they watched her, sensing the urgency of whatever was transpiring in the half of the conversation they could not hear.

Sherriff's Deputy Lucas Ellis yawned. The long fingers on his hand covering his mouth. He readjusted his knockoff aviators, placed his hand back in its 2 o'clock position on the steering wheel of the patrol car. Cropped blonde hair, so light in color his head almost looked bald, shone in the sunlight streaming through the Taurus's driver's side window. A tan hat with a wide, flat brim rested in the passenger seat. There wasn't much traffic in the late afternoon. There was never much traffic any time of day.

Ellis couldn't sleep. He hadn't had a good night's rest for years, between nightmares and memories, many of the dreams qualifying as both. Sometimes he dozed for a minute or two, radar out and ready to catch anyone speeding around the blind corner after the turn off the river bridge on the east side of Flynn. Coin's Corner. Named simply for the Coin Family who lived beside it a hundred years before, their homestead since demolished for pastureland. It was notorious for catching folks speeding in the middle of the night, underestimating how sharp it was until their car was wrapped around a heavy duty guardrail protecting from a plunge down a 50-foot bluff. After only a year and half of police work, Ellis had seen three wrecks with no serious injuries, but his whole life he had heard the stories of the horrific scenes of the ones who hadn't been so lucky.

"Dispatch to Deputy Ellis."

The officer jumped. He wasn't actually asleep, instead day dreaming with his eyes closed about how nice his dad's Corvette would look with a new coat of paint over the bodywork on the back fender. Callahan's team had done beautiful work so far, but Ellis was too nice. After it sat in the shop for a couple of months, he paid for what was done and took the car back without a single complaint. His intent was to have them finish it, but day after day passed and he didn't return to the shop. Something kept him stuck, as if completing the car in the way his father meant to would also make the memories of the man come to an end. Ellis knew it was a foolish idea. He was too logical a man for that sort of feeling. But the car continued to stay in his garage unfinished. And feelings he didn't believe in continued to win over logic.

The staticky voice on the other end wouldn't ask directly for him if whatever was happening wasn't happening in Flynn. Flynn was his territory. His *beat,* if you could call it that in the country. And it was his hometown. Regulating right and wrong in the town in which he was born and raised often seemed harder than doing the same thing on the most dangerous road in Afghanistan, where he didn't know a soul or even speak the language.

"Dispatch, this is Deputy Ellis," the young man leaned forward, speaking into the handheld portion of the radio as he held it up to his thin lips.

"Deputy Ellis, we got a report of a suicide attempt in progress. 631 Main Street in Flynn. White. Female. Threatening to jump off a building."

Whoever she was, he knew her. Ellis flipped on his lights and siren. The high-pitched repetitive tone was complemented by the screeching of tires on asphalt as he whipped the modified highway cruiser around 180 degrees.

"You know, before you jump you should at least take your boots off. I've always liked them. Good looking boots. I mean, we can pull them off you once you're dead, but nobody will want to wear them. From my personal experience, nobody wants boots off a dead person. Grandpa died in his boots, so we buried him in them. Uncle Harren, buried him in his boots. Boots taken off and gifted before a person dies is a different story, though. Kale's real nice pair of python boots were left to him by his grandfather. I guess it's just more acceptable to wear them as long as nobody has died in them. You wouldn't want people looking at you thinking, 'Are those that dead girl's boots?'"

"I told you I'm not up here to jump, Pode," Ava shut down his rambling. She still stood at the edge of the roof of the feed and seed building. Even after the arrival of her best friend. Even as the sun finished setting.

"I have to admit that's a little disappointing. Not the you breaking your neck part, but the part where I thought maybe we'd finally have some excitement in this town.

11

Since you're not going to jump, you want to go get a beer?"

From the corner of her eye, Ava watched Pode rise to his feet. He had been sitting on a metal air conditioning unit sticking up from the flat, tarred roof. He strolled a couple of steps toward her, hands shoved deep into the front pockets of his worn work jeans as his wide chest inhaled a heavy breath.

Ava raised her hand and brushed a strand of box-dyed blonde hair out of her face, her arm quickly returning to its place crossing the other. Her breath was even, but shallow. In her mind she went back and forth trying to decide what to do. She hadn't expected to be spotted by anyone, let alone get a rise out of the whole town. Now her best friend was genuinely concerned about her and that added an overtone of guilt to her initial feelings of relief and amusement. The longer she stood on the edge, the more she felt like what she was doing was absolutely pointless. A waste of everyone's time.

A good sized group of people gathered and peered up at the roof through the light from the crimson ball of a sun in the magenta cloud scattered sky. The feed and seed was a plain building. Square windows, square doors were equally spaced in the wood siding, the building differentiated from the other 15 buildings on either side of Main Street by the extra story, wide loading doors in the side, and neatly painted red and white wooden sign that read "Kettle's Feed & Seed." As a child, Ava had been inside the building maybe 20 times, with the excuse of helping her father, but really only to play with Mr. Kettle's basset hound, Barney. It had been well over a decade since she had seen the inside of the building or Barney lying on his side, sunning himself on the sidewalk out front. The old dog must have died, and though Ava hadn't thought about him for years, she felt a pang of sadness.

The voices of the people below her were not quiet. That was usual in Flynn, but Ava was too far away and the wind was blowing the opposite direction, so she couldn't make out what they were saying. Time never meant much to her, but she realized a few minutes before five, when the younger folks in town left work and the older folks made their way to Martha's for supper, was not the least obvious hour for her to choose. Fifteen or twenty people had stopped to see what the commotion was about. Corinne reemerged from the newspaper office and took it upon herself to be the ambassador for the situation. Her shiny helmet of hair bounced through the crowd, filling in new people as they pulled their car over or walked up the street.

Pode even heard the news, despite a corn harvest to finish and a hundred head of cattle always in need of water or food or another form of care. He arrived with Baker in Baker's ridiculous truck. Ava heard it before she spotted it, losing sight of it as it barreled around the corner to the back of the building. The metal rungs of the fire escape ladder creaked and groaned under Pode's heavy boots as he took them two at a time. He was abnormally quiet for the first few minutes on the roof, Ava asking him to stop and sit. Pode only agreeing once she assured him she had no intentions of ending her life this particular early fall evening.

"Man, I had some expired corned beef I found in Mom's fridge for lunch and the way my stomach's gurgling, I'm starting to think that was a really bad idea." Pode acted like it was any of the other conversations they had had that week. Ava stayed silent. This was what he did. He talked too much. It was his way of normalizing a conflict he had no idea how to deal with otherwise and it was working on Ava. Brilliantly.

13

At the edge of town, a big blue sedan, lights flashing, siren blaring, "Flynn County Sherriff's Department" written in white on the doors pulled angled across the street, blocking oncoming traffic from the east. Sherriff's Deputy Ellis's light hair glinted in the last light of the fall day as the tall, thin officer in a meticulously pressed uniform of the same shade of blue as his car, bailed out the driver's side door. Popping the trunk, he hustled around the back and retrieved a megaphone and held it up to his face. The crowd parted like the Red Sea as he made his way to the front, and Ava knew it was time to go. Somewhat enjoying the concern she was causing the onlookers, she had forgotten someone would eventually call the cops. The cops meant Ellis. She didn't know him well, but he seemed like a nice guy. The guilt inside her grew. Ellis was wasting his time and energy trying to get her down from a roof like a cat from a tree. She was perfectly capable of climbing down, but she didn't want to.

"E . . . come dow . . . fr . . . ere," Ellis's electronically enhanced voice cut in and out through the speaker, "Please . . . do this. You . . . ave so much . . . live . . . r."

"Did he say you have 'So much liver?'" Pode questioned playfully, but nervously.

"To live for," Ava answered quickly, embarrassed for the officer.

"Oh, yeah, yeah," Pode nodded his head. "I hate liver. Though I might've taken it over that corned beef from earlier. Man, that stuff . . ."

Ava sighed, "Alright, I'm done."

"Good," Pode's voice changed instantly from relief to slight anger. "Can you tell me, then, what the hell you're doing up here?"

"I didn't think anybody would even notice me. I definitely didn't think everybody would think I was up here to jump." Ava turned and faced Pode. A loud murmur traveled through the crowd on the ground. Pode pulled his hands from the pockets of Levi's and crossed them across his chest. Fittingly, a faint white remnant of the Kettle's Feed & Seed logo was screen printed across the cotton of his t-shirt.

"Not a whole lot of other things people do after they unexpectedly stand on edges of roofs of buildings." Pode raised one eyebrow. Ava recognized it as the same side of his face as the occasional singular dimple, the asymmetry comfortingly familiar to her.

She nodded sheepishly, agreeing with his honest assessment. She took a last glance over her shoulder at the gathered crowd as a shiver worked its way up her spine. Ava tried to pull the canvas jacket tighter. Someone in the crowd, a man named Dean Howard who worked at the grocery store, excitedly pointed as Corrine leaned in to talk to him. Ellis had vanished.

"Look up there at that crazy Schaffer girl. What is she up to now?" She mumbled the things she was certain they were saying, rolled her eyes up to the sky. "Thanks, Mom."

"OK, well, talking to yourself still kind of makes you look crazy, but I guess it's a step up from jumping off of buildings." Pode was trying to joke, but his voice was too full of sincere worry for the sarcasm to properly work. Ava wanted to be mad at him, but couldn't bring herself to be because she knew she should be thanking him for coming after her. Pode followed her to the railing of the fire escape at the back of the building. As Ava swung herself over and onto the steps, she spotted Ellis beginning to climb toward them. His lean legs were quick on the steep metal ladder.

"Officer Ellis! Hey!" Ava yelled. "I'm coming down now. Pode talked me out of jumping."

Pode took a deep breath as he watched the top of his friend's head dip below the line of the rooftop.

"Pode Wagner? I didn't know anybody was up there with you! That's, uh, that's great!" the officer yelled back to her, stopping mid climb. His mouth hung open after he was done talking, as it often did when he was bewildered. It was not the most intelligent look for a man at his level of authority.

Ava gracefully dismounted the final step and flinched away from Ellis's hands as they moved toward her waist in attempt to help her. The people of Flynn were already filtering into the alley between the buildings, led by Corrine. It only took a few minutes from the time Ava left their vision for the crowd from the street to realize the action was no longer on the roof. A quiet murmur swam among them, as they looked at Ava like she was an alien from another galaxy.

"Nothing to see here, folks! Nothing to see!" Ellis shouted the cliché. "Everybody needs to just go home so we can sort this all out," his final words leading his eyes to Pode as he took the final step with a humble apologetic look in the deputy's direction.

"Why were you up there?" Corrine gasped, opening a flow of questions from others.

"Have you gone crazy?"

"Don't you think your mother would be ashamed of you?"

"Corrine, everyone, please," the officer's voice between scolding and pleading as his hand rubbed his forehead.

Ava ignored them. Of course they thought she was crazy. The questions were ones she could not and did not want to answer, though, so she pushed past Ellis and escaped. He wanted to follow her, captured by the sadness in her intense stare, but controlling the crowd was his job.

On the far side of the building, in front of the loading doors that were closed for the day, Ava's 20-year-old Mustang slumped next to the chipped cement curb. It was an ugly car, even when it was new. Ava was sure of this because she remembered the day she sat in the passenger seat while her mother test drove it. The girl watched wide-eyed as the speedometer needle trembled above the red line marking 100 miles an hour. They cruised the potholed county road, past the Goodmans' pig farm and back. Ava was five years old. She had never been so scared in her life. Her mother had never looked so beautiful. The utilitarian cold of the woman's face transformed into something uncontrollable and striking for that lone memory of Ava's entire childhood, and in that moment, Ava already believed she would never be as beautiful as her mother.

"So now you're just getting in your car and leaving?" Pode caught up with Ava as she opened the door to the faded vinyl interior. Standing in the middle of the street, a foot from the nose of the car, he glared at her.

Ava stopped, a hand on the top of the car door, as she looked through his chest.

"What about all the people back there? You don't want them thinking you're crazy, do you? I mean you're not. Right?" Confusion drifted across the young man's face. His lips parted, "Av?"

"No, I'm not. I was—I think—I think I'm maybe, finally, finding sane."

She didn't want to have to explain, to justify, to delve into the reasoning. And he knew her too well for her to successfully lie to him.

Ava slipped into the Mustang and started it with the key she had left in the ignition. The engine heaved itself over, smoke poured from the exhaust, and the vehicle lurched forward. Maneuvering around Pode, who slowly turned to watch her go, a cloud of dry gray dust from the road kicked up around him and the hunk of metal on rubber drove away. The taillights glowed in the distance through the shadowy twilight like the eyes of a frightened, fleeing animal.

\* \* \*

Four bicycles lay in the weeds in the ditch beside the dirt road that wound along the river past some of the Wagners' dryland corn and across the pasture behind the Schaffers' house. The pigweed was full grown, prickly and stable stemmed. Each plant rose defiantly out of the gold turning prairie grass in the cleared acreage before the tangled mess of trees lining the riverbank. There was a trail, not visible from the road, crossing the land and leading to a hidden gap in the thorny trees. A foot wide and four feet tall, the passageway was the exact same size as the average farm kid.

Once through, the bank on the other side was low and sandy, the immediate portion of the river shallow. Cleared of brush and worn from entrances and exits from the water, the dirt was packed down and became mostly sand at the water's edge. The clearing was lined with soft grass mixed with wild yellow sunflowers that were considerably smaller than the ones grown for their seeds by the Johnsons in the fields west of town. Upon dragging a rotten driftwood log into the open space for use as a bench, a private beach hideaway had been created 1,400 miles from the nearest ocean.

Shannon was spending the night with Ava. Baker was spending the night with Pode. They planned it that way, so they could sneak off together after they arrived at their respective slumber party location. For the girls it was easy.

18

Neither of Ava's parents were home and her little brother had locked himself in his room with a book after only a vague and soon forgotten threat of tattling. For the boys the mission of evasion was much harder. It was time to pick up irrigation pipe and Pode's father spent the day before hinting at using his son and son's friend for the labor. They didn't greet him upon hopping off the school bus, though they knew he must be in the machine shed because his pickup was parked beside it. The boys weren't willing to risk being tricked into work. Instead they ran to the garage, too quick for Pode's little brother to follow them, and jumped on bikes. Baker groaned and moaned about again having to ride a sparkly pink cast off that had once belonged to Pode's older sister but he silenced his complaints as Pode challenged him to a race. Pode always won, the bigger, the stronger, the quicker, the smarter, of the two kids, but the bets had not become any less appealing to the future gambler, perpetual loser, Baker.

"Where is your dad living now?" Shannon asked, chewing on the sleeve of a secondhand blue hoodie with a Jayhawk on the front of it. She sat beside Ava on the rotten log. The boys, shoes abandoned and jeans rolled up, waded into the cool water a few feet from the girls.

Ava shrugged her shoulders. "I don't know. We haven't seen him since he left. Maybe in Salina, with my Uncle Steve." She drug her fingertips through the sand beside her muddy pink and white LA Gears, the lights in the soles of the shoes long ago burned out. The individual grains mushed together, damp barely below the surface even in the lingering heat of the late August day.

"I think it'll be OK, Av," Shannon spoke softly, trying to comfort her friend. "They weren't really very happy together. Maybe it will be better with them not together."

Ava nodded in agreement. "Yeah. It's weird. I don't

know anybody with split-up parents. Well, Audie, but her parents weren't ever married."

"Whoa! You guys got to see this!" Pode yelled. He was standing at the edge of the water, one foot in the river, one foot on the bank. Baker splashed toward Pode, looking at the same spot. Shannon and Ava watched their counterparts, but didn't budge from their seats on the log.

"Shan! Av! Come look at this!" Baker's voice grew higher with excitement. The boy was as surprised as his friend had been upon seeing whatever mysterious thing sat in the sandy mud.

"We're talking! About important stuff!" Shannon yelled back, annoyed. They were past the cootie stage and on to the annoying each other part of the childhood growing process. The differences in the way girls thought versus the ways boys thought was starting to become apparent and would only continue to grow.

"It's OK." Ava stood and walked toward the boys, her curiosity seizing her. Shannon jumped up, the waif with curly dark hair following the blonde who hadn't quite yet lost all of her baby fat. As they approached the boys, Baker took a step back to form a circle. At first it looked like a rock, but then it moved slightly and the girls realized it was a turtle shell, coated in a thick layer of river soot and frozen out of fear of the movement and sound around it.

"Uh, that's an old turtle, Pode." Ava frowned at her friend. The enthusiasm hadn't left his face.

"Wait. Quiet." He demanded of the group and they all obeyed. Nearly an entire minute passed before the tip of the turtle's head peaked out from the opening in the front of the shell, the side nearest Ava. Embracing the situation and risking continuing on, the rest of the turtle's head emerged as well as his legs. It took time to process why he didn't look right, but it hit Ava audibly.

20

"No way. It has two heads," the girl gasped and looked up at her friends, suddenly understanding the boys' excitement.

"That's so cool," Shannon whispered as she knelt to examine him at closer range, but careful not to scare the creature back into his shell again.

"Wish I had Mom's Polaroid." Pode shook his head. They watched as the turtle made a slow movement forward, the eyes on both his head and the head attached to his neck at an odd angle blinked at the same time.

"We could go get a bucket and take him to school Monday," Baker proposed. The other kids considered his idea. Ava slid her feet backward in the sand, making room for the turtle as he crawled forward a labored few inches.

"I don't know. I'd hate to move him around. I mean he's made it this far on his own. What if he got hurt accidentally?" Pode crouched, then sat in the sand behind the turtle, his knees in front of him, his arms wrapped around them.

"Yeah," Shannon nodded. "I'm with Pode. I think we should leave him alone."

"But nobody will believe us." Baker looked around the circle from Pode to Shannon to Ava.

"We'll believe us," Ava smiled. Smiles spread across her friends' faces, too, and the four kids silently watched for a long time as the turtle scooted across the clearing and disappeared into a clump of thick prairie grass.

# 2

Steve Miller Band blared from the jukebox in the window next to the front door of Martha's. Puny rays of late fall sun forced their way through years of grime built up on the glass. Men already dressed in flannel winter attire gathered around a row of green velvet-lined pool tables. Bud Light in one hand, pool stick in the other, a couple of them glanced up at the sound of the front door creaking open. Ellis strutted in in his full cop ensemble, gun at his side, posture too perfect, and took the last seat at the end of the bar.

"What can I get you, honey?" Martha smiled. A tooth on each side of her mouth was missing. She pulled her nearly 300 pounds up off a shabby stool that had been retired from the public side of the bar years before. Above the bar namesake's post, a black and white television with fake wood grain side panels and a knob for channel changing buzzed so loudly the audio for the sports commentary show playing on it could barely be heard.

The woman's face was heavy, but somehow still youthful after 60 plus years of life, 30 of it spent in the dingy dive. It required someone young at heart to run the only bar in town, and her extra weight was simply a byproduct of eating every meal there. It was no secret Martha fried with lard.

"Coke, please, Martha. Thank you." Ellis smiled back. His white horse teeth gleamed.

"Anything for early supper?"

"Maybe in a bit. I ate a late lunch. Helped the Petersons chase some cows around half the afternoon. After we finally got them back in, Mrs. Peterson heated up leftover turkey gravy like I have never had. My lord that stuff was good." Ellis leaned back in his chair and patted the tight royal blue cotton of his shirt and the six-pack sculpted stomach underneath it. Five years in the military had made him lean and strong and now a solitary life and long shifts of police work kept him that way.

"Mrs. Peterson's a fine cook," the next man at the bar nodded, raising the last sip of watery light beer in a heavy glass mug to his lips. "Helped them with harvest a few years back, man, do I know why her boys is all so big."

"Need another one down there, Rodg?"

"Well, yeah, I'll take another, since you're twisting my arm," he laughed, a booming laugh that overpowered the rest of the noise in the room. Starting in his round beer belly and rippling up through his thick throat to his double chin, Rodg may have been the only person to ever laugh at his bad jokes, but he made every ground-shaking laugh count. As this most recent chuckle ended, he took off his green Pioneer Seed cap and rubbed the few hairs left circling the crown of his head, then put the hat back on.

Martha sat a chipped plastic glass of pop and a foaming over beer on the cigarette scarred oak bar in front of the two men. She put her hand on her hip and leaned back against the refrigerator for support, shifting it a few inches to the right. "Officer Ellis, now I don't mean to pry, but I wondered if you have any idea what Dora May's daughter was doing up on Kettle's roof yesterday afternoon? The whole town's been talking and I'd rather know the truth than the guesses folks take about things they don't know nothing about?"

Ellis shook his head and pushed the corners of his

mouth down. "I don't know, Martha, I really don't. People have been asking me all day and I haven't been able to get ahold of Ava on the phone, so I don't know any more than you do."

"It'd be hard to blame the poor girl for anything she does," Rodg spoke up. "No good drunk of a father ran that farm into the ground. Brother left town soon as he could drive a car, and we all know Dora May couldn't have been no dream to take care of for all those months while she lay on her death bed. Poor girl's had a rough few years."

"She sure has," Martha sighed. "I remember taking care of Momma before she passed on, God bless her soul. It wasn't no easy thing to do, and I was 45 with a couple grown kids. I went a little crazy, you know."

Quiet fell over the conversation. Thoughts of loved ones lost heavy in the fronts of their minds. The jukebox whined a George Jones song, something slower, softer, and disconcertingly suitable for the moment. The front door opened with its familiar sound and slammed shut. Pode and Baker, with his arm around the much shorter Audie, her clothes two sizes too small on her wide frame, her hair shoulder-length waves of shimmering auburn surrounding her pretty round face, entered the front of the bar and beelined for a freshly vacated pool table.

Ellis cleared his throat and sipped from the undamaged side of his cup, watching Ava's friends from the corner of his eye. The cup's stained fleshy color and rutted texture reminded him of goose bumps on human skin. "I'll stop by her house sometime, check on her. Make sure she's doing ok."

"That'd be real nice of you." Martha's eyes went to the TV as it suddenly grew louder, the soundtrack to a commercial for fast food tacos buzzing out of the speakers. "This is also none of my business, but I always thought you two'd make a real cute couple."

"Oh, I—," Ellis laughed nervously. His face tinted the slightest pink.

"My goodness, Martha, I think you're putting the cart before the horse there," Rodg's laughing bellowed up from his lungs again. Ellis had dreaded his seating choice at first, but now he wanted to toss his arm over the drunk's shoulders.

"Ava's very pretty," Ellis regained his composure. "But I barely know her."

Martha grinned broadly, revealing one more missing tooth way in the back of her mouth.

Audie and Baker watched as Pode careened drunkenly down the street. They talked him out of driving, but weren't honestly sure if walking home was safe for him. He insisted on going alone, though. Pode checked his phone all night, stepped away to make a call once, but came right back. Audie would have put every cent she had on the fact it was Ava he was trying to reach, but she and Baker kept playing pool and flirting and not saying anything about it.

Grabbing the plastic handle on the interior roof of Baker's giant truck, Audie hauled herself into the passenger seat and used both hands to slam the door shut. The alley behind Martha's was absolutely deserted, like it should be for midnight on a Thursday. Baker laughed as Pode stumbled off a curb, taking three running steps and narrowly avoiding falling flat on his face.

"When he gives me shit later because he bloodied up a knee and ruined a good fucking pair of jeans, you got to vouch I tried my hardest to give him a ride home."

"He's never taken a ride home from anybody but Ava," Audie mumbled.

Baker went on, "What do you suppose she was doing

up on that fucking roof yesterday? Do you think she really was planning on jumping?"

"I don't know," Audie shrugged. "She hardly ever gets out of her house anymore and when she does she doesn't talk. Who knows what's going through her mind?"

"I could see why she'd want to do it. I can't deny I ain't thought about doing something like that. Getting out of this world while I'm still fucking young. Not having to suffer through another sixty years of this shit."

They sat in the empty midnight of a small town. Watched until their friend turned the corner of 6th Street and they could no longer make out his red plaid flannel shirt in the darkness. Audie slid across the leather seat of the pickup until the side of her body was pressed up against Baker's. She was ready to change the subject, bored with his fatalistic imagination. Her breath smelled like cigarettes. He felt her lips, warm and wet, on his neck.

"What are you up to, lady?" Baker whispered, frozen with his hands in front of him on the leather-wrapped steering wheel.

"Nothing," Audie lied. Her hand slid into his lap and he held his breath as he felt her fingers searching for the zipper of his jeans.

Baker laughed nervously, "I don't fucking, uh . . ."

"Come on, Dougie," she kissed him on the lips, but he didn't kiss back. "A little fun never hurt anybody."

"Audie, I don't know if this is a good idea. Fucking anybody could drive by. Martha's probably about done cleaning up in there. We've been friends a long time . . ."

"I know. And I have no idea how this hasn't happened yet. Trust me, I know what I'm doing." With her last words, she placed her other hand on the back of his head and pulled his face toward her for another kiss. She knew exactly what she was doing and Baker tried to put the idea of all of the practice she had had out of his mind. He leaned his head back, felt her hand on his stomach as she undid his belt and the button on his jeans. As she bent between him and the dash, he breathed in time with her movements and registered no more protests.

"Grrree . . . SCREEEECH!" The 20-foot red barn door slid open with a deafening sound. The last light of the sunset burst in, fully blinding Ava. She raised a hand to her forehead to shield her eyes. She knelt beside a metal sculpture, paintbrush in her hand, dirt and vivid color smeared across her white undershirt and jeans with sizeable holes in the knees. She continued to paint without looking up to see who intended to interrupt her work. Gently turning the welded steel and setting it back down, Ava dipped her brush into a recycled soup can full of burnished red paint, stopped for an instant to study, and then touched the loaded bristles to the piece.

Shannon, in billowy hospital scrubs, silhouette of black in front of the orange glow seeping through the wide doorway, crossed her arms across her chest and tilted her head to the side. She stepped from the light and walked through the maze of metal sculpture on paint stained concrete floor until she was standing behind Ava, watching. After a time of silence, Shannon deliberately coughed and Ava hesitated. She stopped working and stood to face her guest. Ava was as curvy as Shannon was thin. Her hair was as blonde and straight as the other woman's was dark and curly. Even the clothes they wore were in great contrast, Ava's stained and tight, Shannon's spotless and loose.

"Hey. I've been trying to call you for a couple days. Thought I'd stop by instead."

Ava met the bright blue eyes staring her down and didn't answer.

"Why were you standing on the roof of the feed and seed the other night? Are you alright, Av? Cause the whole town is talking and they're worried about you. And I'm worried about you."

"I don't know," Ava said as she broke away from Shannon's stare.

"Do you need to talk? Do you need to cry? You know I've got ears and shoulders you are welcome to use?"

"No. I'm fine." Ava walked around her friend to stand beside one of two tables made of plywood stretched across sawhorses. Dirty brushes lay in a pile beside paint thinner and mangled tubes of enamel paint and a welding helmet. Unscrewing the lid on the metal bottle of paint thinner, Ava poured some into an indigo tinted mason jar and began working one brush at a time against the glass bottom. The artist's concentration was officially broken for the day.

Shannon's voice was as soft as the flowing curls in her brown hair. "I haven't seen you break. I've barely seen you cry. Not at the hospital, or the viewing, or the funeral, or after. I know good people, Ava, if you want to talk to someone. There is no shame in it. I can't begin to imagine what you're going through. It's awful. Unfair." She searched and couldn't find a better word. "Shitty. And if you need help of any kind I'm here. We're here. Me. Kale. The girls."

"Thank you, Shan. Really, I'm doing alright. You know, not great, but it's getting better."

"I think you should come eat supper with us tonight. We're making homemade pizza. The girls love it when you come over." Shannon took a couple of steps closer to Ava.

"I thought we had a rule about you using your children to guilt me into things."

Shannon smiled, "Sometimes I feel like that's the only

reason I had children. They are guilt machines. You wouldn't believe the breaks people at work give me when they find out I have three little girls at home. My coworkers are going to loathe the sight of Girl Scout Cookies before I'm done with them."

"That's not the only reason." Ava beat the wooden handle of a brush loudly on the rim of the jar. "You had children because you drank too much beer in Kale's truck after a basketball game."

"Just the first one, in my defense," Shannon pointed at her friend, her smile gone. "And nice job turning this around on me, but let's get back to why my until yesterday very sane best friend threatened to jump off a roof on Main Street a few months after her mother's funeral. I didn't come over here to lecture you or fight with you or whatever you're trying to push me to do right now. I could have done any of that over the phone and saved the gas of driving out here to the middle of nowhere. I came over to make sure you are well. And safe."

"And thanks, but I'm fine."

"Ava. Ava, goddammit! Would you say something real?" The words came out much more forcefully than Shannon meant for them to, but even with deep frustration behind them they still didn't seem to have any impact on her friend.

Ava stopped cleaning brushes. She let go of the jar and took a single step back from the table. She made eye contact with Shannon, who was now standing straight across from her at the other edge of the plywood. The words that came from her mouth were so direct and rehearsed it was like Ava was again reading off the same script she had written weeks before. "I wish Eddy could have stayed longer. I wish he wasn't with that horrible girl. I wish I could talk to my father. I miss Mom. A lot. More than I could have ever imagined missing anyone.

29

Especially her." Ava's face was vacant. "There. Is that what you wanted to hear?"

Shannon wiped an exasperated tear out of the corner of her eye and sighed as her lips flattened together. It was the same expression her face displayed when she was overwhelmed by the strains of motherhood and one of her young daughters wouldn't tell her the truth. She walked around the table and gave her friend a quick hug, but Ava stood as stiff as a board.

"I'm so sorry, Av. I didn't mean to yell at you. I love you. And I'm worried about you." Shannon's tone was gentle again. "I wish you would move back to town. Or you could come stay with us. Or I could come out here and stay with you a couple of nights a week. Or I bet Pode . . ."

"I'm only eight miles from town," Ava interrupted. Shannon had suggested the same things before, and they were the worst set of ideas Ava had heard since her mother's death. With Shannon she would be relegated to a house full of noisy, dirty children and an unemployed, self-loathing husband. In a house in town, she wouldn't have enough space to work. And she wanted distance from everything. Everyone. Even Pode. "I'm fine here. Work's here." She scanned the barn of artwork. Welded, painted, metal objects she had created at record rates, day in day out since her mother died. "It's good for me to work. And I need the money. You should go. Don't you have pizza to make?"

"You can't hold this inside forever," Shannon whispered. "It'll all come spilling out one day."

Ava looked at her friend square in the face. Shannon saw the same face in her earliest memories of life, talked to it, played with it, cried with it, told secrets to it. It had changed, though, recently. She couldn't pinpoint when. Maybe earlier, when Dora May found out about the rapidly growing, all-consuming cancer. Or maybe in the days Ava cared for a mother who was unable to get up, feed herself, bathe herself, go to the bathroom herself, sometimes not even have enough strength to form words and talk. It could have even been after the death, the funeral. Shannon didn't know when the change first occurred, how long it took her to notice it. Now she was trying to get Ava to open up to her, but why should she? How could everything just simply return to normal? Shannon finally conceded this to herself.

They had grown apart since the moment they walked across the stage in the Flynn High School gymnasium to accept their diplomas and hugged each other and promised to never do so. Shannon was already the mother of a toddler and would become one twice more. A wedding and a move to El Dorado came quickly. She went to school to become a nurse while Kale went to school to become a football player. Then a move back to Flynn, where she found herself the sole breadwinner of a family of five. Her time was stretched between work and family so much so she rarely ever saw Ava and never was it arranged. Usually they ran into each other on the street or at the grocery store or at Martha's.

Ava moved to town, had her own house, planned to leave, but was never able to for taking care of one family member after another. First she made sure Eddy was fed and had a place to sleep until he graduated two years after her and took off for college. Next Dora May was sick, and Ava found herself stuck doing everything in her power to keep her mother away from the hospitals they both so loathed. All the while, she dropped groceries off at her father's house and desperately created art. She searched out dealers, vendors, stores for her work and had a following by way of a gallery on the East Coast. While trying to hold what was left of her family together, she churned out pieces and sold them to pay to live.

Shannon repeated the same thing she had requested of her oldest friend many times before, but it seemed feeble facing the facts of their faltering relationship. "If you need anything . . ."

"I'll call you." Ava finished the sentence for her.

Shannon took a step back and then hurriedly walked away. She was angry, but forced a hollow smile and a wave to the best friend she felt like she barely knew. As the poppy-colored minivan backed up and turned in the driveway, Ava's artist's mind criticized the awful color of the vehicle. She naturally judged its unremarkable, style-lacking design. Before she went back to her cleanup efforts, she squinted to pick out a car breaking the plain. It passed the van in the distance at the edge of the blue meets brown nothingness of the horizon many miles away. White letters were printed on the side of it. Dirt and rocks kicked up from the long driveway as it approached and stopped in almost the exact spot Shannon's van had vacated in front of the machine shed.

"Really?" Ava asked herself out loud, not attempting to hide the irritation on her face as she watched Ellis, chest first, climb out of his car. "Nobody told me the parade route cut through my yard."

"Ms. Schaffer!" Ellis smiled, his teeth too big for his face. "Ava. Hey. Hi."

He removed his hat as he approached her and was reminded of the conversation from the day before. Calling her "very pretty" didn't come close. With her blonde hair tied back, pieces of it escaping around her face, tight worn jeans and black lace bra he could see every inch of underneath a paint and dirt stained white men's undershirt, she was amazing. As unpredictable and beautiful as a prairie snowfall in September.

"Hi," her voice was cold.

"Passed Shannon Troskey heading out your drive," he continued, not letting her glare thwart his attempt to make small talk. "She has three darling little girls, doesn't she?"

Ava didn't answer. Ellis's fingers nervously worked along the brim of his hat, rotating it. "I, uh, well, I'm sure you can guess why I'm here. I had to open a file on you at the station and I'd like to close it, but I need to do an interview first. I have to make sure you don't need a psychological evaluation or anything like that. I mean if you want to talk to somebody I can definitely recommend a great guy. In Wichita. He used to work for the military. Helped me a bunch when I got back, but he's got his own office now, so . . ."

"Thank you," Ava stopped him out of fear he may drag on until the darkness of the evening settled in around them. "Thank you, Officer Ellis, for your concern, but I can assure you that I am fine."

"OK, well," the officer uttered an ironic laugh. "Please don't threaten to jump off of any more buildings." He was flustered, in over his head. Rubbing his smooth cheek, he looked down at his shiny black boots as if this might save him from the unbearable awkwardness of the conversation.

Ava watched him, fascinated a man who exuded such composure in the variety of other situations she had seen him in was reduced to this bumbling, shoe-studying fool. Something about the way he acted around her challenged her, flattered her, and repulsed her all at the same time. Mostly throughout her life men had disregarded her, convinced after meeting her she was too odd to pursue. It was something Ava, the girl, never minded and became quite comfortable with. After watching her father and mother's bitter end, romantic relationships terrified her, and Pode's friendship provided her with any need for companionship she had ever had. Ava, the woman, however, was at conflict with Ava the girl, and she found her thoughts wandering other places and wanting certain things the fervor of her art and friendships could not fulfill. Ellis wasn't a bad looking guy.

"Well, I guess I'll head back to town." He looked up. "I'll close that file tomorrow. If you need anything, though . . ."

"Have you ever shot anyone?" The words came out of her mouth, but Ava wanted to take them back the second her ears registered them floating through the sound barrier.

The question made him jerk his head up. His mouth hung open. Ellis was speechless.

"Sorry," Ava apologized. "I'm sorry. That's an awful question. You seem like such a nice guy. I can't even imagine you pointing a gun at someone, let alone actually shooting them."

"Well," he narrowed his eyes, thinking hard. "You do what you have to do. In certain situations. So you make art." He abruptly changed the subject, glancing around the concrete floor of the shed.

Now Ava was caught off guard. Assuming the brash honesty would drive him away like it did nearly everyone else who didn't know her well, it drove him to ask her an equally hard question to answer. And that impressed her. "I do."

Ellis bent over, admiring a scrap chunk of metal. "What do you call this one?"

"Trash."

"That's, uh, interesting."

Ava frowned in attempt to not laugh. "No, it's scrap metal leftover from another project."

"Oh," Ellis smiled, his the fair skin of his cheeks slightly flushing. "I don't know anything about art."

"I can see that." Ava crossed the wide open

workspace, motioning for Ellis to follow her to the corner of the shed where a tall, aggressive form of welded, painted automotive parts stood nearly as tall as Ava. "That might be a good thing, though. Tell me what you think."

"I, uh, don't . . ." Ellis was terrified to say the wrong thing. His confidence was nowhere near its normal level.

"Look at it for a while. What does it look like? What does it make you feel? What stands out? How? Why?"

Ellis stood side by side with Ava. He glanced at her, completely bewildered by her request, but absolutely intrigued by her assertiveness. Her eyes were alive and bright and strong with passion representative of her creation. She was not the same girl from the roof, and he wanted to play along, to embrace her excitement, but he had no idea what she wanted him to say. Hands on his hips, he tilted his head to the side and looked at the abstract form of the hunks of metal fused together, choosing honesty over an attempt to please.

"It's," his mouth hung open. "It seems—aggressive. The bright green is—bright. It's," he closed his mouth. "Is it a woman?"

Ava beamed. "Yes."

"With crazy hair?"

"Yes."

"The snake hair woman, uh . . ."

"Yes. Medusa. It's an interpretation of Medusa."

"Yeah." Ellis was impressed with himself. "Why? Why Medusa?"

The question was perfect, and Ava eagerly answered it. "I can relate. To looking at people and they turn to stone. The way everybody in town gets quiet when I'm around because they were talking about me. Or Mom. Or Dad. Or Eddy."

"I get that." Ellis nodded his head, completely understanding. He experienced similar things. Everyone fell silent when he was around, too, afraid to step out of line and get in trouble. He was well aware of what it was to feel like the odd man out in a room of people he had known his whole life.

Ava walked away from the sculpture, back to the rest of the brushes in need of cleaning. "Thanks for stopping by to check on me."

"Oh, sure." Ellis broke out of the shock he felt in finding something in common with the bizarrely eccentric Ava and refocused on his characteristic unreal level of professionalism. "Sure. If you ever need anything, anything at all . . ."

Ava met his eyes and felt her heartbeat pick up. "Anything?"

Ellis seemed to read her thoughts as he raised his eyebrows and repeated her question as an answer. "Anything."

Years of combat experience, strength training, police work, couldn't stop what happened next. Ellis turned to leave, proud of his quickness in the exchange, took exactly three steps and tripped over his own feet. He tried to land on his knees and when he failed to turn himself the right direction, his arm and then his face became the impact points of his fall partially on the concrete, partially on the sandy gravel drive. Spitting dirt from his mouth, he leapt to his feet, not bothering to check for injury and glanced over his shoulder to see if Ava had witnessed the epic fall, though he was already certain she had.

Ava's hand covered her mouth as she gasped. She took a few steps forward, a dripping paintbrush still in her other hand. She bent and retrieved his hat, crushed beneath his body in the fall. She held it out. Ellis took it from her and retreated to his car without another word. He was thankful the windows of the police cruiser were tinted so Ava couldn't see the warm blood he felt flowing out of his face from the large gash in his forehead where it had struck the metal rim of the sliding door track.

\* \* \*

Ava stopped, dish towel in her hand, between the halfway open decorative glass pocket doors that when closed divided the dining room from the living room. Dora May sat in the corner, in the oak rocking chair, but it didn't rock. Unfocused, her eyes looked out, beyond the quilt-like squares of browns and greens of the fields across the road from the farmhouse. If her mother had ever looked fragile in her entire life, this was the moment in which it was happening. Her thick dark hair was gone. Her bald head shone translucently. Like a snug rubber glove, the skin was so tight and thin you could see every bump, every curve of the skull underneath it. A deep brown three-inch scar above her right ear, from a fall from a tree as a child, was so evident it looked fresh, as if it had happened the day before.

To think of her mother climbing a tree, or even being a child, was a stretch for Ava's active imagination. To think of her mother as anything but power dressed in perfectly pressed polyester slacks and clunking penny loafer heels was impossible. The woman in the rocking chair, streams of sun streaking her beige fleece robe, highlighting her swollen face and hands and feet, was someone, something Ava did not know. The fierce confidence had been killed along with the cancer cells by the liquid poison the doctors pumped into Dora May's blood three times a week.

"Mom?" Ava spoke quietly. Ten years earlier she would have been scolded for speaking so softly.

"I'm not raising a mouse," Dora May would bark at her teenage daughter, shaking her head with frustration.

37

"I'm raising a woman, a woman who can take care of herself. A woman who will stand up to a man. A woman who is loud and lets people know she is in charge." She never understood her daughter. She never understood Ava's flighty artistic nature. Her eleventh hour way of thinking. Her lack of a business mind. How she had given birth to such a creature challenged her and proved to her there was only so much nurture could do to win over nature. She reminded Dora May too much of her father.

Dora May answered in her own soft tone. The bass was still in her voice, but there was a tired cast over the words. "I always wanted to stand up on the top of the roof of the feed and seed."

Ava's eyes scanned the room and then landed again on her mother's face.

Dora May continued to gaze out the window as she talked. "You know it's the tallest building in Flynn County? I always wondered what the view would be like from up there. The land's so flat. I wonder if you can see Dodge City? Or Wichita? I thought about moving there. After high school. To Wichita. Your grandmother and grandfather didn't like it. They refused to help me if I went. It was a different place then. Thirty years ago. Then I started dating your father."

The only real memory Ava had of her mother's father was a Christmas dinner in which her grandfather was ill. Yellowed from liver failure induced by a lifetime of drinking, the man was even more cantankerous than usual and young Ava was terrified of him. By the time the food was served he had reduced everyone in the room to tears, with the exception of her mother. Dora May told him to go to hell and stormed out into a blizzard and walked two miles through frozen countryside before someone checking their cattle spotted her and picked her up and brought her back.

She felt like she should say something, but Ava had no idea if any words would make any difference. Her mother didn't believe in living in the past, or sometimes even the present, the future was where her mind was normally pointed. She stayed especially focused on the earning potential of the future. To hear her speak of history, to see her grow nostalgic, was not charming. It was concerning. Ava was afraid her mother might be losing her mind from the intake of so many drugs and the endless hours without stimulating activity.

Pill bottle after pill bottle lined the vanity in the single bathroom built onto the back porch of the 90-year-old farmhouse. At last count, there were 16 different oral medications and a package of injections. They all had warnings, neon orange tabs with bold fonts and a series of X's. The messages were all alike. They warned not to touch the pills unless they were prescribed to you and then to wash your hands thoroughly after use. Ava wondered, if she shouldn't even touch the containers, why her mother could swallow the capsules, let them slide down her throat, and land in her stomach where their contents spread throughout her body from the inside out. Don't touch them with your fingers. Do ingest them and allow them to disperse throughout your body. This didn't make any sense to Ava, except in the way that meant her mother was seriously, horribly sick. The kind of sick where all caution is thrown to the wind and the side effects of the remedies are far worse than the symptoms of the illness. There was a reason the doctors always referred to it as "cancer treatment" and not "cancer cure."

Dora May had leukemia. A cancer of the blood. Ava knew the type and subtype and could reel off the information she memorized from the pages and pages of text the doctors gave them at the time of her mother's diagnosis. At first it was comforting to be able to give it a name and predict its symptoms and know the courses of treatment. She stayed up all night for the first few weeks searching pamphlets from the hospital and hundreds of websites for information, statistics and facts, and finally, success stories. An artist, with no formal education beyond a high school diploma, Ava knew the disease frontwards and backwards and during one appointment corrected an oncologist.

The section of information the articles left out was how the days between diagnosis and prospective cure would drag on. How in the intermediate it didn't matter how much anyone knew about the disease because nothing was certain. After hundreds, even thousands, of years of recognizing what cancer was, the doctors were still guessing. It became a waiting game. Do this at this time, do that at that time and wait to see if the cancer cell count goes down. Then do it again and hope that the count disappears. If the cancer goes away, Dora May would definitely be young enough and strong enough to go through a bone marrow transplant. Then they would all wait again. Finally, after a year and with no cancer in sight, she would be declared "cured." Cured for now, anyway, as the truth was no one was ever really cured. She would wait the rest of her life, check every year, to make sure this cancer hadn't come back and a new kind of cancer hadn't developed.

"And I always wanted to start a bar fight," Dora May's top lip twitched as she made the admission. She fought a rare smile.

"Really, Mom?" Ava didn't try to hide her surprise. The second-to-last thing she could ever image her mother doing, right before climbing a tree, was getting into a fight in a bar.

"Yes," Dora May smiled weakly at her daughter. Her teeth were dull like the whites of her eyes, gums swollen red. "A big brawl. Like in a movie. Throwing punches. Breaking glass."

"Have you taken your temperature today?"

"I'm fine, Ava. There are things," she trailed off and restarted. "Things I wish I had done."

"OK." Ava shook her head at her mother, crossing the room and sitting on the loveseat beside the rocking chair. "None of that. I'm not going to tell you again. You are not dying, and I don't want to hear any more feeling sorry for yourself bullshit. Next year, when all of this is over, Pode and I will take you to Martha's and we'll all get trashed and we'll start the biggest fight Martha has ever seen. We'll find the meanest person in the place and pick on him until he throws you through the front window. Then that new skinny town deputy will arrest us all and throw us in jail over in Clay for the night, alright?"

Dora May nodded her head and tried to laugh, but only coughed. Ava drove her mother four hours to Wichita for treatments and appointments, sometimes as often as three times a week. She collected the information, paid the bills, helped Dora May to the bathroom, the bedroom, the rocking chair. The mother would have never dreamed her daughter would be the one to pull her through. That it would be Ava who would be the rock. She had completely underestimated the quiet strength, the humble work ethic, the unconditional love of the girl she had so detested raising. Their approach to dealing with life was vastly different, but maybe, Dora May realized, when it came to stubbornness, to intelligence, to survival, she and her daughter were not absolutely unalike.

# 3

The bloodcurdling screams of little girls forced Ava to lean back in her chair and close her eyes. At the kitchen table, six second graders giggled and pointed as Julia held a sparkly pink box up in the air. A set of Disney Princesses dressed in pastel ball gowns with unnecessarily tiny waists and thick flowing hair danced across the box lid.

"You got me the princess game! You got me the princess game!" Julia screeched. "Oh, thank you, Mom! You do listen to me sometimes!"

Shannon laughed at the honesty of her oldest daughter. She leaned against the kitchen counter, behind her a mess of discarded yellow plastic cake plates and half-empty Solo cups of pop and a thousand dirty forks. On the other side of the room in the doorway that led to the rest of the house, Kale held a video camera in front of his face. He grinned ear to ear as he filmed the festivities of his child's eighth birthday party.

In the corner, beside the refrigerator, Ava sat in a folding chair placed there just for her by Julia a couple of hours before. The girl told "Aunt Ava" she wanted her to be able to see, but to not be in the camera view, since adults hated pictures. Ava obeyed and sat in the chair, an empty cake plate and fork in her lap. Somewhere behind Kale, a door opened and shut and Kale nodded his head to greet Pode, who held a poorly wrapped purple package in his hand. It looked like it had attacked him on the way and Pode had no choice but to strangle it with a ragged string of curly white ribbon.

"Oh, good. Another gift," Shannon joked, smiling at Julia. "Just what you need."

Pode stepped forward and placed the package in front of the girl, glancing briefly and awkwardly at Ava as he did so.

"Thanks, Pode!" Julia's high voice proclaimed as she threw her arms around his neck. He hugged her back. Children loved Pode. Everybody loved Pode.

"It's so pretty." She pulled gently on the ribbon curls before ruthlessly ripping into the paper. Ava laughed, intrigued by the difference between what children and adults assess as beauty. "Oh, cool!" Julia held up a clear plastic package with several bottles of nail polish and fancy silver lettering on the front declaring it to be a "Manicure Kit." The group continued the pattern they had followed with the dozen other gifts and squealed back at her and passed it around the circle to be admired.

"OK, girls," Shannon crossed the kitchen to collect wrapping paper remains from the table. "I think that's it for presents. Jules, why don't you pick out one of your new movies and put it in in the living room?"

"OK!" Julia looked over the toys and clothes and DVD boxes scattered across the table, "Um, this one!" She grabbed the box, hopped out of her chair, and led the other girls at the table around the corner and down the hall. Their little sock-covered feet making muffled padding sounds as their clarion voices talked and giggled and screamed some more. Kale followed them.

Ava crossed the kitchen and added her cake plate to a towering stack. She knew her way around, retrieving the trashcan from under the sink and a new dishrag from a bottom drawer. Separating forks from plates, Ava threw the plates in the trash and the forks in the sink. Pode and Shannon talked behind her as she worked.

"Oh, you don't have to help, Pode. Do you want a piece of cake?" Shannon waved him away as she knelt to pick up the wrapping paper he was reaching for on the faded linoleum floor.

"That's OK. I don't mind." He held a gift bag open for Shannon as she stuffed a wad of shiny pink and purple remnants into it. "Meant to drop her gift by earlier, so I wouldn't crash the party, but the steers I've got behind Dad's house knocked part of the fence down, so we had to go catch them. I hope she likes it. I made Wren pick it out."

"Trust me, she'll have every fingernail and toenail in this house painted by the end of the weekend. Herself, all six of those girls, me, Kale, her baby sisters as soon as Grandma drops them off tomorrow, you, and Ava if you guys stick around long enough. How is Wren? I saw her at the hospital, oh, I guess it's been a week or so ago now and she looked ready to pop."

"About a month left. We keep joking with Jack, telling him they missed a baby or two in the ultrasounds and she's going to have triplets."

"Shan!" Kale's deep voice carried over the girls' twittering. "Do you know where the remote to the DVD player is?" Instantly, Shannon disappeared, the finder of things in a house full of husband and children. It was her job, and their dependence on her search and rescue skills was less annoying and more endearing as the years went by. She couldn't remember a time when she hadn't spent hours each day searching for lost device remotes and left shoes and toy accessories.

The kitchen was quiet, except the occasional sound of a fork clinking against the stainless steel basin of the kitchen sink. Pode pushed his mouth to one side of his face, exposing his single dimple and watching as Ava diligently rinsed silverware and sorted it by type into compartments in the dishwasher.

"Av?"

She stopped and faced him, soap suds dripping off of her elbow.

"You're not going crazy, are you? Cause I'm not sure what I'll do in this podunk town if you go crazy and they put you away somewhere." She smiled, but it was a defeated smile. A sad smile. A smile like someone smiles when they don't know what else to do.

Ava reached for a towel and used it to dry her hands. Taking a couple of steps to the side, she swung the fridge door open and stole a six pack of Coors Light cans from the lowest wire shelf. "You got an hour?"

Pode nodded. "If you mean to talk to you and drink that, I got forever."

Pode tossed his empty beer can through the open sliding glass window stretched across the back of his red Ford and immediately reached toward the floor for a new one. The can landed with a hollow rattle and rolled the length of the scratched pickup bed. He sat in the driver's seat, window all the way down, arm hanging out. In the passenger seat, Ava propped her boots on the dash and reclined her seat as far as it would go. Her window was rolled down all the way, too. Air with the dry cold of fall rushed through the truck. Paperwork from Pode's last purchase of seed, tucked under the wide armrest between them, rustled. Escaped strands of hair from Ava's ponytail blew across her face.

Parked on the highest hill in Flynn County, out the windshield they could see thousands of acres of mostly empty fields lining the river. Straight as a ruler on three sides, each rectangle's fourth side, border formed by the curves and juts of the riverbank, cut in and out at odd angles. On the edge of town near the U.P. Bridge, the silos of the grain elevator reached up into a sky of sparse wispy white clouds. The fat gray cylinders, small from the distance, bunched together like a giant package of Duracells. Another mile off the highway out of town the other direction, the giant white blades of electric wind farm fans swooped in constant graceful motion.

"I've been thinking about New York," Ava spoke quietly, fiddling with the tab on the can she held between her knees.

"You have somebody there who wants to buy more stuff? That's great, Av."

"No." Her soft brown eyes focused somewhere Pode couldn't see. "About moving there."

Pode coughed mid sip and wiped dripping beer off his face with the shoulder of his t-shirt. "You're really thinking about it again?"

"I don't know. Yeah." Ava pulled the band out of her greasy hair and ran her fingers through it, pushing it back over her shoulders. Reaching around her thigh, she opened the glove compartment and rifled around until she found a smashed pack of Marlboro Reds. She shook one out and offered the pack to Pode, who nodded his head "no," but stretched to reach into the front pocket of his jeans. Ava leaned across the console as he produced a lighter and lit her cigarette for her.

"What if it turns out to be just more people in another place? Nothing different from what we have here?"

"It might, but I have to see for myself. You know?"

"Yeah. I know." She hated that he knew her so well.

Pode drank and Ava smoked. The only sounds were of the wind and a single relentless cricket somewhere underneath the truck. It was too early in the day for a cricket. Twilight was still hours away. It must have been disturbed, awoken, and driven from its home. Or hungry. Or mating. Or dying. It was too early in the day for a

46

cricket.

\* \* \*

Ava turned around and the heavy, wet rope hanging down from the handle of the sliding door of the rented moving truck slapped her in the face. Blinking and recoiling, she wiped the dirty water from her cheek, climbed over an extraneous box hanging off the edge of the bumper, and jumped down onto the gravel driveway. The ground was soft from a heavy overnight rain. Ava crossed to the sidewalk where the last remaining odds and ends leaned against each other in piles. Pode stared at the stuff, a beer in his hand, though he was three months away from being legally able to consume one. Behind him, the door to Ava's square, five-room peach-colored house was propped open with a broom handle stuck through the broken screen door hinge. On either side of the prefab set of cement stairs, flower beds full of purple petunias and orange marigolds and white geraniums lifted their bright heads toward the sky, happily quenched.

"Alright. What next?" Pode asked. At first he had tried to orchestrate the packing, but quickly realized it would be better to take a step back and let Ava tell him what heavy thing to carry. Everything he put in the truck, she moved and put somewhere else. Both patient people, only a single yelling match had occurred so far.

"Um," Ava looked around at the few items that were left, a laundry basket of cords, a five foot tall metal floor lamp, a banker's box of notebooks, then up at the few empty spots in the back of the truck box. She breathed heavily. Large rings of sweat formed under her arms and on her back. It was early spring, but in the high eighties by noon. The summer was already predicted to be an especially hot one, though every summer Ava could remember had been an especially hot one.

Inside the house, the rotary phone on the kitchen wall rang. Its harsh metal bell jarred Pode and Ava out of the exhaustive trance they had both fallen into while trying to make a decision about what to do next. The phone rang five times, six times, seven times, and Ava shielded the sun from her eyes with her hand as she frowned at the backdoor.

"I guess somebody wants to talk to me."

Pode nodded and took a seat on the front steps as Ava skipped past him. Through the living room, to the kitchen, the phone kept ringing, eight, nine, ten. On the eleventh ring Ava picked up the heavy lemon yellow receiver and held the top of it to her ear. "Hello?"

"Ava?" her mother's voice was recognizable, but somehow distant. It was as if she laid her phone down on the floor and talked at it from somewhere across the room. It wasn't only physical distance, but emotional distance, too. Words came from the woman's mouth, but their typical conviction was gone.

"Are you OK, Mom?" Ava asked the question before even thinking about it. She wasn't sure she had ever asked her mother if she was "OK" before. There was something wrong. Something so wrong it wouldn't have required the woman's daughter to sense it. A stranger would have been able to tell.

"No, I'm not," Dora May answered, the honesty expected by her daughter, the give in her voice at the end of the statement not. "I have cancer."

The three words didn't compute in Ava's brain. She scrunched up her face, sounded them in her head, repeating only the last one out loud, "Cancer."

"I'm in the hospital in Wichita. They wanted to start my treatments right away, so they sent me straight here." The matter-of-factness that was her mother was back.

Dora May was simply relaying a message in third person. It could have been about anyone and happened to be about herself.

"I'm not there," Ava whispered, guilt filling her. "I didn't know you were sick."

"I didn't know I was sick, either. I thought I had the flu or an infection or something. I didn't say anything to anyone. And it doesn't matter now. It is what it is." There it was, finally. Her mother's stiff rational had fully returned to normal levels.

"I'm so sorry, Mom. I'll be there as soon as I can. I'm on my way right now. Did you call Eddy? I can if . . ."

"No. No, not yet. We'll tell him at some point, but I don't want to worry him with it. You know your brother doesn't handle things like this well, and he has summer classes and an internship and whatever the hell else."

"But he should know."

"He will. Someday. Don't worry about it, Ava. I mean, I don't even want you here, but the doctors say I'll probably need the help. They've already put me in a room. They wanted to start treatments right away. Get here when you can, and if you bring me extra clothes, I would appreciate it. You know I didn't have anyone else to call or I would have called them."

Like a punch in the gut, Ava wasn't her mother's first call. She was her mother's only choice. It shouldn't have been a surprise after a lifetime of selfishness, but somehow it still was. Her mother didn't want her there in what could turn out to be the hardest moment of both of their lives. Ava wished she could blame it on the shock from the serious diagnosis, but knew better than that. Dora May probably thought Ava would get in the way, like she always had. First in the way of Dora May's dreams when she found out she was pregnant with her oldest child. Then in the way of Dora May's day-to-day

49

life as Ava grew to have absolutely nothing in common with her mother. Finally in the way of becoming a disappointment, as Dora May had always hoped her daughter would become a doctor or a lawyer or at least a business partner at the real estate office. Ava had no interest in any of that, though. She would much rather sit in her room and draw all day.

"Well, that's it, I guess. Bye."

"Love you, Mom," Ava whispered, but the line was already dead.

She held onto the telephone receiver long after her mother hung up. Staring into the space in front of her, Ava tried to think of anything she knew about cancer. It was a word mentioned by people when they talked about how their grandparents died. There were so many different kinds. Ava hadn't thought to ask what type her mother had, and Dora May hadn't offered. Ava wasn't entirely sure it even mattered.

"Av?" Pode's voice made Ava jump and drop the phone. It clunked into the wall loudly, swinging from the end of a once coiled cord and leaving a nick in the oak baseboard. He overheard enough of the conversation, read the expression on Ava's face, and made a terribly accurate educated guess about what it all meant. Across the kitchen in three quick steps, Pode's arms went around Ava's frozen body. He held her while she cried.

# 4

Pode gripped the arm rest attached to the passenger door of Baker's truck. His right boot pushed down on the floor as if it might break through, as if he could somehow control the speed of the vehicle with the action. The tires screeched around the curve in Highway 94 and popped over the river bridge at the edge of Flynn. Stomping on the brakes at the very moment the front of the truck aligned even with the pole holding both the city limit sign and a 25 mile per hour speed limit sign, Pode's body lurched forward and he thought he might fly out the windshield and onto the wide, seamed concrete of the bridge.

"Jesus Christ, Baker. You trying to kill us?"

Baker man-giggled, a clear, high hooting. "I had to slow down. Got to obey the fucking law, Wagner. You want Ellis to pull me over?"

"No, but you're going to wreck this thing if you keep driving it like this."

"Shit, what happened to you? You getting fucking old, Pode? You sound like an old man. We only got so many years on this earth. We got to live every fucking one of them to the fullest." Baker barely tapped the gas, and the truck roared like it was angry about the new slowed pace.

"We don't have to live every damn one of them at a thousand miles an hour. What if a dog or something ran out in front of you?"

Baker shook his head, ran a hand through his hair, and ignored Pode's question. "God, life's short. God, it is fucking short. Do you think about that?" Baker didn't wait for Pode to answer before he went on. "I am twenty-four fucking years old and I ain't got nothing. No job. About a million fucking dollars in college loans. Live in a fucking trailer. All I got's this truck. And I wouldn't have it if it weren't for getting laid off from the wind farm and getting that good ol' government check every month."

"Yeah, lots of things gone to shit in the world right now." Pode watched out the window as a couple of boys tackled each other over a football in a front yard of crunchy brown grass. He refused to take an active role in one of Baker's habitual doom and despair dialogues. Baker's parents weren't rich, but they did all right and he may have lived in a trailer, but it was the only trailer house in town with a 42-inch flat screen and a leather sofa.

"Hey, how's Ava doing? You talk to her since the roof thing?"

Pode nodded. "Yeah, yeah, we talked. She's dealing with a lot of stuff, like always, but she's doing better."

As they hit the second block of Main Street, a dusty red car came into view and Baker laughed. "Speak of the devil."

Stopping in the middle of the street, Ava pulled close so her window lined up with Baker's.

"Hey, Av, how the hell are you doing?"

"Good. Heading to Martha's for supper. What are you guys doing?" Ava yelled over the revving engine of the truck. Pode smiled as their eyes connected. She looked better, rested. Her eyes were brighter than they had been the night after Julia's birthday party, and he felt some worry lift. Worry that he hadn't consciously realized was in his mind until it wasn't.

"Gas and beer at the Quick Stop, then country cruising. You want to come?"

Ava hesitated, forgetting both happy and sad, "Yeah.

Let me turn around."

The vehicles pulled away in separate directions, the out-a-car-window, middle-of-the-street form of communication almost as common as a phone call in Flynn.

Entering through the loose swinging glass door in the front of the lone gas station in town, Pode held the door for Baker and Ava as she caught up with the men. Short shelves of candy and miniature bottles of ketchup and motor oil and packages of diapers and crackers filled most of the space inside the red and white tiled building. Two red wooden booths stood against a wall filled with windows overlooking the parking lot. They had recently been vacated by the afternoon coffee drinkers, gossiping the latest news as they played cards.

Baker stopped at the front counter. A rail-thin blonde with a red apron tied across her body looked up from a ragged *Cosmo* with someone else's name and address on the mailing label. Penny McEwing's crystal blue eyes smiled before her baby pink lips did. "Hey, Baker. Hey, Pode. Hey, Ava."

"Copper Penny," Baker joked, the teeth in his smile stained with tobacco, giving the girl grief. Like an older brother to her, Baker had grown up next door. He was the only person she didn't mind calling her by her childhood nickname.

"Doug the slug!" she fired back with a flirty grin.

Pode and Ava headed to the back of the store to a single tall cooler of beer, both of them waving to Penny as they passed.

"Uh, forty in gas. Can of Skoal. Pretty please, pretty Penny." Baker dug through his worn leather wallet until he found three bills and threw them on the counter.

"I'll need to see some ID for the chew." Penny put her hands on her hips, her eyes narrowing. "Cause you don't look old enough."

"Listen, here, young lady." Baker bent across the counter, his face close to hers as she tried to not giggle. "I remember the day they brought you home from the hospital. I seen your little pink face all wrapped up in a blanket. You know what your mama whispered to you when they let me hold you?"

Penny propped her pointed chin on the hands. "Don't let me ever catch you with that Baker boy. That boy is nothing but trouble."

Baker stood up straight. "Damn. You don't really remember that, do you?"

"Nope. She just still says it all the time."

Baker laughed loudly. "She's right. Your mama's dead on right."

Pode and Ava returned to Baker's side, Pode setting a case of Bud Light on the counter for the girl to ring up. Penny took Baker's money and flipped the switch to turn on the pump. The door swung open and Cort Wagner, a slightly taller, considerably skinnier version of Pode strutted through. His jeans were too tight, belt buckle too shiny, chip on his shoulder too big.

"Same goes for Wagners," Baker joked, taking his change and chew from Penny. "Cort . . . land!" Baker playfully punched his friend's younger brother in the arm as he walked out the other door to get his gas.

"Ah, God, why the hell's he got to do that?" Cort rubbed his arm, joining Pode and Ava at the counter. Penny leaned out over the counter and Cort smiled as he matched her lean with a kiss.

"Gahh! Uhh!" Ava and Pode groaned like they were disgusted by the sweet public display of affection. "Not over the beer." Pode slid the cold cardboard case over. He took off his filthy ball cap and whacked his brother with it.

"What time you off?" Cort grinned like an idiot.

"Starla called out, so 8:30 or so. I have to close." Penny frowned.

Pode waved his hand between the kids' faces. "Excuse me, young lovers. May I please bother you with the purchase of this alcohol?"

"Dammit." Court ignored his brother. "How is it she always gets to stick you with the late shifts?"

Ava reached around the couple and stole the magazine out from under Penny, flipping through it as she rested her hip against the counter.

"I don't know. I'm too nice, I guess." Penny shrugged her shoulders and tossed her hair.

Pode glanced back at Ava, who had settled into reading and enjoying watching Cort and Penny be in love. In her mind she could still see them as little kids, trying to follow behind on their bikes. Left in doorways of houses and corners of sheds as lookouts. Sent on missions to steal cigarettes from purses and beer from garages in exchange for passage into forts.

As the pair stole another kiss, Pode sighed, made a fist, and slugged his brother in the same spot Baker had.

"Ow! Goddammit Pode!" Cort took a step back, glaring angrily.

Penny laughed. She passed a hand-held scanner over the barcode on the back of the case of beer. "Nineteen seventy-seven."

"Thank you." Pode over smiled, one dimple appearing, as he handed her the exact change in his fist. "You two have a lovely evening." He nodded to the girl and then his brother, winding his arm up like he might punch Cort again and thoroughly enjoying Cort's flinch away. Ava, her nose in the magazine, followed him out of the store with a backhanded wave.

"Ain't she beautiful, Av?" Baker held a shiny new 12-gauge shotgun out in his hands as gently as if it were a newborn child. Ava glanced up from the magazine spread across her lap. She sat at the end of the tailgate of the black beast reading by the red glow of the nearest tail light.

"Yep. Looks gun-y." She was less than impressed by Baker's most recent unnecessary purchase. "OK, question twenty!" Ava yelled the *Cosmo* quiz to Pode. "Have you noticed your boyfriend/husband kissing differently or wanting different things in bed?"

"Hell yes!" Pode kidded. He drank the end of a can of beer and underhanded it as far as he could into the center of the manmade pond he stood at the edge of. A hundred yards away and with his back turned to Ava and Baker, Pode stuffed his hands deep into the pockets of his jeans.

"I think your man's cheating on you! You scored a nineteen and fifteen to twenty means 'definitely!'"

"I knew it! Bastard." Pode kicked the ground playfully.

"You doing alright, Av?" Baker's voice was as soft and sincere as Ava had ever heard it. "I mean, after the roof thing?"

"Yeah, yeah." Ava closed the magazine and leaned her shoulder against the side of the truck bed. "I miss her. I hate her. And I miss her. And I'm not sure what to do with all of that. But, yeah."

"Well, she was all you had. I mean, outside of us, and God knows we're all fucked up."

"Loveable fucked up."

Baker nodded his agreement with the statement and Ava went on. "How're you doing?"

"Eh, alright. Don't know what the hell I'm doing with my life. Wish I could be OK with that."

"If it makes you feel any better, none of us do."

"Baker! Twenty dollars if you hit that can with your

new toy in one shot!"

Ava looked up and watched the can glitter in the moonlight as it bobbed into the center of pond, pushed by a cold night breeze.

Baker grabbed the gun around the barrel and jogged up the incline to Pode. Ava threw the magazine behind her, into the bed of the truck, and stood on the tailgate to better see the can as it floated to the far bank, slowly filling with water. Looking the gun over, Baker seemed confused so Pode took it from him, popped the safety off, and handed it back. Laughing at Baker, pulling one hand out of his pocket and using it to rub the whiskers on his chin, Pode yelled over his shoulder, "Av, you might as well sit back down and pull up another beer! We could be here all night!"

"Shut up," Baker hissed at Pode, holding the gun up to his shoulder. Pode stopped laughing. Crickets chirped out a constant high rhythm. Toads did the same, only in a lower tone. The breeze moved through the few remaining leaves stuck to the oaks and mulberries along the road with a whirring and rustling. A coyote howled far away, answered immediately by the barking and baying of a pair of hound dogs. Ava closed her eyes and inhaled deeply, as if she might breathe in the sounds as they traveled through the air.

"Bam!" Her eyes shot open in time for her to see circles drift out from the place the bullet pierced the water's surface. Baker missed by five feet. The can sat where it had been, only slightly disturbed as it took a single dip to the side, hit by the last of the radiating waves.

"Ahhahaha!" Pode overreacted, slapping his knee as he bent in half. His laughter now the only sound, the exploding of the shotgun silencing the animals and even, it seemed, the ever-blowing wind.

"Fuck!" Baker stood up straight and held the gun

cockeyed as he examined it. "Fucking sight's off. You spend good money on a thing, it ought to work. A hundred dollars says you can't even hit it."

Pode pulled his hat off and tossed it on the ground. He took the gun, tucked it under his chin, and without hesitation pulled the trigger and hit the can. Gurgling, it disappeared beneath the surface instantly. Pode grinned at Baker and drunkenly took a side step as he held the gun out. Trying not to laugh, his smile flattened into an awkward smirk. "Sight looks alright to me. Might be operator error."

Baker shook his head as he begrudgingly refused to take the shotgun and climbed down the dike. "Fucking keep it!"

Ava jumped off the edge of the tailgate. She rolled her eyes at Pode who followed Baker at a safe distance. It wasn't the first time she'd watched Pode best Baker at shooting, but Baker still hadn't learned in 20 years that Pode was the better of the two at almost everything.

"I can stop by for that crisp green Franklin tomorrow. If that's alright with you," Pode jabbed.

Baker stopped, scowling at Pode over the bed of the truck. "You want to walk back to town?"

"Or, whenever." Pode finally let his one dimpled smile go in the light from open passenger side door and Ava laughed at the boys. "I know you're good for it."

A giant green dinosaur lumbered through soft brown ground, dragging behind it a machine that held compartments full of teeny tiny seeds. Millions of them were plunged into the upturned earth, unassuming specks ready to burst open with life after receiving enough nourishment from nature to sustain their growth. Despite the replacement of the horse with the tractor, the continual advancements in the machinery it pulled behind it, and the biologically engineered improvements in the seeds, the actual plan was as simple as it had been hundreds of years before. Plant a seed. Pray for rain. Watch it grow.

The tractor came to a halt as it rounded the outside corner of the small 60-acre field it was planting. The door swung open and a large man in standard issue farmer jeans, plaid flannel shirt, and Carhartt jacket gingerly departed the ladder of steps. Ed Schaffer pulled his boots up, stepping high through the moist dirt, so as to not sink and trip, more athletic than he looked for his age and build. His brown eyes were flecked with gold, like Ava's. His dark hair highlighted with gray and his face framed by thin crevices. The wrinkles left behind from a long, trying life of heartbreak and addiction.

"I brought you a hamburger and apple pie!" she shouted, holding up a white paper sack.

He smiled a big close-mouthed smile bordered by lines that had been deeper when he was younger and thinner. Ava could barely make out the handsome he had once been. The handsome that she saw in pictures in family photo albums she snuck up from the basement of the farmhouse when her mother went into the office to work on Saturday mornings. Those forbidden albums were all over the living room floor now. No one was around anymore who would deny their existence or force her to put them away.

"So you're a cook?" he joked. The closer he got the stronger the smell of whiskey grew.

"From Martha's," she added. "I have no plan to poison you."

"Phew," Ed smiled again, taking the bag from her and leading her around to the bed of the truck. He lifted the latch and let the tailgate drop, revealing a few bags of wheat seed, odds and ends of tools, and a 40-gallon garbage bag's worth of empty, smashed Keystone cans.

Ava turned her back to the truck and bent her arms at the elbows to lift herself onto the scratched up surface of the tailgate beside her father. "The one with the 'X' on it is mine."

The man handed her the foil-wrapped sandwich on top and then went to work unwrapping and eating his own. They ate in silence. Small talk was of no use to Ava or her father. Among the traits she had inherited from her father, only using words when absolutely necessary was the most obvious one. He was a thinker, mulling over things in his mind for hours before finally speaking and then never saying quite as much as he intended to.

He was done eating first, popping open the plastic container the piece of pie nestled into, holding it out to Ava, though knowing she wouldn't take any. She shook her head, plucking the pickle off the last fourth of her burger and crunching it between her teeth. As the apple pie disappeared one greedy forkful at a time, a question or more a statement rose inside of her until she finally found the nerve to say it. He would be the only one, except maybe Eddy, who understood. If he did.

"I miss Mom." Every time she said these three words, in this sequence, it was like the power of them plunged a knife into her heart.

"She was . . ." His hesitant words twisted the knife, dug it around inside of her until she began to feel imaginary warm blood drip into her stomach.

"What?"

He didn't respond. Instead he pulled a flask out from the inside breast pocket of his jacket and took a long swig. Then a second long swig. Ed gazed at the fieldwork he needed to finish. Patting his daughter on the knee he smiled. "Thanks for lunch." He slid off the tailgate and struggled back through the loose dirt to the John Deere beast.

Ava watched him plod away from her. She had tried talk to him about serious things throughout her entire life with similar results. Dodging, ignoring, offering no reassurance, no words of hope or love, Ava came to a point where she even wished he would grow mad, judge her, criticize her. They had both loved the same woman. They had both lost her, in different times, in different ways. Emotion, though, was not a medium her father dealt in. Why should she think this time would be any different?

Ava strained to see in the glow of her ancient laptop. Tired eyes trying to make out the numbers in the corner of the screen. 1:35 a.m. She knew she should go to bed, but she wasn't tired. She was on a second or third wind and afraid of the strange dreams that took over her resting hours. They didn't make any sense. Her mother, her father, her brother, Pode, other people from town wove in and out of scenes of nonsense. Familiar faces that were not at all scary to her in life haunted her dreams, more in feeling than in action. She could not describe the nightmares or even always remember who was in them. When she woke up alone in the darkness in the middle of the night it was in a cold sweat, a panic attack. Her heart raced, head spun, a full state of distress took over her body and she wouldn't sleep again. She would lay awake in bed for hours, until the sun peeked through the floral print purple curtains in her childhood bedroom.

The screen in front of her listed New York apartments. Queens. The Meat Packing District. Upper West End. She didn't know what any of it meant and no matter how much she read about each area, studied maps of it, there was no way the internet could tell her which part of town was best or if a move to the vast city was the right thing to do. And there was a tight budget to consider. She had $9,000, the value of her mother's possessions split in half after she and Eddy sold their mother's late model Buick. The cancer had bankrupted Dora May, even with decent insurance. The copays and the unforeseen costs and simply living day to day for years without income, the tenacious land and real estate buyer and seller, who spent her whole life in pursuit of success and wealth, died broke.

Ava had an unreliable source of income. Selling her sculptures online, she was discovered by an art gallery in New York that now served as the middle man reselling her artwork. They took 20 percent, so with pieces selling for $300 or $400, once or twice a month, Ava would never be rich. Still she shipped work east, and they deposited money into her account at the State Bank of Flynn. She didn't need much to live on. The farmhouse was inherited, she and Eddy the fourth generation of her mother's family to grow up in it, and outside of food money and gas money, the few hundred dollars a month was enough.

She would speak to the gallery. If they offered her an advance, commissioned work, it would be steady income. She would need a second job, waitressing, house cleaning, data entry. She wanted to live in the city, to be thrown into the whole new world it would present and see if she could survive. The expensive new world it would present, judging from the prices of living choices online. The $9,000 would be depleted in no time, especially if she couldn't find a job immediately, or if the gallery wasn't able to help. And there would be the issue of studio space and supplies and the multitude of other costs involved in starting again in a new place.

The phone rang. It didn't just ring, it clanged. Heavy metal wand triggered to violently beat an equally sturdy steel bell. Ava was startled by the sound. No one she knew ever called the house. And it was too late for a salesman or a politician. The number had been Dora May's and Ava didn't give it to anyone anymore. Ava rose from the couch, took her time moving through the dining room to the kitchen, hoping it might stop before she reached it. She would never know who had called for lack of an answering machine and that would be fine.

It didn't stop ringing, though. It continued and she picked it up.

"Av?" Her brother's cynical voice on the other end didn't wait for her to answer, "Hey, I tried your phone, but it's dead or something. I thought I should call and tell you I'm getting married. I asked Mindy earlier tonight. Actually, she thought I should call you, before you hear it from someone else. Will you tell Dad for us?"

"Oh, Eddy. Wow." Ava didn't know what else to say. The first time she had met the petite blonde was at their mother's funeral a little over four months before. She was quiet, nervous, cried a lot even though she had never met Dora May. Ava had no doubt in her mind that their mother would have hated the girl and she wasn't sure if that made her like her brother's girlfriend more or less. "How long have you been together?" It came out in a different tone than Ava meant for it too, almost accusatory.

"Fuck, really? Really, Ava? Long enough. And no, she's not pregnant, if that's the next question." His indignant reaction was a common one, whether or not Ava said something regrettable.

"I didn't mean it like it sounded. I—I wondered . . ." Ava tried to backtrack.

"Well, anyway, congratulating me would have been the right thing to do there. I can't believe you still haven't gotten any better at this human interaction thing. Anyway, we're thinking next June. At Mindy's father's house in Aspen. You're invited, but if you can't make it, that's fine."

"No, I want to go. I want to." She had never understood her brother. He was all of the parts of their mother and father that confused her mixed together and amplified. He always seemed to be scolding her for something, but she could never figure out what she had done to bring on the contempt. "Congratulations."

"Thanks. Listen, I'm standing out front a bar in the middle of Denver and it's snowing. I need to go back inside. We're here with *friends*." He overstressed the word "friends" either to brag that he had friends or for fear she wouldn't believe him. "Bye."

"Bye," Ava echoed, "Love you." But it was too late. He had already hung up the phone.

Trucks backed up in a row around the edge of Pode's pasture pond, full of folks sitting on tailgates, talking, drinking. It was dark and chilly, but with enough taillight glow shining through the night, artificial twilight could be recreated and with enough cheap beer settled in a stomach, artificial warmth. Baker's truck was in the middle of the row, the windows rolled down, the enhanced stereo booming out a mix of aggressive rap filled with profanities and the rare Willie Nelson tune.

Nearest the pond, in the back of a hopped-up, chromed-out, turquoise 1957 Dodge pickup with gray patches of unfinished body work on one of the rear fenders, Cort and Pode lifted a silver keg shaped like a giant bullet up with bent knees and strained backs. Resting it into a plastic tub, ice crunched and broke and spilled over the sides and into the bed of the truck.

"Whew." Pode put his hands on his hips as he stood up straight. "Either I'm getting older or those damn things are getting heavier. And more expensive." He watched as his brother went to work, skillfully tapping the top of the keg.

"Old," Cort confirmed, without looking up. The keg released with a hiss, ready to be consumed. "Old as shit."

"Goddammit! Old! Fucking! Old as shit!" Baker shouted, overhearing Cort as he approached. The first to pick up the nozzle at the end of a short tube leading to the keg, he helped himself to a red Solo cup of the gold flowing liquid.

"Oh, hey, Shan, looks like we got here just in time." Kale laughed as he threw his arm around Baker's shoulders and grabbed a cup.

"Fucking, Kale! Shannon! Good to see you guys." Baker elbowed Kale in the gut as he slopped beer onto the ground and into the outstretched cup. Filling it to overflowing, he sat his own down and pulled another off the stack. "Shan, I got one for you right here."

"Yeah, we don't make it out much anymore with a house full of little ones. Trying to, though." Shannon smiled as Baker forced the beer into her hand. "Thank you, sir."

Pode hopped off the edge of the tailgate, side arm hugging Shannon as his boots hit the hard ground. "Baker's always been real good at giving away my beer." Shannon and Kale laughed. "How you doing, Shan? Kale?" Letting go of the brunette, who seemed to get prettier every time he saw her, he shook her husband's hand and took a cup for himself.

A crowd started to form around the keg, as word of it traveled the row of tailgates filled with farm kids. Kale and Pode broke away from the throng, sipping from their cups, free hands deep in the pockets of their jeans, shoulders hunched against the wind.

"Good to see you and Shannon." Pode spit into the

dried dying grass. The water in front of him shone in the moonlight leaking out between ragged dark clouds as they moved fast across the sky. "How you been doing?"

He was careful to pose the question so Kale could answer it as vaguely or as honestly as he wanted to. Pode had always looked up to the man. Kale was a couple years older in school, the star quarterback, the leading rebounder, the state track hurdler, the popular, good looking guy. Who was now without a job, or a plan, but with a family of five to take care of. The guy Pode picked up the tab for at Martha's a month earlier, when Kale revealed the 15 bucks in drinks he drank weren't in his wife's tediously planned budget.

"Oh, alright. Alright," Kale answered. He paused, then changed the subject. "You guys done picking corn?"

"Yep, finished about a week ago. Need to get the cattle moved to Mom and Dad's then settle in for a long cold winter of football watching and crockpot cooking."

"You think it'll be a bad one?"

"Yeah, they predict it will be. Grandma says she can feel it. Lot of snow and ice. I can't complain, though. We'll take moisture in any form. Ground needs it." Pode kicked the dirt with the heel of his boot. Dust rose from the spot.

"Thinking about seeing if they'll hire me on at the new jail they're building over in Clay. Shan wants me to try. I hear they pay decent. Drive's not too bad."

"Yeah, might be alright for a while." Pode recognized the reluctance in his friend's voice. He could understand why Kale was balking at the notion of becoming a prison guard.

"Shan's cousin runs the used part of the Ford lot. Selling used cars. She wants me to talk to him, too, but God, I just can't see myself doing that, either." Kale gulped his beer, faster, polishing off the entire cup and wiping his mouth on his flannel sleeve.

"You going stir crazy in the house?" Pode kept his vision forward, over the spring-fed pond. The moon was between clouds and the still water glittered like polished glass where the white circle reflected on the surface.

Kale felt all of his pockets until he found a can of chewing tobacco in his shirt. He fished out a dip and shoved it deep into his lip. "I love my girls, but I shouldn't be the one raising them. What are they going to think of me someday? Playing Mr. Mom? Doing the laundry and cooking and cleaning while Shan supports us all? What are they going to think of their dad?"

"I wouldn't worry too much about that. I think they'll probably just see you did what you had to. You might have swallowed your pride, but you did it for their sake, you know."

"I got sparkly pink toenails right now, Pode."

"I would worry about that." Pode laughed, envisioning the big man in a plush robe with cucumbers slices over his eyes while his three daughters meticulously worked on a pedicure. The ultimate emasculation of the high school football star and former most desirable bachelor in town.

Behind them the sound of an engine as another vehicle pulled into the pasture fell into harmony with the murmur of voices and laughter. Suddenly, shouting, a honked horn, interrupted the peaceful calm. As Pode turned around, he watched two men fall to the ground, a crowd of folks quickly gathering around them. Some trying to break them up. Some trying to egg them on.

"Dammit," Pode said under his breath as he and Kale rushed toward the crowd. Pushing through the circle, Pode's hand went to his forehead as he realized the men on the ground were his brother and his best friend. Blood covering Cort's face, from a nose that looked like it might be broken, he rose to his knees and swung and missed

Baker, who caught the younger man's fist between dirty bloodstained fingers. Twisting his arm, Baker threw Cort to the ground where Cort landed with a thud and a stir of dirt.

"What the hell's going on here?" Pode shouted at the men as he stepped between them. Shorter, but wider than both, carrying strength in his shoulders and chest, Pode solidly stood his ground. Cort paced away then quickly tried to dart around his brother for another round with Baker. Pode caught Cort at the waist with one arm, wrapping the other around his arms, clearly the stronger of the two. Across the oblong circle of friends, Kale was by Baker's side, holding onto his upper arm, ready to pull him back if he tried to get anywhere near Cort again.

"What the hell happened here? What the hell is wrong with you?" Pode let go of Cort with a shove away from Baker and Kale, toward the water. Looking from one bloodied face to another, Pode tried to calm his racing heart as he repeated his question. "What the hell is wrong with you?"

All four men were breathing heavily. Baker held his hands against his chest, left knuckle busted open from the punch delivered to Cort's face. Blood gushed out of Cort's nose, rapidly soaking his shirt. He spit a mouthful of it onto the ground, coughed, and once again made a pass in Baker's direction. Catching him from behind, Pode lifted him and tossed him as hard as he could over the edge of the pond. Rolling down the bank and splashing into the water and weeds, it took Cort a second to climb to his feet. He shook water from his head and arms and he leaned over, hands on his thighs, exhausted and finally ready to give up.

Penny emerged from the crowd, her blue eyes even wider than normal, tears and cheap black mascara streaming down her face. She looked at Pode without speaking a word and he could tell from her expression that whatever transpired between the men involved her.

"Your fucking arrogant ass of a brother grabbed her arm. Yelled at her! I didn't like the way it was going down, so I hit him in the fucking face!" Baker yelled, taking a step forward. Kale tightened his grip.

"You need to mind your own goddamn business!" Cort shouted back in a nasally voice filled with pain.

"That girl is like my little sister." Baker raised his hand, pointing and yelling, "You hurt her I will fucking kill you!"

"Whoa, whoa, whoa." Pode waved his arms, shook his head, not sure if he was more mad or disappointed. Taking a step closer to Cort and Penny, Pode frowned. "You hurt her?"

Cort's tough exterior faded as his older brother's stare bore through him. He had never seen Pode in a fight, but he had watched him break up a good 20 of them. He had never even seen Pode really angry. And he didn't want to. "No. I—I—might of grabbed her arm or something."

Penny jumped in in his defense. "He was mad at me. Pode, he was mad at me and he had every right to be."

"He grab your arm?" Pode asked.

"Maybe—not hard. It didn't hurt."

The older brother turned on the younger one. Cort stumbled backward a couple of steps, one boot splashing into the water. "You don't touch her, or any other woman. You understand me? We were raised by the same the father and he taught us the same set of rules, and he will be absolutely disgraced if he ever finds out what happened here tonight. I don't know what the hell she did, but it don't matter because if I ever even hear about you laying another finger on her, Baker won't be the one threatening to kill you. You understand me?"

Cort looked terrified, believing every single word that

came out of Pode's mouth. The pain in his nose was sinking in, too, and making him nauseous. "Yeah. Yes, Pode. I got it."

"Apologize to her."

Fighting the urge to vomit, Cort's hand went to his face and he talked through his fingers. "Sorry, Pen. I'm so sorry."

Penny nodded her head, accepting his apology. She rushed to his side to take his other hand. Pode looked up, eyes shooting around a crowd that rapidly dispersed as a result of his glare. Face set, Pode reached for Cort and helped the girl pull him out of the pond and across the open space to the row of trucks.

"Wait," Cort slurred as he stopped and took a step away from them both. Doubling over, he threw up beer and black blood mucus. Wobbling as he stood back up, Pode grabbed his arm and steadied him. In the light from the vehicles, he used the sleeve of his own shirt to wipe Cort's face and examine his nose. The bottom half of it protruded out at the wrong angle and Pode himself felt queasy.

"Shan?" Pode called, but she was already at his side.

Shannon squinted in the darkness to see Cort's face better. "It's out."

"Yep, looks like it."

"Let's sit him down somewhere in case he passes out. You hold his head, I pop it back?"

"Yep." Pode swallowed hard.

Baker's truck was the nearest to them, but Pode tried to steer Cort past it. Cort's body sagged to the side as if he might collapse, though, and Pode managed to lean him back on the Chevy before he had to pick the younger man up off the ground. Baker was already sitting on the tailgate, guzzling whiskey from a bottle someone produced after the fight. A couple of handkerchiefs and ice from the keg bucket were bound tight around his hand at Shannon's instruction.

Cort blinked a few times and sat, coming to a bit as he felt the cold metal of the tailgate on his legs through the denim of his jeans. Baker took another long swig of the liquor and without a word swung the bottle out, into Cort's chest. Cort dropped his head, his eyes glazed over. Struggling to take it, he managed to wrap his hand around its neck and raise it to his lips, gulping as if it were water. He was at least still alert enough to realize it would help numb the pain.

Making eye contact with Shannon, Pode took the bottle from Cort and set it between two bumps in the tailgate. In one swift movement, Pode held the sides of Cort's head at the same exact same time Shannon grabbed Cort's nose with her fingers and wrapped her other hand around the back of his neck and jerked the head and the nose in different directions.

"Ahhhhh!!" Cort yelled, flailing his arms and falling over sideways into Baker's lap as Pode and Shannon jumped back. The hurt, punctuated by a moment of unbearable intensity, was now easing into a duller ache as the bones in his nose fell back into alignment with the rough coaxing from Shannon. Cort groaned as Baker elbowed him back into a seated position. Penny, who had been standing back a few feet to give the nurse room, rushed to hold Cort's hand.

"If that doesn't stop bleeding, he needs to go to the hospital." Shannon looked at Pode and Penny with concern. "Penny, you find something to fill with ice and hold on there?" Penny nodded and took off toward the keg.

"I'll take him home with me, watch him tonight." Pode picked up the bottle of whiskey and wiped the rim with the hem of his undershirt, the only piece of clothing he could find not coated in dirt or blood. He handed it to Shannon, who took it, tipped it back, and drained it without so much as a cough.

Weaving across the center line and back to the ridges in the asphalt on the shoulder, Ellis recognized the dented white pickup from a mile away. If there was one saving grace to the almost certainly drunk driving, it was the speed at which it was barely happening. Eight miles an hour probably wouldn't kill anyone on the deserted stretch of road, but the swerving might catch someone coming from the other direction off guard.

The officer flipped the switches on the dash of his cruiser for the lights and the siren and pulled out of the dirt drive off the highway. Catching the pickup in no time at all, Ellis followed at a safe distance, patiently waiting for the man behind the wheel to notice. Pulling to the side, barely, the back half of the truck still in the driving lane, it crawled to a stop and lurched forward as the driver took it out of gear.

Ellis left the lights in the police car on to signal to others who would be staring into the setting sun as they came around Coin's corner on their way into town. Marching down the shoulder, Ellis could smell alcohol through the open driver's side window. Ed cleared his throat, grabbed the front of his jacket to straightened it, looked forward through the windshield, and acknowledged the officer's approach with a slight tilt of his head, but no direct look at Ellis's face.

"Mr. Schaffer." Ellis knew the stories. Ed's parents were killed in a car wreck when he was barely out of high school. Dora May was the love of his life, but she cheated on him with nearly every other man in town. Ed hadn't been the luckiest soul over the years, and the deputy sympathized. To cope with his losses, he drank too much, but he did usually stay home. Ellis had never seen him behind the wheel in this state.

"You were swerving all over the road, there. Going way under the speed limit."

"Sorry, Officer," Ed mumbled. He looked 70 years old. His complexion was pitted, shoulders bent. Addiction added 25 years to his looks and was without a doubt taking 25 off his life span.

"You been drinking, sir?"

"Couple of beers, maybe."

Ellis put his hands on his hips and looked up into the sun through his dark shades. "You know you can't drive after drinking." Ed nodded his head in agreement. He seemed beaten, ashamed. Ellis felt sorry for him and more than anything, he felt sorry for Ava. "Tell you what, why don't we leave your pickup here and I'll give you a ride down the road to your house? You can walk back and get it when you're sober."

"Thank you, officer." Ed nodded again and opened the door to climb out. Following Ellis back to the squad car, Ed hesitated and Ellis motioned to the passenger side. Easing into the front of the car, the older man watched as the younger man drove his truck completely off the road into the ditch. Ellis joined Ed in his police car and then cautiously pulled out onto the empty road.

They rode in silence, the mile down the highway and the three down a dirt road leading off the highway at the city limits of Flynn. The driveway to the modest beige house was long and bumpy. There was a time when it was grated and covered with rock, but now deep ruts stretched the length of it, only missing in a low washed-out spot. Ed never called the landlord for anything and so the landlord assumed he was taking care of it himself, or didn't care as long as the rent checks came on time. And even when they didn't, there was forgiveness, since Ed was renting from his second cousin.

A pile of red brick, pieces of leftover ironwork, and a barren patch of dirt from a forgotten flower bed decorated the front yard. The house was plain, even ugly. The front window too big and set off-center, a later addition with different framing than the other windows and the front door. Originally, it was a modular home. One built at a factory in Wichita and brought in in two pieces on a flatbed truck and set on a poured concrete foundation. Over the years several changes were made, a washroom added to the back, the living room in the front elongated. They were cheaply, crudely done, though. The paint peeled from the siding on the newer parts exposing flecks of shiny metal, and the roof leaked at the seams.

The police cruiser turned into Ed's driveway, and both men spotted the Mustang at the same time. Ava stopped in front of the house and stepped out of the car. Ellis parked a foot from its bumper. He and Ed exited the car in starkly contrasting fashion. The officer stood straight and tall in a clean pressed uniform. Ava's father hunched in dirty ripped jeans and a faded jacket.

Ed stumbled past Ava without a word to her. Watching him go, both Ava and Ellis cringed as Ed tripped on the top porch step and caught himself against the metal screen door. A groan emanated from the man, a loud creak from the door. Ava sighed, turned back to her car, and leaned the driver's seat forward, stretching to reach paper bags of groceries in the back. Setting one on the ground, she retrieved a second. Ellis hustled to her side and reached for the sack on the ground the same time Ava did. Awkwardly holding both bulky bags with her body, she swung her hip into the open car door and it slammed shut.

"I got it," Ava said as Ellis's outstretched arms tried to relieve her of the load. "Thank you, officer." She talked as she crossed the yard. Ellis followed her like a puppy. "And I don't know where you found him, but I guess I should thank you for giving him a ride home."

"Oh, you're welcome. You're welcome. Let me get the door." He tried to beat her up the steps, but Ava was already on the porch. She used the wall to prop up the heavier of the sacks as she held the shiny dented door with the toe of her boot.

"Or not." Ellis took a step back. "Well, I guess chivalry is dead."

Ava stopped halfway through the doorway, not used to having a man's or anyone else's help. She was the hard worker, the protector. She took care of herself and her own and didn't ask for anything from anyone. Even Pode knew better.

"Chivalry is dead? You should have arrested him. Thrown his ass in jail. Letting somebody wreck and kill people isn't very chivalrous."

Ellis pulled off his glasses under the shade of the front porch. "I, uh—it ain't that easy, Ava."

Ava met his eyes. Squinty, somewhere between annoyed and thinking, his ivy eyes conveyed the other side of the story. She had never thought about how many people in town he had probably pissed off by enforcing a rule instead of letting something slide. The man surely had no friends.

"Sorry. For being so critical. I wouldn't want your job for anything in the world."

Ellis smiled, his mouth closed, but deep, knowing lines forming on either side of his face. She had seen him smile before, but this was the first one that felt genuine. "Huh, yeah. You, Ava Schaffer, might be the most honest person I have ever met in my life."

Ava scrunched her lips to the side, hiked the bag in her grasp further up her hip. "Sorry. For that, too."

"No, no. I like it. It's—refreshing." The police officer's mouth hung open, enthralled with her in a way she didn't know how to react to.

"At the risk of being too honest, again, these bags are really heavy."

Ellis jumped and reached for the door. She let him hold it for her.

Ava escaped into the house. Through the partially open door, a smell hit Ellis, of dust, mold, rot. Peering into what had once been a living space in the house, all he could see were piles of papers and objects and trash. A path snaked across the room, not much wider than Ava as she returned through the overwhelming clutter. Trying to pretend like he hadn't been staring at the mess, Ellis pulled the door open again, and Ava let him hold it for her a second time.

"Do you . . ." Ellis tried unsuccessfully to form a cohesive sentence. "Are you free sometime? Friday? I'm off and I wondered . . ."

It was painful, but somehow charming to watch the tall man so nervous. Ava helped him. "Want to grab a drink at Martha's?"

"Yes."

"Sure," Ava shrugged her shoulders. "What time?"

"I'm off at 7, so I'll need to go home and shower and change and," Ellis stopped. He was talking to himself, not to the woman standing in front of him. "You don't need to know all that, do you?"

"No." Ava raised her eyebrows. "So, 8 or so?"

"Eight." Ellis let out a heavy breath or relief and smiled wide.

Ava smiled back. "See you then."

Ellis tipped his hat to her, which at any other time would have been a move Ava would have laughed out loud at. Old fashioned, ridiculous. He was trying so hard, though, and seemed to live by a different set of rules than the other men she was ordinarily around. Just because she wasn't accustomed to "chivalry" as he called it, didn't mean she didn't like it.

As the cruiser backed into a Y-turn, Ava reentered the maze inside the house. Breathing shallowly through the musty awful smell emanating from the piles, she unpacked the grocery sacks on the small space of kitchen cabinet that remained clear. Opening the refrigerator, she shoved a mix and match package of lunchmeat rounds and a carton of milk onto the bottom shelf, shifting the bottom to top hoarded food over. She stared at the mess, wanting to take an arm and sweep it across each shelf and into a trash bag and carry it away to the dump. The silent wrath of her father, from the last time she had that same urge the week after her mother was diagnosed was more than she ever wanted to tangle with again, though. He locked the door. Wouldn't let her in. Wouldn't talk to her. Avoided her in town. For an entire month.

Ava pulled boxes of cereal and a loaf of bread and other items out of the second bag and left them to fill the open counter space. She folded the paper bags and looked around hopelessly before tossing them on top of the nearest overwhelming stack. Moving through the narrowed hallway to the back bedroom, Ava stopped and watched from the doorway for a moment before entering.

A fortress he had created for himself by walling in every other part of the house, her father's bedroom was tidy. This was where he lived. All of his time spent in this one room. When he was not working in his workshop out back or eating at Martha's or drinking at the VFW Club, he could be found in his burgundy arm chair, watching the television propped on top of an antique dresser. Outside of a basket of dirty laundry in the corner and a Playmate full of ice and beer, the floor in the room was clear. Ed zoned out, a half-empty Keystone can on the nightstand beside him.

"I'm taking off, Dad," Ava yelled over the deafening sound of the television.

He nodded his head. He still hadn't looked at her.

Ava started to leave, but remembered Eddy's call. "Oh, Eddy's getting married. To that girl he brought back to Mom's funeral."

Ed's brow furrowed. "The redhead?"

"No, he's not with her anymore. This one's blonde? She cried a lot at Mom's funeral? They're having the wedding in Colorado next summer."

Her father nodded slightly, never looking away from the screen. She couldn't tell if he had actually taken in the knowledge or not in his foggy alcohol haze. In Ed's defense, Eddy did go through girlfriends pretty quickly, and a couple of the previous ones had had red hair.

Studying her father, she began to feel pity for him and that was how she knew it was time to leave. "Love you," Ava mumbled as she left, twisting her way back through the piles of junk and out of the house.

Kris Wagner, a petite woman of 45 with colored brown hair carefully sculpted into a dated hairstyle, stepped back from the kitchen stove. Except for the few wrinkles that popped out when she laughed or smiled or strained, her face was still full of youth, though it had been decades since she herself had been a child. Married to the love her life the weekend after their high school graduation, she was a mother seven months later and a mother of three by her twenty-third birthday. It was as if she had grown up with her children. Her family was her life, keeping her young in her heart even as her first grandchild was only weeks away from entering the world. Using a kitchen towel to wipe sweat from her brow, Kris fork tested the tenderness of the boiling potatoes in the pot in front of her. They were ready to strain and mash with butter and whole milk.

Her daughter, Wren Baker, leaned uncomfortably to the side in a kitchen chair. An orange t-shirt that belonged to her husband stretched over eight and half months of pregnant belly. Dark eyes and hair, the younger woman's porcelain pale complexion was dull and tired. She was in the kitchen to help her mother, but a few minutes into the peeling of the potatoes, she was exhausted and had to sit. A trashcan, topped with a layer of yellowing brown peeling strips, still sat in the middle of the kitchen floor beside her, and Wren found herself with barely enough energy to observe her mother assemble the rest of the meal.

"Couple minutes more for the gravy and then I think we're ready," Kris chirped happily.

Thick white goodness dotted with pepper bubbled in a skillet beside the pot of freshly mashed potatoes. After cooking three meals a day from scratch for two and half decades for a husband and three kids and the many, many people welcomed into her house, it seemed she should hate it. The cooking had morphed into another form of love, though. Not a woman to gush sentimental thoughts into a handwritten card, Kris instead poured her love into the filling in the legendary apple pies she dropped off on front porches and left on passenger seats of cars of neighbors she knew were going through tough times.

"I'll go tell everybody," Wren's voice strained as she used the side of the table and the back of a chair to hoist herself up.

"Oh no, dear. Rest. I can."

"I need to walk, Mom." Wren ambled across the kitchen. She used the doorframe to balance as she climbed down the steep steps off the back porch of the two-story farmhouse. The young woman's initial excitement over her pregnancy with her first child was wearing thin. Now each day seemed like an eternity. Every muscle in her body ached. Everything she did, she did with great effort and strict limits—sleeping, sitting, walking. She didn't want to wish away time, but the enthusiasm she felt over meeting her son was so all consuming she could not think of anything else.

The men were standing at the corner of the drive, beside an enormous gray metal shed where her father and brother kept their farm machinery. A dusty red combine sat beside the open side doors. The corn header was attached, but ready to be disassembled and cleaned and put away for the winter. Pode pointed as he talked, though Wren couldn't hear what he was saying. Henry Wagner, their father, was nearly identical to his son in stature, with extra width across his shoulders and chest. They also had the same kind face, but the elder Wagner's forehead and cheeks were traced with deep lines around his mouth and eyes. And his eyes were not soft gray like Pode's, but instead a deep, black-brown. Dark eyes his daughter, but neither of his sons, had inherited. His hair was still brown, except at the temples where it was speckled with gray and cut short to neatly frame his tanned face.

Henry's hands were in the pockets of his jeans, button-down long-sleeve shirt tucked in. A thick belt and polished boots both the same color of sable brown seemed a bit too dressed up for a farmer, but like other professional men, Henry took pride in his work. He dressed with respect for his role.

Wren's husband, Jack Baker, looked especially tall and thin standing between the two Wagner men, a striped polo shirt hanging off his shoulders. He followed Pode's pointed hand with a pointed hand of his own. Wren crossed the gravel drive and placed herself between her husband's body and his outstretched arm. Jack looked down and smiled, wrapping his arm around her and squeezing her tight. The mother of his future child smelled wonderfully maternal to him, a mix of the scents of vanilla hand lotion and raw vegetables.

"Mom says lunch is ready."

Henry pulled his hand out of his pocket and consulted his watch. "Noon. On the dot."

"You could set your watch by the woman." Jack smiled.

"I set my whole life by her thirty years ago." Henry nodded to his son-in-law. "Smartest thing I ever did."

Jack's smile grew as he pulled Wren closer to his chest. "Couldn't agree more, sir."

The group set off back toward the house, unwilling to meet the wrath of Kris if they weren't ready to eat when she was ready to put food on the table. She got up at dawn, made three pies, drove into town and attended church and sang in the choir, labored for two hours in the kitchen while they drank coffee and read the morning paper and walked around the farm enjoying the crisp fall air. The least they could do was be on time for Sunday dinner.

Grumbling into a lower gear as it turned into the Wagners' drive, the Mustang cruised slowly past. Ava parked between Pode's old red Ford and Cort's older blue Dodge. Slamming the door shut, she waved to everyone and smiled specifically at Pode as she joined them on their hike up the long sidewalk.

Ava and the three men stopped on the porch to remove their boots and Pode his cap. Like clockwork, they went to work helping Kris, no need to be asked or instructed. Wren and Jack picked up plates and forks and

81

began setting the oak dining room table in the next room. Pode walked through the dining room, to the living room in the front of the house to help his grandmother, Granny Wagner, out of the blue floral upholstered glider in the corner. It was where she spent the majority of days, alternating between watching television and nodding off. Ava carried glasses of water back and forth through the arched doorway between the kitchen and dining room, placing one at the top of each place setting at the table. Henry helped his wife with the food. Kris followed him, throwing a flower-adorned stone trivet under each hot dish so they wouldn't scar her great-grandmother's table.

"You know where your brother went to?" Henry looked up and around the room, the first to realize they were missing Cort and Penny. Nobody could remember having seen them for a couple of hours.

"No," Pode answered simply, supporting the barely there weight of his fragile grandmother as she eased back into a heavy wooden chair at the head of the table. "That good, Granny?" Pode asked loudly as he pushed the chair under the table.

"Yes, yes, thank you, dear." The woman, who was fast approaching 90, spoke solidly. Her voice in great contrast to her fragile looks.

"I'll go see if I can find him." Pode nodded to his father, stopping to put his hand on Jack's shoulder. "But if there isn't any chicken fried steak left when I get back, somebody has some explaining to do."

Jack laughed. "Hey, no promises, buddy. We're pregnant, so I'm eating for two right now."

Wren rolled her eyes as she finished the last place setting.

Pulling his boots back on, Pode didn't bother to unbunch his jeans from the tops of them. He skipped down the back porch steps and stopped at the end of the drive, hands going into his pockets as he tried to figure out where Cort and Penny might be. He also wondered which extreme state he might find them in. Fighting or fucking. Either way it was probably not something he wanted to walk up on.

"Cort!" Pode yelled, rounding the corner of the machine shed and taking the dirt road past the pasture a hundred yards. As he crossed the clearing between the road and the hedge brush, Pode heard the wind rippling the river before he could see the water through the prickly tree line of crab apples and thorny pines. Fall had already forced most of the leaves to the ground. Only a few stragglers clung in clumps on trunks.

"Cort! Penny?" Pode turned sideways and slipped through the storied opening in the underbrush. He spotted Penny sitting on the petrified tree trunk in the faux beach hideaway that had seemed to him so much grander in childhood. Pode had wandered to the clearing to sit on the same trunk a thousand times, usually to contemplate life and often with Ava or Baker or Shannon for company.

At the edge of the creek, Cort stood with arms straight at his sides. The expression on his face paired with the remnants of two black eyes, was hauntingly blank.

"Penny?" Pode could see tears on her face. "Penny, you alright?" He glared at the back of his brother's head.

"Goddammit, Pode. We're sort of in the middle of something here," Cort spoke quietly, but aggressively.

"Everybody's inside. We're ready to eat. Dad sent me after you guys. You know he'll be pissed if you don't make it up to the house in the next couple of minutes." Pode looked from Cort to Penny and then back again.

"We might as well tell him." Penny's voice was ragged. Dark circles under her puffy, bloodshot eyes made her look as if she hadn't slept for days. Cort was silent, so

Penny went on. "Pode, I'm pregnant."

"And I don't even know if it's mine." Cort's words were strangled. He put his hands on top of his head and paced away.

"It is." Penny stood up adamantly repeating an argument Pode could tell she had already said many, many times. "I screwed up. I flirted with a guy in Clay last month, but I didn't touch him. I swear I didn't. You know how rumors get around, though. Somebody's cousin's friend's ex-girlfriend or something saw us together and word got back to town." She was pleading her case to Pode now, having given up Cort. "Cort's the only guy I've ever been with. I've only ever kissed two other guys before him. I swear. And when I was flirting I was mad. Cort keeps blowing me off to go drink, so I thought I'd get him back and that was a bad idea. I knew it was when I started doing it." She looked right at Cort, directed the comment at him. "I swear I did not know I was pregnant then."

"You're sure? You been to a doctor?" Pode's voice was barely above a whisper. Penny, rising to stand before him, looked absolutely overwhelmed. A 17-year-old preacher's daughter about to learn more about the world in her young life than she had ever imagined she would to this point.

"No. I haven't been to a doctor. But I'm two months late. And I've peed on three sticks and they were all plusses. Cort saw them." She collapsed into sitting on the trunk again, defeated.

"What the hell am I going to do, Pode?" Cort's tune changed, the shock of the facts in front of him finally beginning to sink in.

"Uh," Pode was in a state of shock of his own. "Well, you want my advice? Marry her. See if Callahan will hire you on full time. Save the money you spend on beer and cigarettes. Get your shit together and get ready to be somebody's dad."

Cort and Penny both stared at Pode wide eyed. Two lost sheep. They hadn't processed that far, neither of them once thinking about the future in their entire short lives. All of a sudden it was laid out in front of them. It was terrifying, but it was possible. Millions of people had done it before. Their own parents. Maybe it wasn't the life they would have planned for themselves had they ever actually made a plan, but it was a life, not even a bad life, and they could fight it or they could embrace it.

The brush at the end of the trail from the yard parted and Ava emerged. She yelled from the edge of the mini forest. "Your father isn't too happy with you two. He's been staring at a plate of chicken fried steak and potatoes and gravy for a good ten minutes now. If he has to ask your mother to reheat it, I'm pretty sure he'll kill you all." Nobody talked, or even moved. "What's going on? Pode?"

Pode shook his head, waved her away and Ava realized there was a vicious seriousness about the situation she couldn't see from the distance.

"Uh, OK. We will start without you." Nodding back at Pode to let him know she understood, Ava escaped to the other side of the brush without coming any closer.

Granny was sleeping peacefully. Head lulled to the side. Fork still held tightly in her left hand. A couple of spoonfuls of potatoes and gravy and a bite of a roll eaten. She shifted, but didn't wake at the sound of the back storm door slamming shut. Everyone else was nearly done with their food, the Sunday dinner conversation sparse with the obvious emptiness of three seats. Pode entered the dining room first, sitting down heavily between Ava and Wren. Reaching for the worn stainless pot that held the mashed potatoes, he filled his plate, pretending he was unaware of the rest of his family at the table and their fixated eyes.

Pode was saved as Cort and Penny took the two empty spots across from him. Handing the pot across the table to his brother, Cort was now the one not noticing the quiet and the stares. Offering the potatoes to Penny, the girl didn't move. She looked at her lap, upset beyond functioning. Scooping out a big hunk of potatoes and placing them on her plate for her, the pattern of Pode taking something, passing it to Cort, and Cort adding it to Penny's plate without her assistance continued until all of their plates were full.

Eating as if nothing was wrong, Pode pointed. "Av, could you please hand me that tub of butter?"

Ava picked up the yellow container with the smiling Holstein cow on the side of it, happy to end the awkward hush. "Sure, here you go."

"Thank you," Pode nodded as he took it from her and used his steak knife to cut and butter his roll.

A few more almost unbearable moments of utter silence passed, and suddenly Granny jumped, her movement surprising everyone. Forks clattered against stoneware plates. Henry's knee hit the underside of the heavy table. Jack coughed into his hand. Granny frowned, her narrow eyes slits under her heavily wrinkled forehead. She focused her attention on Cort, then Penny, who had finally begun to pick at her steak, eating bits of crusty coating fallen off the whole.

"What did I miss?" The old woman tilted her head slightly to the side, and spoke directly to Penny. "You know, dear, there's far worse things in this life than having a baby."

Wren and Jack looked at each other. Kris gasped. Henry spit water onto the table in front of him. Penny's head went into her hands. Cort froze, open mouthed, looking at Granny with disbelief. She hadn't missed a thing.

"You hand me the salt and pepper, Av?" Pode asked, breaking the tension.

"Sure." Ava reached for the glass shakers sitting in front of Wren.

"Thank you."

"You're welcome."

Pode gazed vacantly at the black and white television above the bar and absentmindedly twirled an empty shot glass with his left hand. He could barely hear it above the crowd noise of Friday night at the only bar in town and the screen was blurry, but he didn't know if it was the age of the television or his fifth shot of tequila that made it that way. A seat sat empty between Pode and Rodg who was also hunched over staring at the TV. Fatter, older but otherwise alarmingly similar to Pode in the way he sat and checked out from the world. He was drunk, too, but beer drunk, not liquor drunk. Philosophical drunk, not sloppy drunk.

"Petrichor."

Pode scowled at the TV, the young drunk not taking the conversation starting bait from the town drunk.

"Smell after the rain," Rodg continued. "Word of the day in the *Eagle* this morning. How do you suppose I lived fifty-two years and never heard that word?"

"'Cause it don't ever rain here,'" Pode answered, his words beginning to grow slurry.

"Ha, hahaha!" Rodg's booming laugh filled the noisy Friday night bar. He shook his head, glanced at Pode, and shook his head some more.

Martha tottered back and forth behind the bar, bringing with her several bottles of booze from the locked rear storage room. Pode turned his attention to her, intently watching as she pulled pour spouts out of empty bottles, rinsed them in the deep stainless steel sink and popped them into new full bottles of liquor. Martha looked up, feeling Pode's eyes on her. "You got a ride home tonight, Wagner?" Her tone was not that of a lecturing mother, but instead a good friend, who had seen him drunk enough times to know when to intervene.

It took him a second to realize she was talking to him and then, shaking himself out of the alcohol induced fog, Pode tried to focus. "Auh, yah—"

"I'll give you ride home if you need one," a sickening sweet woman's voice interrupted. Pode turned his head with great effort and found an alarmingly scrawny Tina leaning into the space between himself and Rodg. Greasy hair fell into her face. A lit cigarette perched between the fingers of her left hand, a fresh gin and tonic balanced in her right. She had graduated high school the year after his mother.

"Tina, you leave that poor drunk boy alone." Rodg looked from one of them to the other, "Unless he don't want to be left alone. Then—uh—never mind me."

"Hey, baby, you want to get out of here?" Tina leaned in to whisper in his ear. Her breath reeked of Pall Malls and Seagram's and made his gag reflex contract.

Pode had fought her advances before, but he had never been quite so drunk around her. Or quite so lonely. He planned to stop for supper and maybe a couple of drinks then to head home to watch the game, but one drink led to another and another and another. Now the young man was content to watch the scenery spin around him as he guzzled alcohol and forgot about all of the pressing commitments in his life. The news of his little brother's baby, the lack of moisture in the ground, how he would feed the cattle all winter, most of all, the thought of Ava leaving town, floated away down a river of Cuervo.

Tina grabbed his thigh. Pode jumped, though his reaction time was considerably slowed. "Come on, sweetie, we can walk to my house from here." Her thin dry lips pecked him on the cheek.

Across the bar, the front door opened and shut, but no one noticed because the crowd swelled to a wild, yelly mess. Ava scanned the room, but didn't see Ellis anywhere. She fought through the crowd, pulling her canvas jacket off along the way. In one swift move, she adjusted the cleavage peeking out of the top of her tight kelly green dress as she pushed the straps back up on her shoulders. Her hair was down, straight, eye makeup thick, dark, earrings huge, sparkly. From the knees up she might have been able to pass for a club goer in a big city. On her feet, though, were the jet black boots, doing their best to confuse the rest of the outfit.

"Ava," she heard his voice behind her as a hand wrapped around her forearm. She turned around to find her chest an awkward few inches from his face. Ellis sat at the table she had been standing with her back to. "Saved you a chair."

She took the chair, dodging an out-of-control cue ball as it bounced off the edge of a pool table and rolled past her feet. Immediately she noticed the tall glass of ice water in front of her date. "I hope you haven't been here too long. You should have ordered something without me."

Clocks had never mattered to Ava. Times were suggestions to her, guesses. She guessed she was 20 minutes late, but Ellis knew, from the wrist watch he never took off, it was closer to 35.

"Oh, no, you're fine. I'm not much of a drinker, anyway. I thought I'd wait for you," he smiled, revealing his row of pearly whites. "You look beautiful."

Compliments about her looks never set well with Ava. Generally she put them off by ignoring them or quickly changing the subject. Tonight, though, she found it nice to hear a compliment and didn't deflect it. For almost three years she had barely left the house, forgot about things like jewelry and make up. Ava wasn't sure if she remembered how to cross her legs in a skirt without flashing everyone across the room from her, but she was about to find out.

"Thanks, you look nice, too. In something other than the cop—stuff," Ava answered his smile with a smile of her own. "Oh, my God. Is that from . . ." she reached out toward the fresh scar on Ellis's forehead, but stopped short of touching it. The hat he'd worn the day she saw him at her father's house must have been low enough to cover it. It looked painful and raw, in the beginning stages of healing.

The light skin of his face flushed a bit. "Yeah, it looks worse than it is. It didn't really hurt."

"I have to be careful where I leave my invisible shovels." The corner of Ava's mouth twitched, but the joke fell flat and drifted past the officer.

"Hi, guys." A high school girl Ava vaguely recognized as someone's younger sister plopped two menus in front of them. "What are you drinking?"

"Oh, let's see, I think I'll take a . . ." Ellis's voice faded away as Ava recognized Pode's back at the end of the bar. The most disgusting woman in town was putting her hands all over him and though he didn't encourage, he also didn't push Tina away. Ava stood without thinking and crossed the room with intent that forced the crowd to notice her. People in her path grew silent, stepping out of the way. Behind her, Ellis turned and he and the young waitress watched. Tina's head jerked up, like a surprised rat caught in the light by a late night kitchen raider, at first not recognizing the pretty young thing in the bright colored dress.

"Pode?" Ava placed a hand on his arm and he looked at her, his eyes fuzzed over. As he focused in on her, he stopped spinning the shot glass on the bar and held it still in his hand.

"Av?" Her beauty sobered him for a moment. "Damn you loonice. Whyeryou so dressed up?"

"I'm here with," she said the name with hesitation, "Ellis." It sounded stranger out loud than it did in her thoughts over the past few days. Pode dropped the shot glass and it bounced loudly on the bar, flew over the side and smashed into a million shards of glass on the concrete floor below his studded leather barstool.

"But if you need a ride home . . ." Ava stared Tina down. They stood at either of Pode's shoulders.

"He's coming home with me," Tina's little voice squeaked, defiantly. The beady eyes and the croaking voice and the hooked nose were more rat-like than Ava had ever realized.

"That's probably a bad idea." Ava lowered her voice and leaned in close to Pode's ear, "To go home with the town whore."

"What did you say?"

"Layadies, lades," Pode drawled, unsuccessfully trying to stand between them and instead flailing back, into the bar. Rodg reached out a hand, ready to use it to steady Pode if he needed to.

"Did you call me a whore? You bitch!" Tina screamed at the top of her lungs, coming at Ava with a terrifying drunken rage. Ava moved at the last second to let her crash past, into a pool table. As Ava would have guessed, though, this wasn't the first fight for the train wreck of a woman. She was tough. Tina pulled herself up, running back at Ava, this time a stick on metallic blue fingernail gouging into Ava's forehead as she caught a clump of Ava's hair and pulled. Ava grabbed Tina's arm, digging her own nails into the flesh on the underside while she used her other hand to hold the much smaller woman far enough away that she could only kick at her boot shaft covered shins.

Just as quickly as it started, it was over, to Tina's disappointment and Ava's relief. Two men from the Friday night pool league locked Tina's arms behind her, the woman out of breath from wrestling and emphysema. Ellis, alone, had his arms around Ava, gentle, yet forceful, as he pulled her back toward their table. She could feel the warmth of his body against hers, the softness of his shirt, the smell of his aftershave. It was a magnificently masculine smell. As he let go of Ava, she added in her head how many years had gone by since she had been wrapped up in a man's arms. She had forgotten how good it felt, even under the strangest of circumstances.

"Are you OK?" Ellis asked, impatient. Ava nodded her head and touched the bare spot on her scalp, then moved her hand to her bloodied forehead. The fake fingernail was sticking out of the wound. Ava pulled it out and her stomach flipped over as she realized what it was and shook her hand violently to fling it away.

"I've never had to arrest my date before."

Ava frowned. "What? You're arresting me?"

Ellis shook his head. "No. No, but I should. For assault."

"She came after me first."

"What did you say to her?"

"Only nice things." Ava raised a single eyebrow.

"Yeah, it's a joke. All a joke. I'm going. You can stay, get trashed, and fight and whatever the hell else you want to do, but this isn't what I want to do with my night. I'm leaving." His face was full of disappointment, hurt. Ellis threw a couple of ones onto the table from his wallet for drinks they never ordered and stormed out the back screen door into the alley. It banged hard after him. Ava flinched with the sound of rippling metal. She wanted to follow him, attempt to explain her way back into his good graces, but Pode was still slumped over at the bar.

"Ava, dear, why don't you take your friend home before there's any more trouble." Martha made a rare appearance around the public side of the bar, sweeping glass and ice and hair into a dustpan as she spoke. Fights happened now and then. It was something Martha understood as a hazard of the job. She also understood, though, that getting all parties involved out of the bar as soon as possible was always a good way to not have to call county.

"I'm sorry, Martha," Ava genuinely apologized, going to Pode and putting his arm around her shoulders.

"It's alright, love. I'm really not the one who needs apologized to." The wise woman glanced at the back door.

He was heavier than she remembered, though it had been quite some time since she had been in this spot, so she thought maybe she'd forgotten. Balancing her half-passed-out friend against the side of the Mustang, she opened the door, folded the passenger seat as far forward as it would go, and heaved Pode inside. He knew the drill and clumsily pulled his legs in after himself so Ava could close the door.

The engine took four tries to start. Ava almost gave up before the fourth try for fear of flooding it and having far larger problems on her hands than a passed out drunk best friend in the backseat of her car and an owed apology to man she liked and didn't know why. The junker did start, finally, and she rubbed her hands together as she waited for it to warm up in the freezing night.

Illuminated by a 200 watt light on the top of a 15-foot pole, a five-room blue house with white trim and no shutters stood back off of Oak Street nearly a hundred feet. The house beside it had been demolished a few years before. A plastic "For Sale" sign staked into the ground since, but it still sat empty, effectively stranding the house last on the dead end street. The Mustang lumbered into the familiar driveway and came to a stop at the center of the circle of light from the pole. Ava pushed the car door open and jerked the seat forward, shivering in the darkness as she waited for Pode to realize they had stopped.

"Pode, come on. It's cold out here," she said, crossing her arms tight across her chest. "Pode!" Ava leaned over and shoved him hard into the torn vinyl seat.

"Wha, I don', where . . ." His words were labored and hard to understand. He sat straight up, looking all around himself through eyes struggling with the brightness of the car's dome light. It took him three tries to hoist himself out of the back seat and then pure momentum from falling forward out of the car forced him down the sidewalk and up the steps to the cement porch. Ava followed close behind, fumbling with her keychain, her hands so frozen she could barely feel her fingers.

"S'not locked." He sagged into the door, turned the knob and pushed, but nothing happened. "Oh, yeah, it is. Huh, forgot."

Ava reached around him and put her copy of his key in the door. She grabbed Pode's arm and directed the big man inside, through the living room, and to the back of the house. Once in the bedroom, Pode collapsed face first, sideways across the bed, snoring immediately. One of his boots was already hanging off, so it wasn't hard for Ava to pull it the rest of the way. The other, though, was stuck. She tugged on it for a while, finally freeing it with a whole-body heave backward. Pode stirred, raising his head to look at Ava. He stared at her, perplexed at first, and then slowly realized why she was in his bedroom.

"Thans for ride. Sorry I ruined yurdate," he mumbled into the corner of a pillow.

"It's OK. I don't know—I don't know what I was doing, anyway."

"You look pretty. Downright purdy." Pode's eyes were closed. He was a single deep breath away from dozing again.

"Sleep," Ava whispered as she sat beside him on the bed. She rubbed her face with her palms and pushed her hair back behind her ears. With a yawn, she tugged her own boots off and stood. Crossing the bedroom, she closed the door and retreated to the living room.

The cold on Ava's bare arms and legs was almost gone. Rubbing the last bit of it out of them, she dropped her boots by the couch and locked the front door. A hand-sewn quilt identical to one she owned and a creation of Pode's handicraft gifted mother, crumpled up at the end of the couch. Ava reached for it and tossed it out over herself as she settled into the familiar broken-in leather. She tucked the blanket in and curled into a ball, wishing she had sweats pants. She could borrow a pair from Pode, but didn't have any desire to go to the work of digging through his dresser drawers. She could go home, but driving out into the country in the middle of the night, exhausted from night after night of broken sleep, seemed like an open invitation for a deer to dart out in front of her and total the already less than dependable Mustang. If that happened, and she knew Pode was passed out drunk, she wasn't sure who she would call to come get her at this hour of the night.

Through the closed bedroom door, Ava could hear Pode snoring, deep constant guttural sounds. The couch wasn't uncomfortable and the quilt was warm. It didn't take long for her to close her eyes and fall into a light but calm slumber.

\* \* \*

Ava hated house parties. They made her anxious, as if her social ineptitude was on display for a bunch of strangers to analyze. Everyone insisted she go, though, it would be one of only a few times Baker had the house to himself, with his parents out of town on vacation and his older brother Jack away at college. The fact that it was Baker's house and a bunch of people she knew made it better, but not ideal.

Somehow a keg had made it into the kitchen despite most of the crowd still being in high school. Ava stood in the open space between the well-lit kitchen, where Baker and some older guys, a few she recognized, a few she didn't, poured themselves Solo cups of beer, and the dimly living room, where the stereo boomed out thuggy rap and a couple grinded on each other clumsily while others stood along the wall drinking and watching.

She didn't drink. Yet. She didn't have a desire to after watching it tear apart her father's life and her family. At 17, Ava already found it hard to be the only one in her friend group who didn't. Shannon didn't drink either until recently, until she started dating Kale, the senior football star. A friend who didn't drink made it easier for Ava to avoid it, too, but now she was simply the odd man out.

Tired of watching Baker and the scene in the kitchen, Ava fought through the bodies in the crowded living room. She picked Pode up on the way to the party, but lost him somewhere along the way. Guessing he was outside smoking, Ava pushed the screen door to the patio open and walked out into the cold. A few people sat in lawn chairs, stood in the yard, shared lighters, and passed cigarettes and joints back and forth. Straining to see in the dimness from the back porch glow and the stars overhead, Ava couldn't find him in the backyard. She wanted to leave, to get away from the eyes and the smoke. She would much rather be sitting in her room, alone, sketching her next project. If she left without him, without even saying anything to him, she would feel guilty.

Back inside, Ava stopped beside Baker as he took a swig of beer. He was already drunk. "Baker!"

"Hey, Av, grab a cup!" he shouted back.

"No thanks! Hey, have you seen Pode anywhere?" They had to scream to hear each other over the ridiculously loud music. It wouldn't be long before the neighbors complained and the cops from county showed up. Ava definitely wanted to be gone before that happened.

"Uh!" Baker thought out loud. "Oh, fuck, yeah. I saw him headed upstairs a little bit ago!"

As Ava walked away Baker caught her by the arm. "What?"

"You probably shouldn't . . ."

"What?"

"He was . . . uh . . . he was with Audie!" Baker, though impaired, still understood the ramifications of the situation, and Ava was more than thankful for his warning.

She nodded, letting Baker know she understood what he meant.

"Stay here, though! You don't have to drink, but hang out here in the kitchen with us!" He waved his cup of beer toward a short guy with messy dark hair over his eyes. "Do you know Chance? He's from Clay."

Ava smiled at the solemn kid. She was genuinely appreciative of her friend's offer, but not interested in staying. Crossing the kitchen and stopping in the back hallway of the house, Ava looked up the staircase. Placing her hand on the oversized knob on the last banister, she considered her choices and then turned from the stairs and reentered the living room from the hall. Accidentally bumping into someone as they took a step back, she shouted "Sorry!" over the music and fled the house, not stopping until she was beside her car. With a look back, Ava knew she and Baker might be wrong about Pode and Audie. That they might not be doing whatever two drunk 17 year olds do in a bedroom at a party, but the knot in Ava's stomach told her they weren't.

# 5

The police cruiser rounded the corner of 5th and Oak, creeping down the street like a predator stocking prey. Inside, a heavy-eyed Deputy Ellis sipped black coffee from a Styrofoam to-go cup with a blue and turquoise firework design on the side of it. He squinted through his dark shades against the first rays of daylight sun. Approaching the empty lot and the last house isolated at the end of the street, he spotted her green dress as she exited and closed the front door behind her. Ava froze on the bottom porch step as she looked up.

Ellis put the car in park in the middle of the road and rolled down the passenger window. "Good morning, Ava. Just cruising through town, making sure everybody I saw at Martha's last night made it home safely."

Suddenly self-conscious of her wrinkled dress, matted hair, and new forehead wound, Ava answered, "We did. Pode's fine. Hell of a hangover, when he wakes up. But that's nothing new to him." It was brightly sunny, but cold enough her breath formed a cloud at the edge of her lips as she talked. The shape of her clumsy words lingered in the air as she spoke them.

"Great. Good to know everyone here's OK. Have a good day."

As the automatic window crept up, Ava's mouth opened, but nothing came out. Not even a weak and necessary "I'm sorry." She closed it as she watched the police car pull a quick U-turn at the end of the dead end. Ellis drove past her in the opposite direction without another look at her. Two blocks away, most of the McEwing family piled out of the brick two-story Methodist church parsonage, beside the white house with blue trim Baker had grown up in. Pastor McEwing waved quickly, but Sandy McEwing glared at Ava as she helped the youngest of her four children buckle himself into the back seat of the family's champagne-colored SUV. Ava felt like she could feel the pastor's wife's judgment crawl under her skin, despite the four inches the middle-aged woman's skirt seemed to be missing on the cold morning. Penny apparently wasn't going on the family excursion. Her car wasn't in the driveway. Ava wondered if the preacher's wife knew what she did, feeling it leveled the contrition playing field.

Drafts of air flowed down the hall from the broken kitchen window where crusty aged duct tape no longer covered a quarter-sized hole in the middle pane. Its stickiness wore out over its years of use. Plopping into the deep two-sided porcelain sink, the fibers in the wad of tape mixed with the water from the ever-dripping faucet, creating a mushy gray paste. The color of the dying tape was similar to the color on the walls and 10-foot ceilings of the farmhouse's kitchen. Once upon a time painted stark white, they were now dingily stained from years of greasy frying and burning baking.

On either side of the porcelain sink, nondescript wooden cabinets ran the length of the wall, topped with white vinyl flecked with metallic gold. A nearly empty bottle of Jack Daniels sat nearby, the lid lying beside it, not replaced. Across from the cabinetry an almond-colored refrigerator hummed, "waah, waah, waah." It pumped cold air into a space that held only the end of a flat two liter of Coca Cola, some string cheese, and a half a bottle of outdated Dorothy Lynch. The front of the fridge was filled with faded four by six snapshots developed long before. Magnets covered all four corners of each, keeping them from curling and falling, but carefully placed so as not to cover the smiling face of a little blonde girl with big insightful dark eyes and a brother with darker hair and narrower eyes.

Ava felt the cold air leak in the kitchen from her post in the living room underneath the quilt gifted to her by Pode's mother. Open photo albums rested on the floor all around her. Whiskey and Coke in a heavy glass highball perched on the edge of a side table. Stalks of wheat were etched at the base of the glass, matching the bunch of wheat carefully inlaid into the oak accent table it sat upon. Tucking the quilt over her legs and in between the side and the cushion of a baby blue La-Z-Boy, she shivered. On her lap sat a liberally used sketchpad and a cracked mechanical pencil. The page of the sketchpad Ava worked on was full of designs. Many crossed out brutally. A select few with giant circles of acceptance drawn around them.

Outside of an occasional creak as the foundation settled and the whistle of the wind through the screens of the back porch, the night was eerily still. Ava stopped drawing for a moment, closed her eyes, and attempted to visualize her next move. A picture didn't come, though, so she opened them and reached for her glass. She coughed as the liquor and stale sugar hit the back of her tongue. This current drink was unintentionally much stronger than the previous four, her ability to properly measure impaired by the beginnings of drunkenness. Her mother drank whiskey, never beer, which made sense to Ava in reflection. Dora May never did anything halfway. She didn't want to feel buzzed, she wanted to get drunk. She didn't want to live well, she wanted to be rich. She didn't have cancer, she had an aggressive, incurable form

101

that would become untreatable. She didn't get sick and get better, she got sick and died.

Tears were streaming down Ava's face, thoughts overflowing her mind. She folded the cover of the sketchbook over her work and guzzled the end of her drink, using a corner of the quilt to wipe a portion that had missed her mouth off of her chin. Pulling her legs up to her chest she took a deep, sobbing breath and let go. Crying. Sobbing. Wailing. Until her sides hurt and she couldn't see through the puffiness of her eyes. It seemed like it might never stop. But it did, finally, hours later, as Ava passed out into sleep, exhausted.

An extra black shade of dark settled in due to thick cloud cover overhead. The prediction was rain, but the clouds only crawled east, low and heavy, doing nothing more than simply looking threatening. The farmers in Flynn, their expert advice highly valued, guessed if anything did come from the sky it would only be a light shower, at best an inch or two. It wouldn't be enough moisture to do much good for the wheat already in the ground, but it would probably be enough to make the corn fields muddy in the morning, to prevent the larger landowners from finishing up the last of the harvest.

The rain laden clouds brought an extra damp cool to the air and created the perfect temperature for a bonfire. No one needed to be told where or what time. It was learned through being and living. Like a pilgrimage, a line of vehicles headed west on Old Highway 94 for six miles, turned left at the Wagners' pivot, drove two miles to the river, past Baker's parent's house, and parked in the clearing. Everyone then walked 400 yards south along the riverbank until a gap opened in the trees. It was where a homestead used to sit, but the name of the folks who had settled the property was forgotten. The property had belonged to various branches of Pode's family for the better part of a century. Too uneven to farm, it had become pasture, grown over now with a thick tangle of trees, mostly ancient oaks who easily outlived the people who planted them.

The house fell in on itself, and all of the good burning wood had been pulled off for kindling by Pode's father and his friends. Limestone blocks from the foundation were drug away and placed in a circle around a pit of dirt. A garden shed stood nearby, built a hundred years after the farmhouse and recently reinforced. It kept firewood and matches and cases of spare beer dry. Pode and Baker and whoever else got away from their day of work early, built a fire in the ashy pit. By the time the sun sank and the rest of the party showed up, flames had been expertly coaxed into a low, steady burn. Heat radiated out across the clearing as if it someone switched on a furnace, and even the coldest night became quite pleasant.

Ava stopped the Mustang in line with a row of trucks abandoned in the designated spot by the river. With both hands, she struggled to jerk the parking break back into its locked position, envisioning the car rolling and plunging over the edge of the bank into the river. She leaned to the center of the car, checking her reflection in the oblong rearview mirror, considering a wispy layer of bangs she had cut into the front of her hair an hour before. Swept to the side, the hair satisfactorily hid the half-moon-shaped wound left behind from Tina's errant fingernail.

The rich, smoky smell of the bonfire grew as Ava picked her way through underbrush that had regrown over the path during the summer. No one wanted to sit by a fire by a river full of mosquito swarms in 110-degree weather, and for Pode and the other farmers, summer was the busy season. He worked from dawn until dusk in a field caring for crops or in a pasture caring for cattle.

Reflecting off the eerie darkness of the tree cover, the fire cast wicked, angled shadows on the ground and foliage walls of the clearing. As Ava pushed the last few branches out of the way with her elbow, she entered the clearing and scanned the crowd. It was already good sized and she recognized every single face.

"Av!" Audie jumped up from her seat at the circle of rock. A bottle of beer in her hand, she threw her arms around Ava in an overdone hug. "Come on, let's get you a beer."

Ava was happier to see Audie than she had been in a long time, because Audie was drama walking. If she wasn't living any, she was causing some. With her old friend around, maybe no one would remember the roof incident. Or the bar incident. Audie had surely either topped them both by now or was working very hard toward doing so.

Across the clearing, on the far side of the fire, Pode and Baker held bottles of beer and laughed. Pode looked fresh. He was cleanly shaven and dressed in a crisp plaid pearl snap and a pair of newish jeans. A different guy from the one at Martha's the past weekend. Baker looked haggard in head to toe dirty camo. A stained brown camouflage shirt under green camouflage overalls tucked into his muddy black boots. Beside them a metal horse trough overflowed with fresh ice, necks of bottles sticking up through the sparkling square crystals like pigweed in an unsprayed field of milo.

"Hey, Av!" Baker smiled his goofy smile, his focus completely on avoiding Audie as she reached in front of him for a bottle of beer and handed it to Ava. Ava twisted off the cap and slipped it into her pocket. Pode took a step away, not looking up at the women. He took a long final swig of the beer he was holding and tossed the bottle in an already sizeable pile at the edge of the clearing.

"Oh, hey, Baker. Sorry. Didn't see you there at first," Ava joked.

"Yeah, you didn't have to dress up for us," Audie followed Ava's lead.

"Fucking hilarious. Both of you. I was in a tree stand all day. Didn't have time to go home and change before I came over here to help Pode with the fire. You're welcome for the warmth and beer, by the way."

"Wearing camo isn't going to be enough to hide from deer if you're in that beast of a truck. Scare the shit out of every living creature in a 20-mile radius," Pode added and fished another bottle out of the ice.

"Laugh. Go ahead and laugh, but when it starts pouring and you need somebody to pull your fucking Ford out of the mud, don't ask me. And I ain't giving anybody a ride later."

"Wow, party just started and Baker's already looking for someone to ride him later?" Kale's loud voice boomed as he entered out of the darkness on the other side of the clearing. He held a handle of Jim Beam around the neck, about half of it gone. Close behind, Shannon followed, tossing her mass of frizzy black curls over her shoulder. Her face was set in hard lines, exhausted or angry, Ava couldn't tell, but as soon as they made eye contact, the lines faded into a smile.

"Ava!?"

"Audie called me four times this afternoon." Ava motioned toward their friend, but she was caught up in a flirting match between the boys. Kale's arm wrapped loosely around her waist.

"Good." Shannon reached around her friend and pulled a beer out of the ice. "I don't usually like anything she does." She frowned at the woman as Audie rubbed Kale's arm. "But I'm glad she convinced you to come out."

"She didn't really convince me as much as beg me. Then threaten. Then she almost cried, I think."

"Oh, lord."

"Yep. I think she was afraid it would all be high school kids and she'd need somebody to hang out with. Well, you know, for like ten minutes until she ditched me for a random guy."

"You suppose she'll ever stop sleeping with other people's husbands?"

"As soon as other people's husbands stop sleeping with her," Ava answered before thinking.

Shannon quickly changed the subject. "Why's Pode so quiet?"

He was at the edge of the darkness, not part of the group Audie entertained. Ava shrugged her shoulders.

"I heard you drove him home the other night after the bar fight."

"Nothing goes unnoticed in this town, does it?"

"Well, no story that starts with a bar fight. Which becomes more epic every time I hear a new person tell it. Whether they were there or not. I think you're in a cast with a black eye now, at least in the last version I heard."

Ava nonchalantly fixed her new bangs. "Ugh, what a mess. I don't know what I was thinking. Ellis threatened to arrest me."

"You were there with him." It wasn't a question, but instead Shannon was confirming parts of the story she had heard that she wasn't sure were true.

"Yeah, I met him for a drink. He stopped by the farmhouse after the roof thing and then he gave a Dad a ride home the other day. He asked me out and I . . ."

"Hey, you don't have to justify anything to me, Av. He seems like a nice guy. Nice to look at, too. I bet he's got really good abs."

Ava laughed. "Yeah, it doesn't look like I'll ever

know."

"So do I get to hear the story? I mean the real story?"

"It's not that exciting. I walked in to Martha's and Pode was sitting at the bar. Tina was all over him, and he was so drunk. He couldn't stand up straight or talk. When I was trying to get him to leave, I sort of called Tina a whore and she heard me. Some of the pool league guys and Ellis broke us up. Ellis took off all pissed off, and I gave Pode a ride home. That's it."

"And spent the night there."

"Was this on the front page of the *Tribune*?"

"Half the people I work with saw your car in his yard the next morning. You weren't exactly discreet about the whole thing." Shannon called Ava out, like she used to in years past when their hanging out at parties together was a common occasion. There was a sense of normalcy to it, to longtime friends and brutal honesty. No kid gloves because Ava's mother had died, just tough love between two friends as they talked out their problems with each other.

"I used to stay there all of the time. Why is this worth talking about now?"

"Because you and Pode have been inseparable since he had his arm around you at your mother's funeral. Because you met Ellis for a drink and ended up staying the night at Pode's."

"OK, OK, I see it now. The story gets better. Or worse? When I walked out of Pode's house Saturday morning, Ellis drove by in his police car."

"No!" Shannon couldn't help but laugh.

"Yes. I don't know if he was staking out the block, or has perfect timing, or what, but he stopped me and asked if everything was alright. I was standing there in the freezing cold in the middle of Pode's yard in the same dress I had on the night before. Except it's all wrinkled and I didn't realize until I got home and looked in a mirror that I had this sexy mix of eyeliner and blood smeared all over my face."

"Oh, my God! Oh, Av."

"I know," Ava laughed with her friend at herself. It felt good to laugh at herself, like it was releasing the humiliation and guilt. "I have no idea what I'll do or say the next time I run into him."

The last couple of the words were too loud, because everyone else had grown quiet. Both women realized they were turned away from the clearing and so engrossed in discussion they had forgotten about the party happening behind them. Across the pit, the flickering firelight reflecting off his badge and belt buckle and gun, Ellis nodded a greeting to folks seated on rocks beside him.

Sensing the awkward silence, Ellis politely nodded at the group standing around the beer as he approached. "Hey, I'm not on duty as of," he looked at his watch, "Ten minutes ago. I'm not arresting anybody. Just wanted to drink a beer by a bonfire on a beautiful night." He reached into the ice and stole a beer, popping the top off and taking a sip. Everyone looked away from the police officer, to the person standing next to them and conversations slowly began to start again.

Ava, in a state of shock, was brought back into the world with the sound of Shannon's whispered voice. "Ava, if you want to get out of here, I'll go with you. Kale can find his own ride home."

The idea was tempting, but Ava decided against it. "No, I'm staying. This town's so small I'm sure I'll run into him again tomorrow. Might as well get it over with now."

"There's a lot of people here. We might be able to avoid him."

Shannon was right. The crowd swelled to 50 or 60

people, laughing, loud talking. All Ava had to do was stay on the other side of the fire. It might be hard, though, as whatever attraction she had felt before the debacle at Martha's was still strong. She wanted to run to him, apologize for the fight, explain that nothing happened with Pode, but the chance of Ellis believing her seemed unlikely. And whoever was standing nearby would hear the whole thing, and Ava would be the star of a whole new round of rumors dictated by how he reacted.

Ellis smiled and waved to someone as he took a seat alone on the chalk rocks. Ava felt her eyes glued to his face, her stomach twisting at the sight of his smile.

"Ah, shit," Kale's voice grew louder with each shot he took from his bottle of whiskey. "Shan!"

She looked up at the sound of his voice calling to her and crossed to where he stood with Baker and Audie and a collection of other people. Ava followed close behind, her back purposely turned on Ellis.

"What?" Shannon asked as her husband clumsily threw his arm around her shoulders, more to hold his drunken self up than out of affection.

"What the hell's the name of that steak place we ate at with your parents?"

"In Kansas City? Benton's?"

"Yes! That's it."

"Ah, no, we ate at the restaurant in the casino." Baker shook his head. Kale offered up his Jim Beam. Baker took it first and guzzled a long swig. He handed it to Audie, who did the same and then tried to hand the bottle to Ava, who denied it with a nod.

"Was that a raindrop?" Audie asked abruptly, wiping something off her cheek and looking up toward the sky.

"It rained earlier when Pode and I were getting the fire going. For maybe a minute or two, then quit. We had to go get fucking dry wood."

"Ha!" Kale threw his head back laughing, pulling his wife over with him. "You had to go get dry wood, hey?"

"Are you thirteen?" Shannon rolled her eyes at him, disgusted.

Ava felt a cold drop hit the hand holding her beer.

"Fuck!" Baker cursed up at the sky. "Maybe it'll just be a little sprinkle."

Shannon leaned toward Ava. "You want to go sit in the car and wait it out."

"Oh, yeah, we should do that." Kale was too drunk and consequentially horny to realize his wife was talking to her friend and not him. He grabbed his lady around the waist and drug her toward the path. They were gone before Ava could reply. The rain was falling consistently, but fairly lightly and the crowd was thinning as people ran to their vehicles for shelter. Ava hurried down the path and as she passed the rock Ellis was sitting on he stood up and spun around and thrust a shoulder into her face.

"Whoa! Oh. Ava? I'm so sorry."

"No, you're OK."

Their hands were locked around each other's arms, Ellis reaching for her so she wouldn't fall.

His face was hard to read, surprised and confused, but painfully polite. Suddenly he let go and took a step back. "I didn't see you here when I walked up."

"I didn't see you either," she lied. "A lot of people." As she made the remark, she realized they were the only two left standing in the clearing. The rain had grown stronger, stifling the fire completely.

"We better go before we're soaked." Ellis's words were sterile. Neither positive or negative, happy or sad. They were simply words put together to state the obvious.

Monsoon sheets of water began plunging to the ground, creating an instant muddy mess on the path. Ava stopped and looked over her shoulder. The whitewashed

shed was the only thing visible in the tree shadows and utter darkness. Her car seemed so far away and the chance of it making it up a road prone to flash floods beside a river without getting stuck or stalling out was not good.

"I think I'm going to wait for it to let up in there," Ava yelled over the crashing sound of thunder and pointed to the shed.

Ellis nodded. Wiping water off his face, he watched as Ava picked her way through patches of dead grass between puddles of mud and slipped through the slight gap the shed door hung open.

Baker slammed the door to his truck shut against the weather. He stepped on the clutch and turned the key. Letting the truck run, he watched in his rearview mirror as trucks and SUVs backed from their spots and crawled up the grassy trail to the river bank and lurched onto the rutted dirt road. His threat from earlier not true, he planned to bring up the rear of the slow processional, ready to get out and help if anyone became stuck in the quickly rising water. Only able to see a few purposely deserted cars and Pode's taillights, Baker shifted his truck into gear.

Surprised by the opening of the passenger side door, Baker hit the break. Audie climbed in, soaked head to toe, her hair matted to her head, black trails of her thick eyeliner streaking her cheeks.

"Whew. Wow. It is coming down out there." Audie closed the door hard and the dome light faded off. She wiped her face with the sleeve of her jacket and smiled wickedly at Baker.

"Hey, Aud. Car stuck?" Baker tried to pretend he didn't know why she was in his pickup.

"I don't know. Didn't try to move it. Sat there for a

111

second. Thought about going home. Or to Martha's. But saw you sitting here and changed my mind." She folded up the middle console and slid closer to him. "Changed my mind because it's rainy and dark and we're alone in this clearing by the river . . ."

"Ain't alone. Pode's still parked over there. Waiting with me to make sure everybody makes it out." Baker sat up straighter and pointed out the windshield.

"Pode doesn't count." Audie slipped her cold hand inside his damp camouflage overalls, and the man's stomach clenched.

"Audie, I don't . . ." Baker leaned his head away from her, avoiding her attempt to plant her lips on his neck.

"What?" Audie pulled back. "What's wrong with you?"

"I'm not—I don't . . ."

"You start seeing somebody?"

"No—but I'm not really—I'm not really feeling this." Baker wrapped his hand around her wrist and pushed it away. Audie frowned, at first confused and then offended.

"I don't get it."

"It's not you. I fucking swear it's me. It's just—it's—I'm . . ." Baker spoke quietly, refusing to look her in the face.

"Yeah, I've heard that one before, asshole. What the fuck is wrong with you?" Audie moved on from offended to infuriated, more from his use of the cliché expression than of his refusal of her advances. "God. Fucking asshole." Audie scooted across the seat and swung the door open and disappeared into the storm.

Taking a deep breath, Baker leaned across the seat and pulled the passenger side door Audie left hanging open closed. He put the truck into reverse and eased it through the mud and onto the trail, spinning out and splattering mud across the back of a deserted sedan. Once on the path, he stepped on the gas, less concerned about traction than speed, and steered the truck down the dirt road, flying and swerving through collecting water and loose gravel.

Once inside, Ava found the shed more watertight than she would have ever imagined it could be. A rusted shovel leaned into the corner opposite the door and a swath of cobwebs stretched across the ceiling. A work bench handcrafted of saw horses and unfinished two-by-fours and thick plywood lined the longest wall. On the makeshift table sat two cases of beer hidden away by Baker during the earlier rain and forgotten by him during the mad rush to cars.

The door creaked open and Ava jerked her head up to see who had entered. Ellis pushed the door as shut as it would go behind him, blocking out a flash of lightning as it struck a tree 50 feet away. He shook the water from the long sleeves of his uniform shirt. "I didn't want you to be out here all alone. It could be a while before the rain lets up."

Ava nodded. Her eyes were beginning to adjust to the darkness and she could make out the same tentative expression on Ellis's face as she was certain was spread across her own. This was her karma, she decided in her head, for ruining their date. Locked in a shed with him all night.

"Well, at least there's beer," Ava pointed over her shoulder.

Ellis retrieved the flashlight from his belt and shined it around the room, exposing further cobwebs and stacks of firewood along the wall by the door. He stopped moving the light as it highlighted the workbench. "Yep, more than we could possibly drink in one night."

"Is that a challenge?" The words came out of her mouth before she could stop them. She was trying to joke, to flirt, but because of the mood, the statement was overshadowed and inelegant. Ellis's mouth fell open. He had no idea what to think of her.

"Pode's a friend. Please believe me," Ava blurted out. She couldn't do it. She couldn't be stuck with him for what could potential be many hours without leaving the truth on the table. Whether he believed her or not was his choice, but either way she had to do it. The words spilled from her. She lost all control over them. "Nothing has ever happened between us. Nothing ever will. He is my best friend. We grew up down the road from each other. We've been friends for as long as I can remember. Before I even met Shannon or Baker or Audie. He knows me better than my brother does. I take care of him when he drinks too much and I make sure he doesn't make any bad decisions, because he's good at doing that when he's drunk, and then I drive him home. And he takes care of me. He fixes my car and helps Dad farm sometimes."

Ava stopped, but Ellis didn't say anything, so she continued. "I'm sorry. That's actually the first thing I should have said. I am so sorry. I didn't mean for that fight to happen at Martha's. I didn't mean to be an asshole or make you look like an idiot. I would never intentionally do that to someone I . . ." she chose the next words carefully, "Like. I really like you. And I am really sorry. And if you don't ever want to see me again as long as you live I completely understand, but please don't hate me."

Ellis stared at her. Staring and thinking. She couldn't tell what he was thinking. Ava wondered if it was a military, police tactic he had learned along the way. She couldn't think of anything else to say and after having stumbled through what she felt was one of the worst apologies she had attempted to make in her entire life, she didn't trust herself to say anything else that would improve the situation.

Silent, Ellis crossed the dirt floor and tore one of the cardboard cases of beer open down the side. He stole two bottles, twisted off their caps, and held one out toward Ava. Stepping forward, she took it from him. The police officer unbuckled his heavy belt, left it on the ground, and hoisted himself up onto the workbench. Leaning back against the wall, his long legs stretched out in front of him, Ellis balanced his flashlight upright so it created a dim lamp effect upon the open rafters of the ceiling. He took a long swig of his beer, his Adam's apple in his lean neck shifted as he swallowed.

Ellis laid his hand on the spot beside him. "You might as well settle in. If this is a challenge, you've got a whole case of beer to drink on your own." He tried not to smile, but failed. It was dark and shadowy in the room, but from where Ava stood, she could see the corners of his mouth twitch upward.

Ava felt relief wash over her as she joined him. She sat close, within arm-brushing range, on purpose. The workbench was so deep, her feet were a foot short of the edge and it made her feel small. She felt like a girl with a crush on the boy sitting next to her in class. Ellis leaned his head back and forth. His neck cracked and Ava blinked hard at the sound. Slowly unbuttoning his uniform shirt, he pulled it out of the waistband of his pants and sighed with the new level of comfort this took him to. He was sopping wet to the white t-shirt he wore underneath, and through the clinging, nearly transparent, cotton, every crease of well-defined muscle in his chest was visible. Shannon was right.

The sound of the rain hitting the thin wooden walls and roof surrounded them. It was methodic, relaxing. It didn't seem like it was going to let up anytime soon.

"How's your—the art—going?" Ellis's words surprised Ava, snapped her out of the trance the steady rhythm of the rain had lulled her into.

"Oh, good," Ava answered. She leaned her head back, against the wall, mimicking him. "How's your . . ." She paused and playfully added, "policing going?"

"Good, good," Ellis answered. He tipped his beer back and guzzled the end of it. He tossed it over the edge of the workbench and it clanked on the ground and rolled away. "I'm winning," Ellis reached for another bottle from the case beside him.

Ava grinned, impressed he was entertaining her initial joke.

"Do you like it?" The question was too intrusive and Ava wished she could take it back. She had heard the story, but she was too young when it happened to remember the actual event. Ellis's father was a police officer. He was shot to death at a traffic stop. Nothing else came into her mind. She couldn't remember any of the details. She wanted to ask other questions, but she knew what it was to lose a parent. If he wanted to tell her, he would.

"Yeah. I like it. I like helping people. And I can't imagine doing anything else with my life." Ellis cleared his throat. "People get stuck here. One obligation or another keeps them here, but I came back. I traveled halfway around the world and came back."

Ava was fascinated. "Why?"

"You can breathe. See all the stars. Go to the middle of the country and be the only other person around for miles and miles."

"I'm thinking about moving to New York." Ava didn't know why she told him, but it seemed right in the moment and somehow safer to tell someone who was almost a stranger than her friends. His opinion would be plain, honest. He didn't know her like they did.

Ellis was quiet for a long time. He drank his beer. As Ava began to believe he wasn't going to say anything in response to her statement, he spoke. "I've been there. You can't see the stars. Too many city lights."

"So I've heard."

They drank. Ava finished her beer and dropped the empty bottle on the ground the same way Ellis had. She sat up on her knees, bent over his lap, and retrieved a new one. Ellis studied the outline of her body. He took a sip of beer and it went down the wrong pipe and he futilely tried not to cough as he choked. He glanced at her, over his shoulder, their height difference vastly apparent as she returned to her seat.

"Only reason I stopped by tonight was because I was hoping you'd be here," Ellis spoke softly. Ava's heart scurried up the wall of her chest and rested in her throat. It was the last thing she expected him to say. "I hate these kinds of parties. I don't waste my time on them anymore. Everybody's the same. It's like they're all still seventeen."

"I know exactly what you mean," Ava matched his quiet tone, happy to change the subject and even happier that he had come looking for her. "Years have gone by, but nobody's changed. With my friends—Audie's still a slut. Kale's still an idiot. Shannon still follows him around like a puppy. Baker's still weird . . ."

"How many years can you stand around in the mud and drink beer and give each other shit?" Ava felt like Ellis was reading her mind.

"Yeah, there's no—nobody changes, grows." She took a drink of her beer and set it down hard on the board beside her, accentuating her point.

Ellis raised his hand to his forehead and rubbed it gently.

"It looks better."

117

"What?" Ellis asked, not realizing he was touching the thin scab that had formed over the slash from his fall in her driveway.

"Your head wound."

"Oh. Yeah. So does yours."

"Thanks. We have to stop this thing. Every time we're together one of us ends up with a bloody face."

Ellis busted out laughing, a deep laugh that Ava had never heard. She laughed with him. As their laughter waned, Ellis took his hand off of his own knee and lightly touched the top of Ava's as it rested on the raw wood between them. His finger traced an outline across the back of her hand as they both watched. Ava felt a shiver run up her arm and spread across her back.

"Are you cold?" Ellis's voice was full of concern as he took her reaction as an opportunity to wrap his big warm hand around hers.

"No, no, I'm fine." Ava found herself looking up again, meeting his wide, green eyes as her speech trailed off. She held her breath, closed her eyes, as he leaned forward the few inches between them and kissed her lips. Ellis pulled away from her and Ava saw that beneath the current cool calm of the man, he was, like her, a frightened kid. Ava drew her body up, into another kiss.

He smelled good, like crisp aftershave and fresh rain. The second kiss was longer, deeper. The warmth of his tongue in her mouth caused goosebumps on her skin and Ellis let go of her hand, wrapping his arms around her body. Ava's jacket was heavy with damp, sticking to her shirt. She undid the buttons quickly and pulled it off with Ellis' help, discarding it over the edge of the workbench. Kneeling, Ava moved so she was in front of him, one knee on either side of his outstretched legs.

A hand on his face and the other flat on his chest, she kissed him, both of them openly desperate for another

118

human's touch. Ellis's hands found the space between her jeans and t-shirt and his hands caressed her exposed lower back as they continued to kiss each other. Ava wanted him. She wanted every inch of her skin pressed against every inch of his skin, but for all she knew about him, she barely knew him. The recklessness of giving in was appealing, but too dangerous and Ellis seemed to think so even more than Ava did. He leaned forward and nuzzled into her neck, holding her close, Ava's body warm in the cold wet air in the shed.

The ground was saturated with dew left from the overnight rain. Each blade of dying grass covered in tiny crystals reflecting the gradually clearing gray of the fall sky above. Though the grass was wet, the brown earth coming through in patches below it was not muddy. Rain hadn't been part of the forecast all summer, which made for a quick corn and bean harvest, but would lead to fear of not enough moisture for the wheat seeds poked barely below the surface of the dirt. Left to incubate through the winter, the little green nubs would struggle to break toward the sun come spring, if they didn't have the nourishment they needed now. Three inches, which had fallen the night before, had already vanished into the earth. Greedily consumed by plant life. And once again the ground was dry.

Pode kicked a clod of dirt at his feet with the toe of his leather work boot. The clod flew through the air a couple of feet and landed in fragments. A short distance from him, a hundred head of cattle were already up for the day. Swaggering along, picking at the hollowed out remnants of a giant round bale of hay. They were a mix of Hereford and Angus. Reds with white faces and blacks with white faces and a few odd all grays, the misfits' physical traits pulled from an indirect part of the bovine genetic lottery.

119

None of the cattle stirred as Pode approached them. They were accustomed to him, his scent. Most of them had known him their entire life. From the time he could walk, Pode had helped his father with the cattle. At first as a small child eager to follow in every footstep his father took. Then as a boy excited by the chance to name all of the new calves and the hope of seeing a live birth so he could take the story back to school with him on Monday to share during show and tell. Then as a lazy teenager shoved out of bed as the sun rose on Saturday mornings because his grandfather was too old to work cattle and another strong man was needed to help corral and haul the steers to auction in Winfield or Enid or Dodge City. Now as owner of the cattle entirely responsible for the care of the slowly growing herd he purchased from his father.

Picking through the cow shit on the ground as best he could, Pode high stepped over the pasture ground and between the gathered cows. They moved aside for him as he touched their flanks with his outstretched hand. Behind him, in the open field, he heard a pickup cruising over the bumpy rows of corn stubble. The shiny new, beige F-150 came to a stop a hundred yards away beside a creek fed by a series of springs on neighboring land that twisted up rolling hills and between trees the entire length of the 300-acre plot.

"Mornin'!" Henry yelled as he climbed out of the driver's seat of his truck.

Pode nodded in the direction of his father in answer. He looked tired. Dark circles formed under his eyes, and stubble spread out over his face. Henry didn't ask; he assumed his son had been out late. Drinking. The drinking he had hoped was a phase. As he reached his mid-twenties, though, Pode only drank more and this worried his father, but even more so his mother since her

120

own father had fallen victim to alcoholism before he was out of his fifties.

"Had almost three inches in the rain gauge this morning," Henry said as he joined his son.

"It's not enough. The ground sucked it right up. Like nothing happened. It needs to do that for a whole week for us to be caught up on rainfall this year." Pode's voice was gravelly.

"You sound like one of the crotchety old men at Martha's," Henry laughed at Pode. "Three inches is better than nothing. Three inches of rain'll change everything. Think about it. We got 500 acres of wheat. If three inches of rain improves the yield by two, that's an extra thousand bushels next summer and an extra fifteen in the bank. It's like we made fifteen overnight without having to do a thing but let nature happen."

Pode understood exactly what his father said, but wasn't in the mood for math or logic or to try to keep up with the chipper mood the elder Wagner was in. The Mustang and Ellis's police cruiser were still parked on the riverbank when Pode finally put his truck in reverse and backed out of the pool of rain water forming. He gave up on Ava and didn't go after her, terrified he might find her and the town cop together.

"Is that her, over there?"

Pode jumped at the sound of his father's voice, wondering if he had fallen asleep standing up. He shook his head "no" in answer and stretched to see over the thickly winter-coated backs all around him. The red and white cow's head was between two bars of the feeder, buried in the last of the alfalfa. She tilted at an extreme angle, balancing all of her weight on her front left leg as she held her front right hoof up unnaturally and curled it underneath her body. The injured foot was swollen with blood and puss seeping out of it. Gnats buzzed and landed and climbed into the open parts of the wound. A mouth full and chewing, the cow raised her head, feeling Pode's eyes on her, "83" printed on the plastic yellow tag pierced through her ear.

"Here she is, eighty-three," Pode shouted to his father, who observed from a distance.

"Footrot?"

"I thought so when I first saw it, but it looks like it could be the leg, maybe a thorn somewhere. Either way I think we ought to take her back to the house. She always has a nice big calf. I'd hate to lose her. Get some penicillin in her, keep her still and see if that helps any."

"Six? Eight?"

"She's probably close to ten. She was one of yours. I got the book in my truck if you want to know for sure. Let's see if we can get her in the trailer?"

Often it felt strange to Pode to tell his father what to do with the cattle. The older man had seen the births of most of these cows and their mothers. They had belonged to him until the day he decided they were too much work. It was either watch them all sell or buy them and continue the family tradition that was now four generations along, so Pode became the boss. He made the decisions and bought the beer to thank his Dad for the help he offered in feeding and watering and catching and trailering and moving and medicating.

The cow inspected Pode as she chewed her cud, somehow already aware she was the target of his visit on this particular cloudy morning. He reached his arms out, trying not to spook the rest of the cattle as he separated her from them. She swung her head nearly 180 degrees to better see him with both of her dramatically eyelash framed dark eyes, but she didn't budge. Pode shifted his body into her forcing her to take a couple of hopsteps away from the bale. He walked her toward the mid-sized silver horse trailer hitched to the back of his pickup. Both the truck and trailer were sparkling clean from sitting outside in the hard rain. A good space away, Henry was prepared to head the cow off if she attempted an escape.

A few feet from the trailer the cow stopped. Suddenly realizing how far she was from the others, she let out an off-pitch bawl.

"It's alright, boss," Pode's voice was gentle. If there was anything he had learned from the beasts it was to stay calm and patient. Cows were simple creatures; the slightest bit of excitement stressed them. A loud noise alone would startle them and cause a bolt in the opposite direction. The cow stopped chewing. She seemed to be contemplating the situation, though Pode knew he was probably giving her too much credit. She might be simply resting because she couldn't go far on her lame leg without taking a break. Pode let her stand near the trailer for a little while before he moved in her direction again. She went along with him for three more clumsy steps and then swung her head back and forth, noticing Henry who had so far been out of her vision.

"Murrrahhhh!" she bellowed from the back of her throat, balking at taking a step up onto the wooden slat floor. Across the field, several of her companions turned toward the action, concerned.

"Come on, cow." The younger of the two men picked a stick up off the ground and used it to tap the ground behind her back legs. She kicked out sideways, barely missing Henry who leapt back in the nick of time. The cow stumbled and nearly fell over. Pode took the rope he had stuck between his jeans and his belt and dropped it around her neck. Letting out one more deep cry, the cow reluctantly moved forward and Pode used every bit of strength he had to pull while his dad pushed. The first step into the horse trailer was the hardest, but with the front half of the beast in, the rear half followed without issue. Henry threw the door shut behind her.

Pode took a deep breath and reached for her neck to take the rope off, certain if he left it she'd get caught on something inside the trailer and struggle and tip over while he tried to drive down the highway. As he shimmied between the wall of cow hide and the wall of metal, the animal shifted her weight onto her back legs, picking one up and stepping right down on Pode's left boot.

"Ahh! Dammit!" Pode yelled as fifteen hundred pounds of cow and calf crushed all of the bones in his foot.

"You alright?" Henry yelled through the open slits in the back door panel.

Pode shoved the cow's flank with everything he had. "Move! Shit!"

She stepped off of Pode and he felt faint from the pain. Sucking in his breath, he pushed the door open into his father and limped quickly away from the trailer. He heard the metal latch screech as it locked into place. Pode doubled over and recited every profane word and anything that remotely sounded like a profane word he could think of in rapid succession.

He felt Henry's hand on his shoulder, "I'll drive you over to Clay. Have 'em look at it. She'll be fine in there for an hour or two."

"No, Dad. I'm fine. Just hurts like hell at first. I'm fine. I'll take her to the house. I got to get that fence fixed by the creek today, too. I don't want them all out in Herman's wheat, and it's only a matter of time before that happens."

"You sure, Pode? That's a damn painful thing, to be stepped on. Might of broken bones." Henry took a step away, trying to read Pode. A man stood in front of him, toughing out the pain, but he would always see a boy.

"Yeah, I'm fine." Pode straightened up. Within his boot he tried to wiggle his toes and felt at least three of them move. "Let's go."

Something tickled Ava's nose. Half asleep, she raised her hand to her face and rubbed the spot. Sticky and coarse, she felt an unidentifiable stringiness to whatever it was. As she opened her eyes she was surprised to see blurry blue fabric in her vision. She was lying on Ellis's arm. His other was wrapped tightly around her waist, their legs tangled together. Across her face and the officer's chest, a nocturnal spider had been daring enough to weave her fragile web. Ava brushed at the web, pulled it away with the tips of her fingers, a look of disgust on her face. Propping her elbow under her, she sat up and looked around the shed. The sun dawned, but not long before and weak after the rain rays of sunlight leaked through crevices between the wet swollen boards in the walls. The dirt floor was damp, rain seeping into it from the surrounding ground.

Ellis rolled to his back awoken by Ava's movement. Without meeting his squinting eyes, Ava frowned and removed the rest of the cobweb from them. He had thrown his uniform shirt and her jacket over them like a hobo blanket and they collapsed into sleep on the plywood table as they waited out the rain that seemed like it would never end. They hadn't said anything more, but found each other a few times throughout the night with hands and lips between sleeping. Ava felt great comfort in the lean, strong arms. She slept a dead sleep of exhaustion, the rising and falling of her lungs in her chest hard to detect.

"I fell asleep," Ava whispered, rubbing her face with her dusty hands.

"I did, too. You—that was amazing sleeping you were

doing a bit ago. I was afraid you stopped breathing." Ellis's voice matched her quiet as he sat up beside her and swung his heavy boots over the edge of the table.

Ava laughed. "That wouldn't look good, would it, Deputy? Waking up beside a dead girl in an abandoned shed in the middle of nowhere?"

Ellis laughed too, embracing her bizarre humor. "I swear, officer, I woke up and she was just dead. I found her like that."

"Have you ever heard that before?"

"No, thank God no. But I think I've heard every other version of lie that exists."

"I can imagine. Wonder if we'll be able to get out of the mud." Ava stood to put on her jacket and felt dizzy, her stomach empty and upset by too much beer. The worst of the hangover was still a couple of hours away.

"Hasn't rained for weeks. Now that it's been a few hours, I'm sure the ground soaked it right up." He jumped to his feet as well, more stable than Ava, but the bones in his back and arms and legs were stiff from sleeping on the hard wood surface. Leaning forward, he pulled the door of the shed open and followed Ava out into the cold morning. Wrapping her arms around her body, she seemed unconcerned with Ellis, carefully treading the worn path, leaving for grass on either side a few times to avoid pockets of mud.

Once at her car, Ava stopped and watched Ellis ungracefully try to take the same route she had. The lightheadedness she felt was beginning to become a headache. Picturing herself covered in mud and leaves and cobwebs, hair frizzy and sticking up, she wanted to escape to recover in a warm shower and soft bed before Ellis saw her again. He didn't seem to mind, though. He grinned stupidly. She couldn't help but smile back.

"Thanks," Ava mumbled, "For waiting with me." She

reached for her door handle and pulled the heavy door open, water streaming off the bottom of it.

"Oh, sure, yeah," the man answered. "I'll see you, I guess?"

"Yeah," Ava looked up at the much taller man. She found him attractive before, but the slightly frazzled version of the usually so-put-together Ellis was somehow even better. Ellis's grin grew into his open-mouthed, big-toothed smile and he kissed her sweetly. Ava sank into her car, her head spinning from more than the remnants of the alcohol in her blood.

Absolutely still, except for his chest rising and falling underneath a light camouflage jacket, Baker waited. Three hours in, he hadn't spotted anything but a large rabbit. The rabbit froze and sniffed the air several times before entering the clearing 20 feet from the deer stand, deeming it safe. It chewed lazily on a bush at the edge of the clearing, tugging branches and leaves free and placing them in a pile, readying materials to make a nest.

The new shotgun's barrel at his side, pointed toward the sky, Baker wrapped his hand around the cold metal. He thought the overnight rain might stir the animals, force them to move around and enjoy the cool wet of the morning. So far only the rabbit had the same idea and with the sun beginning to break the thinning gray cloud cover, daylight was soon to follow. Baker's chance of seeing the 12-point buck he had caught glimpses of near the road was almost over. The big beautiful animal was far too intelligent to be out in broad daylight.

Laying the gun down, the tall man stretched his arms and legs out in front of himself. They were stiff and sore from being folded up into the hidden deer stand for so many hours. His neck popped as he leaned from one side to the other and rotated it around and stopped with his face facing into his lap. Rolling his shoulders, head bowed, he heard a twig snap directly to his right. Careful not to make any quick movements, Baker raised his head and leaned forward to better see the brush beside him.

Bone white and magnificent, the peaks and points and sculptural curves of the set of antlers looked like an unlit chandelier hung from the branches of the wind mangled mulberry trees. The buck was sniffing the air like the rabbit had. His shiny black nose twitched. His broad brown chest breathed in the scents around him. Almost directly above the beast, Baker knew his scent must be obvious. He had the shot. An absolutely perfect shot. At this close of a range one bullet would take the incredible creature down clean. He wouldn't have a chance to run. He wouldn't know what hit him. His life would end so easily.

Tears sprung from Baker's eyes, and he let them creep over his cheeks to his chin before wiping them away with his dirty hand. Without thinking, he cleared his throat and the buck jerked his head back and forth with the unusual sound. He looked directly at the tree stand without seeing it. Baker's heart stopped. The animal's head was perfect, flawless. The dark eyes full of expression and thought.

Baker stood and the buck froze, even the caving of his stomach as he breathed stopped as he held his breath.

"Go away, deer," Baker whispered, but the animal didn't move. "Go the fuck away!" Baker yelled at the top of his lungs. The deer bolted from its spot. The movement in his body and the legs as he fled were unmatched by any other living thing in nature. He was through the brush and miles beyond the clearing before the great buck slowed his pace. Birds nested in trees all around them took to the air and fled the clearing. The rabbit darted underneath brush and disappeared. The other animals disturbed by the sound of a man's voice and the reaction of the buck.

Baker sat. He bent his forehead into hands and let loose a brutal, soul-jarring round of sobs.

The road around Coin's Corner was deserted. The sun was out, but so were heavy clouds, so it was too early to tell if the day would be a sunny one or a cloudy one. Ellis sat in his car, eyes closed, not sleeping but thinking. Of nothing but Ava. His mind wandered to the feeling of her skin, the soft warmth of it, of her lips on his. Her steady rhythmic breathing, the rising and falling of her chest under her worn t-shirt. He wanted to hold her again, as soon as possible. To find her and wrap his arms around her and this time let things go much further.

It was the best night of sleep he could remember in recent history. How he could sleep so soundly with a plywood board as a mattress and wet jackets as a blanket in the cold of the fall night, he didn't understand. Ellis had spent sleepless years in a soft bed in a warm home. It was the comfort he found in having her body next to his. The comfort he felt in holding her and watching her sleep so soundly that finally distracted the overthinking of his mind and allowed him peaceful slumber.

He didn't know if he should call her, if the next day would be too soon. He had returned to overthinking and second guessing and wondering whether it was a one-night event or if she wanted more, too. Without a doubt, everyone in town knew about them already. He would get extra stares in town, now. He didn't care, though, because he knew Ava didn't care and that thought was amazingly freeing.

The faraway sound of an engine forced Ellis's eyes open. As he reentered the reality of sitting barely off the highway on a dirt road in the driver's seat of his highway patrol car, he squinted to see a light blue dot break the horizon to the west of town. It was moving far too fast, coming into view much quicker than it should be. The officer sat up straight and put his car in gear and held the clutch, ready to spring into action and pull over what he could now tell was a pickup.

It was the patched-up baby blue '57 Dodge that was the work in progress of Henry Wagner's youngest son. Ellis couldn't remember his first name. He had done most of the work on the Corvette, a talented kid with cars, but with a lot left to learn about life. This wouldn't be their first run in. Pulled over twice before for speeding, it was no surprise to see him bolting toward Flynn, but Ellis thought the kid should have known better than to go so fast around the corner in the antique vehicle. Close enough to clock, Ellis read 87 miles per hour on his radar and pulled out of the drive, hoping to stop the kid before he reached the most treacherous part of the turn.

Heading right for the truck, on the other side of the narrow highway, the squad car caught up with it in no time, pulled into the nearest drive and headed back toward Flynn, lights and siren on full blast. The truck didn't slow down. The younger Wagner had to see and hear the cop, but he didn't even make an attempt to brake. Riding far too close to the guardrail lining the space between the shoulder of the road and the rim of the harrowing river bluff, Ellis was terrified he would witness his first deadly crash.

The edge of the truck skimmed the top of the metal guardrail. Sparks flew out from between the two and the kid overcorrected, swerving into the wrong lane. Ellis's heart stopped as dumb luck danced the brick of a vehicle across the other shoulder and back into the center of the road without a loss of control. The driver, finally terrified into thinking, stopped the truck roughly in the ditch at the end of Coin's Corner and before the city limit sign of Flynn. The truck itself seemed to be taking a deep breath.

Ellis dropped his head, pulled off his sunglasses. He couldn't imagine what was going through the Wagner kid's mind. Turning off the siren, but leaving the lights on, he stepped unevenly out of his car and gathered himself as he approached the truck. The kid in the driver's seat was wild eyed, confused, like an injured stray dog. He stared at Ellis without fully seeing the cop. The officer expected to smell alcohol through the open driver's side window of the truck, but didn't. The window on the passenger side was rolled down, too, despite the chill in the air and the fact that Cort was only wearing a ragged t-shirt.

"What the hell were you doing there, kid? Trying to get us both killed?" Ellis laughed an ironic laugh, shaken from the event and disregarding all proper police procedure.

Cort's eyes were dilated; he couldn't sit still, glancing up and down and to both sides repeatedly. His right leg jumped. Ellis's hand went to his forehead as he realized what was going on. "Alright, I don't want any trouble, here, Wagner, but I'm going to need you to kill the engine and step out of the truck for me."

Cort hesitated, processing Ellis' request through his brain. Ellis felt along his belt, making sure he knew the exact location of his gun. Taking a step back, he gave the kid room to open the door of the truck and step out. Rubbing one arm with the other, unable to stop moving, Cort slammed the truck door shut.

"Come on back here," Ellis instructed and Cort walked around the back of the truck, his movements jerky. "Place your hands on the top of the tailgate for me, please."

He was following directions. That was a good sign.

The look on the 22 year old's face was full of concern, not anger. "Please don't arrest me, sir. Please don't. I got a baby on the way and Dad's already so pissed off at me for a bunch of things. I can't go to jail. Please don't make me go to jail."

It was pitiful. The young man was absolutely pitiful. Ellis breathed deeply, hands going to his hips as he considered the options. There was true remorse in Cort's voice, but this wasn't one too many beers or listening to the radio too loud and losing track of how fast he was going.

"What are you on, Wagner?"

"Nothing, sir."

"Lying to me ain't gonna help your case any." Ellis walked toward the door of the truck. "If I look around in here will I find anything?"

"No, sir."

"Nothing at all?"

"No, sir. I ain't got it on me. I smoked it at a friend's house. I swear I ain't ever done it before and I will not again. I can promise you I won't. Just, just please don't put me in jail."

"Meth?"

"Yes, sir. But I swear it's the first time I ever tried it and I will not again. It was stupid. Fucking stupid. I can't screw up like this anymore. I got a fucking girl and kid to take care of."

Ellis glanced into the cab of the truck. He didn't bother to search it, fairly certain Cort was telling him the truth. "OK, empty out your pockets and put everything on the edge of the bumper for me."

"Don't take me to jail, sir. I'm begging you. I'm so sorry about this," the younger Wagner pleaded with the officer.

"I'm not arresting you, but you can't drive high like

this. You could have killed somebody or yourself. You understand that?" Cort nodded his head and Ellis went on. "I'm going to take you over to county, put you in a cell, and let you come down from this. Soon as you're able, I'll let you come back and get your truck."

"Thank you so much, sir, thank you. I do understand, I swear to God I do and I so appreciate this and I will never do anything like this again."

"You do I arrest you, have you prosecuted and you go to jail instead of raising your baby, you understand me?" Ellis was firm, but not mean.

"I do. I swear to God I do."

"Good. Now take everything out of your pockets for me."

Cort fumbled through his pockets and produced a beat-up leather wallet and a handful of change and a can of Skoal, then replaced his hands on top of the tailgate. He leaned forward, his forehead touching the backs of hands, his body twitching. Ellis paused and looked at the things before collecting the wallet and leaving the rest. Taking the kid by his forearm, the officer led him up the ditch and opened the back door of the cruiser and helped him inside without handcuffing him or locking the doors.

The girls were tucked into bed. The house was quiet except for the murmur of the television in the living room. Shannon sat at the kitchen table in a split vinyl chair, legs folded underneath her, hair piled up in a massive pony tail of dark ringlets. She clipped coupons from the Sunday edition of the *Wichita Eagle*, the paper saved for her by her mother every week. Wood floorboards under worn beige carpet creaked with her husband's steps as Kale walked down the hallway. He crossed the kitchen and opened the fridge, rearranging juice and formula and yellow Tupperware containers of leftover supper to get to his last bottle of Corona. Without looking at each other or saying a thing, the two existed in the space of their kitchen. Kale popped the top off the gold glass bottle in his hand and threw it away in the trashcan under the sink. The coarse sound of serrated scissors separating pieces of newsprint behind him, the man took a long swig of his beer and started his trek back to the couch in the living room.

"Ellen and Barry are going to Jamaica in January."

Kale stopped in the doorway, his back turned to his wife. Shannon continued to cut coupons without looking up. The words themselves were meaningless. He knew she didn't care about where a coworker was going after the New Year, but she was trying to start a conversation. She was trying to bring up a truth she was afraid to discuss again and so was taking a deliberately passive route.

"Can we talk about this tomorrow?" Kale asked quietly.

"Talk about what?" Shannon played dumb, which instantly infuriated her husband. "Ellen's vacation?"

"Shan, I know what you're doing here. You're stressed out about money and trust me, I am too, but can we talk about it tomorrow?"

Shannon shrugged her shoulders. "Sure. Tomorrow. Sometime between you taking Julia to school at eight and picking her up at three and taking Grace to preschool at ten and picking her up at two and taking Kate to her doctor's appointment at noon and meeting the insurance guy about the roof at four and me making sure everyone eats breakfast and then working a twelve-hour shift and trying to do a couple of loads of laundry and all of us getting to your mother's house by seven for supper. Sure. Tomorrow."

Kale sipped his beer and glared at his wife. She had said everything she had said without glancing up once from her coupon clipping, turning a page and scanning it for discounts. Crossing the kitchen again, he pulled out the chair on the other side of the table from her, sat his beer and himself down hard, and waited to speak until she stopped cutting and looked him in the eye.

"Did you talk to Lou?" Shannon's voice was barely above a whisper.

"No," Kale's was firm, but not much louder.

"Why not?"

"Because I don't want to be a fucking used car salesman. That's like one step up from trash collector."

"No, it's not. And it doesn't have to be forever. Just until you find something else. I think you'd be a good salesman."

Kale shook his head and put his elbows on the table and his chin in his hands. "Why?"

"I don't know. People like you. They trust you." Shannon had pleaded this case before. "And the reality is that we can't float along like this forever. We have been so lucky, but all day at work I see awful things. Car wrecks, kids with cancer, house fires. Awful, awful things. We have nothing, Kale. No savings, fifty-thousand dollars' worth of debt, two cars that are more than a decade old, a leaky roof that insurance may or may not deem is from hail damage. You know neither of our parents can help us and my sister is never going to let us live down borrowing from her even if we pay her back a thousand times over. She mentions the money every time we're in the same room together."

Silence at the table, as both of them considered Shannon's latest list of arguments. She had a good job, but it wasn't enough and he may have been upset with her in the moment, but Kale did wish he could take his wife on a vacation to Jamaica.

"Used car salesman," Kale said to himself. Shannon

studied his face, trying to read which direction his mind was going. "There are worse things, I guess. I don't know if I'll have time tomorrow, but Wednesday. I'll go talk to Lou Wednesday. After I drop Gracie off."

Shannon smiled a weak smile, temporarily happy to finally get an agreement out of him. Kale pushed back from the table and stood up. "I'm watching a really bad horror movie and I got extra room on the couch, if . . ."

His wife's smile grew. "See? Salesman." Uncurling her legs, she rose from the kitchen chair and joined Kale in the living room, wedging herself perfectly into the space between his body and his arm against the back of the couch. Shannon settled in with her hand on her husband's chest, head on his shoulder. They both laughed loudly as a girl ran and tripped through a less-than-convincing dark forest sound stage set. An instant after her laughter stopped, Shannon dozed and Kale bent his head ever so slightly to kiss her forehead.

The Flynn County Courthouse sparkled underneath the sun. From certain angles, the stark white paint didn't look dry. Its wood shingles had been scraped and sanded and repainted over two months before, though, when the summer heat was still in the air. The look of wet to the paint was a convenient joke to the old men who sat in the chairs lining the wall of Lois's Cut 'n' Color across the street, awaiting haircuts and catching up on gossip. They were watching it dry, in the most literal of all senses, underneath the red and white pole that had stopped spinning long, long ago.

A late model metallic crimson Cadillac crept down Main Street and came to a halt in a parking spot at the front doors of the courthouse. Using the doorframe and the mushed-in top of the driver's seat, a huge balding man hauled himself up and out of the car. The entire vehicle wobbled back and forth as he let go. From sitting and sweating and sitting some more, the back of his gray suit jacket creased into deep wrinkles. The three gold buttons on the front wouldn't have closed with the help of a vice and a miracle over the white dress shirt that concealed a belly the size of a prize-winning watermelon.

Inside the barbershop, Spud Cox turned to Max Turner and said, "Looks like Billy James lost weight since I seen him last." The two meddlers shared a hardy chuckle. Each shifted in their chair and continued to read their respective sections of the same day's *Wichita Eagle*.

Billy James lumbered up the courthouse steps and pulled the front door open, turning his body sideways a bit to fit through the frame. The lobby of the nearly hundred-year-old building had red brick pattern sheet vinyl stretching the length of the room. The flooring met with walls of fake woodgrain paneling. On the right side of the small square room, an aquamarine 1972 standard issue office waiting room couch with curved silver arms created a seating area with two identically matched blue chairs. *People* and *Better Homes & Gardens* and *Highlights* magazines perched at the end of the balanced glass on silver frame coffee table between the couch and chairs.

The left side of the room was filled with a large laminate built-in desk and shelves. Behind the desk crowded with family pictures, Kris typed in rhythm with the song on the radio. She looked out of the corner of her eye at Billy James and smiled in greeting as he walked through the office and past her to an opening directly across from the front door that led to the guts of the building.

At the last step before he went out of her sight and into the hallway, the big man stopped. His voice was loud, labored. "Kris, Ava Schaffer's coming in for a meeting with me later on today, if you could send her back when she gets here. You don't need to call me or anything. I don't have much else going today. You can send her on back. Thanks."

"She's coming in again?" The man only offered her a toad-like grimace. "Yes, I'll do that." Kris smiled at him with her answer, the corners of her thin mouth and gray eyes breaking into laugh lines.

Somewhere in the distance the door to the office Billy James rented from the city shut heavily. Country music hummed through the front office. The ancient clock radio sat near the top of the neatly cluttered desk shelves. The music was barely audible, but Kris knew all of the words to all of the Waylon Jennings and Kenny Chesney songs that alternated between commercials for Baker and Sons Lumberyard on Fifth Street and the Ford Dealership in Clay that was desperately trying to get rid of last year's overstocked F-150s.

A half hour or so passed before the front door of the courthouse swung open and Ava stepped inside. Their eyes met and neither could keep from smiling, as Kris jumped up from behind her desk to greet the taller young woman.

"Ava! Oh, how are you?" Kris reached out and held onto Ava's forearms. She seemed thinner even since Sunday dinner the week before and this was something that worried Kris far more than Ava's worn clothes or lack of shampoo use. With all of her kids now in their twenties, the mother knew they didn't take care of themselves like she wished they would. Beer was not a substitute for food. Dirty hair and clothes were not attractive. Vehicle accessories were not wise ways to spend an entire paycheck. Wren and Pode seemed to be headed in the right direction, but despite baby news, Kris feared her youngest still had a long ways to go.

"I'm good," Ava answered. Kris's warmth radiated throughout a room like no one else Ava had ever known. It was something, she realized while still in grade school, her mother lacked completely. The feeling made her love to go and to stay at her friend's house. Pode had the family, the loving brother and sister, the loving parents, Ava desired. Though she would admit that it was jealousy, it was never of the hateful variety, because there was no way she could hate a family who embraced her, welcomed her, and showered her with love like she was one of their own.

"Are you taking care of yourself," Kris asked, though she already knew the answer.

Their eyes met and Ava felt as easy to see through as a piece of glass in one of her works. No matter how many coats of paint she brushed on, Kris's motherly insight peeled it away, layer by layer, until the woman caught a glimpse of what was underneath.

"Well, I guess we should get to why you're here. He didn't give me any details, but Billy said I can send you on back."

Ava left Kris standing beside the desk in the front office without any explanation about the details of the meeting, either. The building was deeper than it appeared from outside. Six doors staggered either side of the hall that carried on the tacky linoleum, faux paneling theme. Two of the doors led to community meeting rooms where everyone from the Flynn County School Board to the Girl Scouts to the local farmers' associations met on their specific nights of the week. One door had a plaque, declaring it the "Flynn County Records Room." Across from it the fourth door led to an empty office, stenciled with the name of a lawyer who had retired from practice in Flynn decades before Ava was born. The last door on the left was a break area, with a sink, table, refrigerator, and doors leading to men's and women's restrooms. The sixth and final door at the end of the hallway was closed, but brightly lit through the frosted window in the top half. On the milky glass block gold lettering read "William A. James, Attorney at Law." Ava slowly read the bold letters to herself as she raised her hand and knocked on the wooden frame around the door's window.

"Come in," Billy James's familiar rasp commanded.

Ava opened the door and peeked around the edge of it. She had sat in the same office a few weeks before with her brother, listening as her mother's 52 years' worth of belongings were itemized and split up. Her last will and testament read to her children by her longtime lawyer and friend.

Billy James rose arduously from his plush genuine suede office chair. "Ava, dear, how are you?"

She met him on his half of the long room, uncomfortable with how much work it took for him to stand and walk and breathe, and took his outstretched clammy hand. Billy James had been a part of her life for as long as she could remember. Dora May was always quite fond of the presence of smart, influential men and being the only lawyer in town, as well as the town's lawyer, lent that sort of power to Billy James. Ava had always wondered if her mother would have been interested in something other than a friendship if it hadn't been for the lawyer's many unhealthy habits. Though a nice man and an obviously intelligent one, Billy James's physical appearance would almost certainly never have lived up to Dora May's level of vanity.

"OK," Ava nodded.

Billy James considered her silently, a look on his round face she couldn't quite read. The flattening of his lips and the lines around his strained eyes made her think he was stuck somewhere in deep thought between a happy memory and a great bout of sadness. She had seen the same expression looking back at her through mirrors over the previous few weeks.

"Should I close the door?" She pointed with her thumb back over her shoulder as she asked. Her voice brought him back to the tile floored, fluorescent-lit room.

"Yes, yes, thank you. Then please, have a seat."

She nudged the door shut and crossed the room again, easing back into an armchair that matched the office chair Billy James settled into behind his oversized mahogany desk. Ava felt small in the room, nervous. She had never been fond of official places like offices and hospitals and courtrooms. Throughout her life they had only signified bad. Divorce, sickness, death, things that would rearrange the landscape of a girl's life. Happy stories happened in happy places like cafes and friends' houses and riverbanks. Sad things happened in places like this.

"Ava, I, uh, I guess I might as well cut right to the chase on this." He cleared his throat, but it didn't relieve it of any of its roughness. "I got a call yesterday from an insurance company. They got a hold of my name because they found out I was your mother's lawyer and I guess they didn't know or couldn't find your information. Do you have a cellular telephone? Or just that house one? You're awfully hard to get in touch with sometimes."

Ava shrugged. "I don't ever answer my phone. Sorry."

"Well, anyway, they sent me documents they had. Explained 'em." He moved his computer mouse and clicked it a couple of times. "I'm sure you know this, but she worked for the hospital over in Clay right about the time she had you, twenty-four, twenty-five years ago. At the time they had supplemental life insurance, which was optional and it was an option she chose. She's been paying for it all this time. Never paid it late once according to all their documents. They just now found out

141

about," he paused between the next few hard words, "Her . . . passing . . . and . . . uh . . . wanted to square up with you on the claim."

"Shouldn't we call Eddy?"

"No. You are the only listed beneficiary."

"But is there a default thing? I mean, so that it gets split between her kids?"

"That would only be in the case that she didn't name a beneficiary or the beneficiary she named died. She never added him the policy."

"Did she forget?" She asked herself the question more than the man sitting in front of her.

"I don't know, Ava. It's odd. I know. She wasn't the type of person who forgot things like this, so I couldn't tell you for sure what happened. She received a bill from them, once a month, that she paid on time, every month. She probably even received phone calls now and then for assurance, to make sure she didn't have any updates to make to the plan, things of that nature."

"Well, how much is it for? I mean, maybe she didn't bother with it because . . ."

The lawyer interrupted, "Half a million dollars."

"What?" Ava's mouth hung open for a few seconds, until she realized and closed it.

"Five hundred thousand dollars," Billy James reiterated.

"Five-five hundred-thous . . ." Ava's voice trailed off.

"Yes, ma'am."

"Whoa."

"Yep."

Ava's mind spun. Why would her mother never put her brother on the policy? Was it an oversight? Did she mean for it all to be Ava's? Was she testing her daughter, like she did so often, in ways she never tested her son? Did she entrust it to Ava knowing Ava would give her brother half, anyway?

Billy James let Ava gather her thoughts before he spoke again. "I have the company's information. They'll need a call back from you so they can verify things and get some information from you so that the funds can be issued to you. Ava, are you alright?"

"I—I had no idea. I mean, I don't know how it was paid for. I paid everything, all of her bills, while she was sick the last few months."

"Maybe she paid in advance, by the year or something?"

"I had no idea," Ava repeated.

"I promise you I didn't either, as her lawyer or her friend. And I helped her write her will and she didn't mention it. Your mother was," he looked for the right word and couldn't find it, "Something else. And your brother inherited every bit of it. If I were you, I'd not tell anybody until you decide what to do with it. And I mean anybody. Cause the way news travels in this town, Eddy will know about this faster than a new pair of shoes can find a fresh pile of dog shit."

"Yeah. Yes. Thank you?"

He went on. "I can email you all the information for the company. They'll need forms signed and faxed back so they can process the claim. It may take a few weeks to go through. You have any questions about any of it, give me a call. Alright, dear?"

\* \* \*

Eddy sighed. His nose buried deep in a book. His wide shoulders on his painfully skinny frame hunched forward over the red gingham clothed table. Ava played with empty sugar packets. She had taken them from the oblong container in the center of the table, poured their contents into her iced tea and was folding the crisp pink rectangles different ways, searching for how to assemble the idea forming in her mind. Eddy looked up, watched her for a second, and then went back to reading, his face full of disgust.

On the other side of Martha's, Dora May swept through the front door, crisp navy suit, matching navy pumps. Their mother always swept, strutted, perched. She didn't enter or walk or sit. Ava was fascinated by the woman all throughout childhood, but now felt a pang of jealously because she already knew she would never be like her. What preteen Ava didn't understand yet was while the mother drew eyes with strong demanding confidence, the daughter would draw far more with gentle eccentric charm.

"Have you ordered yet?" Dora May's deep voice accusatory.

"No," Eddy mumbled, never looking up from his book. "Ava thought we should wait for you."

Dora May rolled her eyes. "We don't have all night. You should have ordered without me."

Defeated, Ava dropped her eyes to the table. Their mother twisted in her seat and looked around the room, spotting a girl behind the bar, filling drinks and placing them carefully on a serving tray. She waved, arm stretched straight above her head, until she was satisfied the girl had seen her.

"Well, how was everyone's day?" Dora May spoke at her children, not to them.

"Good," Ava and Eddy quietly responded in unison, neither of them looking up or meaning it.

"Eddy, for Christ's sake. Could you close your damn book for twenty minutes and at least pretend to have a few of the manners I've forced into you?"

His eyes rose over the edge of his thick plastic-rimmed

glasses. Reading for a few more seconds, partly out of defiance, partly to find a good stopping point, he dog-eared the page he was on and pushed the book to the corner of the table. They sat in silence. Ava played with the emptied sugar packets. Eddy frowned resentfully at his closed book. Dora May leaned back in her chair as she examined a manicured fingernail with a fresh split in the middle of it.

"I showed the house on Cotter today. To a young couple. They're from somewhere around Kansas City. He's the new math teacher at the junior high school."

"Mr. Marks," Eddy confirmed.

"Yes, Marks." Dora May had no idea how to relate to her children. She had never had any sort of maternal feeling toward them. She knew, but would be the last to admit, that they had raised themselves, because she had always been too busy working. Or fighting with their father. A tiny speck of guilt began to grow inside of her, but as she did every other time she felt this same guilt, she forced it away with a monetary resolution.

"I was thinking new bikes." Both sets of her children's eyes darted to her face. "Since we didn't get to take a family vacation this summer."

Ava and Eddy both smiled, widely. They had never been on a family vacation, so the excuse was a joke, but neither one of them dared point it out with shiny new 10-speeds on the line.

"Hi, are you guys ready to order?" the girl from behind the bar asked with a cautious glance in Dora May's direction.

"Yes, thank you, Corrine." Dora May's voice was cool. Ava tried to remember the girl's last name, but couldn't. She had seen her around town, with the tall military guy. Lucas Ellis. She remembered his name because his mother was the school librarian. Mrs. Ellis, or Catherine, because she was one of the cool teachers who didn't mind if you called her by her first name.

"I'll take a grilled chicken breast, like the one you put on sandwiches, but only the breast. And a side salad. No cheese, fat free ranch on the side, please."

"To drink?" As she scribbled on the order pad, an itty bitty diamond on her ring finger caught the dim light in the room.

"Water. With two slices of lemon."

"I want a cheeseburger," Eddy declared. "And fries. No tomato."

"No tomato on your fries?" Ava grinned at her brother. He shot her a look that told her he wasn't in the mood to be made fun of.

Ava focused her attention on the waitress. When she smiled, Corrine couldn't help but return the girl's warm smile. "A chicken strip basket, please."

"Sure," Corrine's seemed nervous. "I'll put this in and be right back with your drink, Ms. Schaffer."

The front door of Martha's creaked as it opened. A sound so familiar no one bothered to look up, because they were so used to it. Years before, the group who played pitch on Tuesday afternoons gave Martha a bottle of WD40 wrapped up as a Christmas present. She refused to use it, though, and instead left it sealed and climbed up on a chair to put it on the highest shelf above the fridge, where it remained untouched, coated in a layer of dust so thick it was hard to tell what it was anymore.

Billy James plodded across the empty floor space between the tables. It was barely wide enough for him to get by without bumping the backs of the chairs. He slowed as he reached the bar and stopped beside Dora May.

"Dor, kids, how're y'all doing?" Younger Ava's imagination always pictured a live frog living deep in the lawyer's throat, causing his murky voice. Slightly older Ava thought that he needed to stop smoking so many cigarettes.

"Oh, hello, Billy." Dora May tried to sound nonchalant, but something in their mother's voice was off. Billy James was the only person Ava had ever heard call her mother anything other than "Dora May" or "Ms. Schaffer." They had been friends for a long time and that was Ava's best guess as to why he was able to get away with it.

"Mr. James?" Eddy was suddenly overcome with excitement, the complete opposite of the boy a few minutes before. "Do you have any good cases right now?"

Billy James considered him, amused. "Still want to be a lawyer, Eddy?"

"Yes. I am *going* to be a lawyer."

"Well, don't grow up too quickly. You'll put me out of business." Billy James smiled at Dora May who responded with a dismissive shake of her head, but was clearly proud of her son's future ambitions.

"Oh, I won't. I am not staying here. I hate it here. There's nothing to do here. I'm going to move to New York or Chicago or somewhere way bigger."

The man chuckled. "Yeah. I've been to those places. This place isn't so bad."

"It's peaceful," Ava spoke quietly. She wanted to be part of the conversation, but was afraid of being humiliated by her brother.

"That's absolutely right, Ava." Billy James was serious. He glanced from Ava to Dora May to Eddy. "Your sister's a smart girl."

"Pffft, whatever. She's like, flunking everything but art."

"There's another lesson in there for you, boy. How well someone does in school has absolutely nothing to do

147

with how smart they are."

Ava beamed. People rarely stuck up for her. She liked Billy James despite the unattractiveness of his taxing voice and his flimsy, thinning blonde hair and his severe weight. He was a good man and always kind to her.

"You all have a nice night."

"Thank you, Billy."

Dora May feigned disinterest as the dysfunctional little family waited for their supper, but continued to covertly watch him from the corner of her eye.

# 6

Every shade of color between orange and pink stretched across the sky in great uneven swaths striped with thin white clouds creeping slowly toward the horizon where the sun had dropped out of sight moments before. Shadows of World War II era wooden houses cast themselves long over the streets of Flynn, busy with Friday evening traffic arriving home from work and school and leaving again to get to Flynn County High School in time to watch the kickoff of the third home football game of the season. In an hour or two the cheering crowd would be heard all across town by the older folks who stayed in and listened to the game on the radio and ate their early suppers and obeyed their early bedtimes.

Pode limped up the sidewalk to the front porch of his house and sat heavily on the top step, ready to relax and soak up the last rays of sunlight left in the unusually warm fall day. He put the case of Bud Light cans tucked under his arm down beside him. Pulling gently at first and then deciding on one swift movement, he jerked his left boot off.

"Holyfuckingshit."

The man closed his eyes, ground his teeth together, and leaned back, enduring the pain coursing up his leg from the foot that had been trapped all day and was swollen to twice its normal size. Pode peeled his dingy sock off to reveal a mass of black and blue only identifiable as a foot by the toes at the end of it. This had been the first day for a week that he hadn't tried to stay

149

off of it. He'd walked two miles looking for the bull and found the creature tangled in a mess of barbed wire and brush. For a reason Pode would never know, the animal bolted into the fence and instead of busting it, entwined himself to the point of lame and gave up.

"Stupid cow." He shook his head. "If that hoof doesn't heal you'll be the best prime rib I ever had for Christmas dinner." Ripping open the side of the case of beer he grabbed three cans. He popped one open and took a long swig. Then he carefully stretched his sock back over the bruises and shoved the other two inside of it on either side. Scooting until his back touched the porch pillar behind him, Pode lifted his throbbing leg and elevated it on the edge of the box of remaining beer.

Squinting into the end of the creamsicle sunset, Pode watched a figure as it turned the corner at the end of the street and continued walking past the empty lot beside his house. He could make out the pattern of the oversized men's flannel shirt Ava had unearthed in an old box and espoused into her wardrobe the previous winter. It made her look sloppy, mannish. As mannish as Pode's pretty blonde friend could look. Ava frowned at Pode's shoeless foot and the misshapen sock stretched over it. She stepped over the cracks in the concrete sidewalk and stopped at the bottom of the steps.

The friends stink eyed each other. Neither of them were quite sure what to say. Finally, Pode was the first to break. "You want a beer?"

Ava tried not to smile. "A foot beer? No, thank you." She leaned over, reaching her hand out toward his foot. "What did you do?"

"Don't touch it." His voice was firm, serious. He leaned forward ready to grab her hand.

"Sorry. I'm sorry."

"That's OK. I got stepped on by a cow. It hurts like

hell."

"That's why you smell like shit. I could smell you all the way down the block."

They were both grinning. There was too much history. They knew each other too well. It was each other's mission in life to make the other laugh. There was no set of rumors, no imagined scenario about a bonfire and a cop, that was more important than 20 years of friendship.

Ava climbed the stairs and stepped over Pode, careful not to disturb his foot or its placement on the caved-in box. Dragging a rusted, turquoise painted, fan-back metal chair from beside the front door, Ava placed it beside Pode and slid back into it. She gazed out at the sky with him as it faded to a black and a blue not dissimilar from the current colors of the man's foot. Night took over and they sat in silence illuminated by the glow of the spotlight on the post in the yard.

"You drop your car off at Callahan's?"

"Yeah."

"Good. Only a matter of time before one of the other motor mounts goes and then you'd be stuck without an engine at all."

Ava shook her head. In his words she caught a glimpse of his father. It was strange to watch the trading of places as it happened. Pode did the majority of the farm work now and his father helped. Both of them were growing up, in some ways forcibly. It seemed too soon. Ava felt too young, but it was the effect of the place they lived in and the way they lived in it. Hard work, resilience, practicality were bred into them like how to point was bred into a good hunting dog. Their friends were getting married, having babies, buying land to farm. In many ways, Pode and Ava were lagging behind.

"You hungry?'

Ava glanced at Pode, surprised by how fast the

darkness had settled in. "Not really. Are you?"

"Yeah. There's a couple of frozen pizzas in the freezer. Do you think you could handle throwing one in the oven?"

"Yes," Ava groaned. Her complete lack of cooking skill was an ongoing joke since the kitchen accident Pode coined the Spontaneously Combusting Oven Mitt Event of '09.

She rose from her seat and as she shut the storm door behind her, Pode yelled, "Try not to catch anything on fire!"

Ava ignored him. She was relieved they could still joke, but Ellis entered her mind, as he so often had during the past week and guilt filled her. She would be careful not to light anything on fire, physically, in the kitchen, but she could not guarantee there would be no emotional fires elsewhere. She hadn't done anything wrong, but she felt like she had. Ellis called her a couple of times, but Ava let it go to voicemail. She didn't know what to say. What to do. What the bonfire night even meant. Her decision to show up on Pode's doorstep was the following of a plan made weeks before. He had suggested she leave her car at Callahan's and walk to his house for a ride. There wasn't any other motive, Ava convinced herself. It was a plan they had made weeks before.

The kitchen had not been remodeled. Ever. Avocado green appliances rested on worn brown patterned linoleum. Around them, darkly stained, flat front cabinets lined three walls, cut out to expose a single small window. Wallpaper of yellow and green damask peeled at the edges and in the corners, scarred black with grease in patches behind the oven. Ava opened the freezer door of the round-cornered refrigerator and dug through it, pulling out two boxes. She read the fronts of both, deciding on pepperoni and shoving the supreme box back inside, precariously, shutting the door against it before it tumbled out.

Ava rotated a knob to kick on the gas oven and opened the box and the plastic that encased the pizza, rearranging the pepperonis fallen to the side. She heard Pode's voice and aimed an ear toward the living room and front porch. A woman's voice she recognized but couldn't place was also speaking.

The oven was instantly hot. A burst of heat hit her in the face as she pulled the door open with the scraping sound of a loose hinge and carefully slid the pizza onto the top rack. Ava closed the door and looked the kitchen over before leaving it, knowing Pode would never let her live down another cooking disaster.

From the living room, the voices were louder and Ava could understand what they were saying. She reached out to touch the screen door handle right as the woman's voice spoke. "Yeah, Rick's at the game, so I was hoping to get your help to move it, but I completely understand why you are out of commission. I'm sure that is terribly painful. Do you need any help with anything? Can I bring over supper, or . . ."

"No, no thanks, Ms. McEwing. I'm good. Sorry I can't help you tonight."

Ava took a step backward and peered out the gap between the edge of the dusty mini blinds and the thick wooden window frame.

Sandy McEwing stood at the bottom of the front porch steps. A fragile woman, petite and thin boned, she looked as if a heavy wind might knock her over. Her once-strawberry-blonde hair was pulled back into a high ponytail. Long stick-straight bangs stopped bluntly above her barely there eyebrows and wide crystal blue eyes. Eyes Penny had inherited. It wouldn't be strange for her to walk across the street for a neighborly visit, but something about the tone of her voice struck Ava as odd. Curiosity sparked, instead of rejoining Pode, Ava paused to listen.

"I feel so bad leaving you like this." The pastor's wife took a step closer, Pode's face eyelevel with her flat chest. She put a hand on his shoulder and he blinked hard. "Do you need help getting inside, at least? I could stick around. Keep you company." With her last few words, she leaned too far forward.

Ava was no longer peeking and was full on staring out the window. She couldn't believe what she was seeing. She had never liked Sandy McEwing and didn't know anyone who did, but could never pinpoint why. It was suddenly clear. Ava had watched her be way too kind to other's women's husbands throughout the years, but it never before dawned on her that there might be another objective beyond the pleasantries.

Where other men might have been speechless in their shock over what was happening, Pode couldn't shut up. "No, no. Thank you, ma'am, but I don't need anything. I don't need anything at all. I would gladly help you move the shelf if I could, but I can't, so I am of no use to you, at all."

"I don't know about that. I bet I could find a use for you." The much older woman smiled crookedly at Pode as her other hand landed on his inner thigh. Ava's hand went to her mouth as she gasped. As entertaining as the horrible awkwardness was, she had to save her friend.

"Hey, Pode," Ava announced as she opened the screen door. "I put the pepperoni in, if that's OK?" She stopped midway through opening the door, pretending to be surprised to see Sandy at the bottom of the stairs. "Oh. Hi. Ms. McEwing."

The woman jumped and quickly pulled her hands off

of Pode. Ava frowned at her, glanced at the back of Pode's head, then right back at Sandy, tilting her head to the side to accentuate her fake confusion.

"Well, um." Sandy reached out and patted Pode on the shoulder a couple of times. She attempted to make touching him look as if it was simply part of a friendly gesture. "Thanks, anyway. I'm sure I can have my *husband* move it when he gets home later. I hope your foot feels better, soon. Good to see you, Ava. You two kids have a lovely evening."

Her pace was just shy of running. Pode and Ava, one as puzzled as the other, watched in silence as she reached her driveway and ducked into the garage through a side door.

"Whoa," Ava said quietly. "Is she always like that?'

"No. I've helped her do stuff before. She's always nice." Pode thought for a second. "I mean, kind of flirty, but she's never touched me before."

Ava busted out laughing. "Your mom would love this."

"Oh, please don't say anything to Mom, Av." Pode rubbed his forehead.

"She would laugh so hard."

"Ugh." A look of dread spread over Pode's face. "I almost puked in my mouth there. I didn't know what to do."

Ava laughed harder, reaching out a hand to help Pode up.

"Nooooo!" Ava yelled, folding her hands together on top of her head, leaning back flat against the living room couch.

"Oh," Pode said indifferently as he reached out as far as he could with his leg propped straight out on the edge of his oversized arm chair. He pulled all of Ava's remaining poker chips, and a bottle cap she had found in the pocket of her jeans and passed off as a blue chip in a last ditch effort, across the coffee table. "I guess that means I won. Again."

"How can somebody be so fucking lucky?" Ava shook her head.

"Uh, between the lame foot and getting hit on by the creepy old lady across the street, I don't know that I'd consider myself 'lucky' tonight. Poker's all skill, actually."

"Then you should move to Vegas."

"Beer?" Pode held his empty can up.

Ava shook her head. "I'm ready for bed."

"Sore loser. Can you grab me one?"

"Yes," Ava mumbled and drug her feet across the living room. The fire she had built in the fireplace earlier in the evening was burned to a few smoldering embers. Outside the window the wind was blowing so hard the walls of the house creaked in resistance to it.

"It's 'Yes, Poker Master Wagner,'" Pode yelled after her.

"I'll shake it," Ava threatened as she returned holding the beer out in front of her as if she might.

"Don't take your losing out on that poor beer. It's not his fault."

"No, but it probably does have something to do with me consuming several of his friends."

Ava gently sat the can on the corner of the table in front of Pode and sank into the couch again with a deep yawn. She closed her eyes and listened as Pode popped the top on the can and drank. She had had four and there were seven left in the fridge, meaning Pode had had 13 beers in the past four hours. It wasn't the amount of alcohol that surprised her anymore, it was his significant tolerance to it.

"What would you do if you had half a million dollars?"

Ava sat up straight. "What?" How did he know? She could feel her heart racing.

Pode frowned at his friend's reaction. He was holding a poker chip up in front of his face. "A half a million dollars? Or a million? Or ten million? Whatever amount? What would you do with it?"

Ava breathed a sigh of relief. Pode didn't know, couldn't know. He had simply picked a number out of the blue. This night had become lucky for him.

"I don't know." She shrugged her shoulders. All day, since Billy James told her about the life insurance, she had mulled it over. The question was much harder when it was no longer fantasy based.

"I think I'd build a mansion in the country somewhere with a game room and a pool. Collect guns and cars."

"That'd be cool," Ava teased. "Then maybe we'd have a real poker table to play on. And some friends to play with."

"Come on. What would you do if you had endless money?"

"I don't know. Travel. See more of the world."

"New York?" Pode already knew the answer.

"Yeah."

Ellis tossed and turned. Finally beginning to doze, three hours after crawling into bed, his phone rang. It was a highway patrolman who lived in the next county over. He was the first on the scene while driving home through Flynn and saw the glow of an intense fire from the road. The clock on Ellis's bedside table read 3:18 a.m. He pulled jeans and a sweatshirt on over his boxers. Socks and boots and belt and gun and he was out the door in five minutes, the cold of the late fall night stinging his bare face and hands.

Paramedics were loading someone strapped to a

stretcher into the back of the Flynn County EMT ambulance as Ellis parked his cruiser in a row with two other vehicles with flashing lights. He recognized the robust profile of Sherriff Beatle standing beside a taller, thinner man in uniform. The men's breath and the exhaust from the vehicles formed clouds that quickly dispersed into the brisk air. Stuffing his hands into the pockets of jeans, Ellis strolled across the road and stood shoulder to shoulder with his boss, peering over the mangled piece of guardrail with a gap in it where the metal and cement and bolts gave. Coin's Corner had claimed another victim. Nearby, the larger fire truck from Clay was being packed up by a crew of four men in heavy yellow fire suits.

The fire smoldered, but it was almost out. The vehicle, or what the officer could make of what was left of it, blended into the scalded trees. Ellis couldn't tell if it was a car or a truck. The back door of the ambulance slammed shut, the sound causing all three dazed men to turn toward it.

"Are they gonna live?" Ellis asked, the words croaky.

The highway patrolman spoke first. "Yep. Actually didn't fair too bad, considering the way the wreck looks. He's burned on his arms and neck, but probably too drunk to even know it."

Ellis nodded. "Can you tell who it is?"

"Ed Schaffer. Suppose I'll go see if I can find his daughter. Poor girl." Sherriff Beatle retreated to his blue F-150, vinyl lettering and a design on the side of it designated it the sheriff's vehicle. "You guys stay here 'til the smoke's burned out, make sure it don't relight."

"Wait," Ellis called after his boss. He took a couple of big steps away from the edge of the bluff. "I have her number."

The sheriff's eyebrows tilted in as he pondered the

Ellis. A dirty smile spread across his face under his graying mustache. "Well, deputy, I didn't know. Alright. Alright, you go find her. I suppose she might need comforting. I'll stay here and watch the fire."

Sherriff Beatle had been married four times. Each time it was to someone ill matched who he'd cheated on with his next soon-to-be wife. The expression on Ellis's face told him all he needed to know about how the younger man felt about Ed Schaffer's daughter, but he didn't think it was his place to question the deputy's judgment. Despite whatever craziness he had heard about her, she was pretty and the sheriff knew that was sometimes all it took.

"Bang! Bang! Bang!"

Pode's solid wood front door trembled as someone knocked aggressively on the outside of it. Ava sat up, instantly wide awake in the dark room, but confused about where she was. She was on a couch. Pode's couch. Under blankets. Retrieved from the closet. In Pode's house. Through the closed bedroom door she could hear movement as Pode stirred in response to the knock.

Ava brushed her hair back with her fingers and wiped sleep out of her eyes. Cautiously, she crept across the room. She looked back at Pode's bedroom door, wondering if she should wait for him, then leaned to peek out the window in the same way she had earlier in the evening during the visit from the pastor's wife. Her imagination ignited and she pictured everything from a murderer with a chainsaw to a drunken, lonely Baker, but instead found Ellis. His hands landed on his hips as he paced away from the door.

Ava smoothed her hand over the front of her flannel shirt as she fumbled with the deadbolt and the door handle. The door blew open on its own, cold wind gusting inside. Ava caught it before it hit the wall. Ellis turned to meet her inquisitive stare. His voice was clouded with dread. "Ava. So glad I found you." He wanted to take her in his arms, tell her it would be OK, but he had to break the news of why he was doing so first. "Shit. There's no good way to say this. Your dad was in a wreck about an hour ago."

She dropped her hand from the door and let it crash into the wall and violently bounce back.

"He's in the hospital in Clay."

"He's alive?"

"Yes."

Over Ava's shoulder Ellis could see quilts and a pillow wadded up on Pode's couch. The concern he held left him. She told him the truth the night of the bonfire. Pode was nothing more than a friend, not a valid reason to be jealous.

"Let's go." Ava jumped at the sound of Pode's voice right behind her. He leaned against the wall trying not to put any weight on his black and blue ballooned foot.

"Oh. Jesus, Wagner. You look like you need a doctor." Ellis's was repulsed as he got a better look at Pode's foot. "You need to rest that, buddy. I'm not on duty, right now. I can drive Ava over there."

"OK." Ava didn't hesitate. She followed the cop out the door, but as the bottom of her bare foot hit the cold cement, she realized she wasn't wearing socks or shoes and stopped. Pode joined her on the porch, holding her boots out to her. She shoved them on without questioning how he had so quickly limped across the room and back. It wasn't until they were out of the driveway and onto the street before she wished she had taken the ride from Pode instead and that she would rather have him with her than Ellis. Glancing back, she could see his shadowy, crooked outline leaning on the middle column of the front porch.

The inside of the squad car was utilitarian. Only the necessary dashboard items existed. Plain white gauges, clearly marked buttons, vinyl seats of generic dark blue. Ava named the owners of the houses they passed in her head, attempting to bring herself back to the reality of where she was going and why.

"What happened?"

Ellis kept his focus firmly on the road in front of him. "I don't know all the details yet. It happened at Coin's Corner. Highway patrolman who lives over in Plata County came up on it about an hour ago or so. It looks like your, uh, your father lost control and went right through the guardrail. Flipped his truck and it caught fire. Got stuck on a tree, lucky for him, so it wasn't too far off the road and the paramedics were able to get to him just fine. Going all the way down the bluff to the river would have been a different story. There'll be more of an investigation in the morning. When it's light out."

He paused, not looking at Ava. "I don't think it's going to be very pretty, Ava. If there was fire there was probably burning. I'm sorry. But I want you to be prepared for the worst."

"No. Yeah," Ava responded, barely above a whisper. "Was anybody else involved?"

"No."

"Was he drinking?"

The officer paused. "I—I don't know. I'm sure they'll do a toxicology test."

She knew he did know and that her father was. It was a dumb question. She didn't know of a time in which her father could be described as not drinking. Whiskey on his breath, stumbling while he walked, a permanent bottle in the pocket of his jacket. He was different, people said, his drinking was under control when he and Dora May got

161

married, but Ava was too young to remember this mythical sober "before."

Ellis reached and placed his hand over Ava's where it rested on her knee. She inhaled a long breath in order to fight back the tears she felt sneaking in. She flipped her hand over and wove her fingers between his and he squeezed them. The police cruiser sailed down the pitch-black highway at a speed well over the limit. Ava closed her eyes.

Hospitals all smelled the same. Looked the same. The smell was bleachy. The look was sterile. Color schemes were whites and blues and greens. Colors proven to be relaxing. Colors that displayed dirt easily, so that the dirt could quickly be removed with something bleachy smelling. For all of the time she had spent in clinics and labs and doctors' offices and hospitals with her mother, Ava had never grown used to the smell or the look, both of which flooded her brain with memories as she walked hand and hand with Ellis through the automatic glass panel doors of the Clay Tri-County Hospital.

Ellis stopped in the entrance, unfamiliar with which way to go. Ava habitually headed for the front desk, pulling him with her. It was staffed by a woman she recognized, but before they were able to speak to her, Ava heard her own name yelled across the lobby. Shannon, in plain pink nurses scrubs, walked quickly toward them from one of the many hallways leading off of the open space.

"He's in the ICU and it's not visiting hours, but I can take you there. I spoke with his doctor." Shannon looked tired, her bright blue eyes framed by dark circles. She had worked at the hospital for years, moved up the ladder to a supervisory role easily. She had wanted to be a doctor in every discussion about the future Ava could remember from their childhood, but the plan was derailed. Three days after her seventeenth birthday Shannon found out she was pregnant. Ava was there when the plus showed up on the plastic stick. Shannon cried for hours before she called Kale. Ava backed the Mustang out of the driveway of Shannon's parents' house as Kale's beater pickup pulled in.

Ellis let go of Ava's hand and allowed Shannon to take her arm. He trailed the women down a hall, the only sound their three sets of swift footsteps on the hard floor tiles. Shannon entered a combination on a keypad next to wide double doors. They slid open without a sound and as they entered an area usually sealed from public access Ava became anxiously aware of the silence. For a moment she wondered what time it was, but didn't complete the thought before her mind shot somewhere else. Leading them onto a large elevator with doors on both sides, Shannon pushed a button. She leaned her head toward Ava's so that their temples touched, but looked up and made eye contact with Ellis. The expression in the nurse's eyes was grimly haunting, communicating more to the officer than words could.

The back doors of the elevator slid open as a faint beep sounded. Ellis and Shannon turned toward them, but Ava didn't move. She was losing herself. She was shutting herself down in order to brace for whatever scene was to come, a trick she learned while dealing with whatever disturbing step of sickness her mother was battling. Ellis touched her shoulder gently and Ava flinched.

"You'll have to wait here, Officer Ellis." Shannon led them to another set of doors, this one flanked by several warning signs. Ellis was not *immediate family* and was *not allowed* according to several of the bold red sets of text. "There's a waiting room, at the end of the hall and to the right." Shannon pointed. Ellis, used to being the direction giver and the rule enforcer, understood that this was not his territory. In a hospital, a nurse pulled rank over everyone else. He watched intently as Shannon used her key card at the doors and led Ava through.

The similarities to this ICU that housed her injured father and the one her mother died in were uncanny. They looked so alike that Ava felt her body cease to move despite what her brain told it to do. She reached for the counter that created a complete circle in the center of the room. Several nurses and doctors were seated at computers inside of it. All around the outer walls, doors led into rooms where machinery and monitors beeped and buzzed and glowed. Most of the curtains were pulled across the openings to the rooms, but in the two or three that weren't Ava saw lifeless bodies lying in steeply tilted beds wrapped tight like Halloween mummies in stark white sheets.

"Av." Shannon put her arm around her friend's waist. "If you can't do this right now, that's OK. If you need a few minutes we can go sit outside." Shannon didn't know what it felt like to lose a parent, let alone be faced with the threat of losing the other only weeks later. She was blessed with a huge healthy family and every single day she was reminded of how fortunate she was.

"No." Ava stood up straight. She pulled away from Shannon. "Which room is his?"

Shannon considered Ava as if she was her nurse, not her friend, deciding for her whether or not to continue. Her hair was greasy. Her face was sunken. Her skin was an unnatural shade of white. Ava looked like she might have wandered in from another part of the hospital, like she should be admitted herself. Her eyes were clear, though. Somewhere inside a momentum carried her. Where it came from, Ava didn't know, but now was the time and the place for it and she had no other choice. Strength—mentally, physically, emotionally—was somehow still attainable for the young woman who had been through so much.

"He's over here. In six." Shannon led the way again, slower this time.

They crossed to the other side of the circle and Shannon opened the concealing curtain. Ava took a deep breath and looked at her father. Then she took a second deep breath out of relief because he looked quite a bit better than the terrible she had imagined. Sheets loosely over him, his arms and chest and face were uncovered and wrapped tightly in bandages that also encased a good portion of his neck and chin. He was sleeping, his face content. Whether it was a natural sleep or induced by the clear bag hanging above the bed, Ava couldn't tell.

"I had them page the on call doctor before I went downstairs. She should be here any minute now to talk to you." Shannon's voice was barely above a whisper.

Not knowing what to do, never knowing what to do in the many claustrophobic hospital rooms she had been shoved into, Ava sat. A chair directly behind her, she sat so hard it scooted back and bashed into the chair rail on the wall. Ava also never knew what to say. She didn't say anything at all, knowing she would only be saying something for the sake of Shannon. The truth was that had this been a barbeque on a sunny day, few words would have been exchanged between the father and the daughter. He knew she was there or he didn't and either way Ava wasn't sure how much it even mattered to him.

* * *

The chair was in the corner. A big bulky thing, the colors of fall, crimson, orange, brown, with an idealized portrait of a white tail deer in a repeating pattern scattered across the fabric. The room was dark. Lights off, orange, polyester curtains drawn closed across oversized storm windows along the front wall of the farmhouse, dusk settling in outside. The television set was loud. Announcers' voices blared discussion of the action in the baseball game on the screen.

He sat in the chair in the dark watching the game. Shiny golden beer cans overflowed on the side table with the wheat design carved into the side of it. They were just the ones he had drunk through the first inning. His drinking had begun earlier in the day, much earlier. At Martha's before lunch, then at the VFW Club in the afternoon, then in his truck as he cruised through the countryside, now in his chair in the living room as he watched TV.

He was already in the chair when Ava and Eddy hopped off the school bus. They skipped down the driveway, raced to the end, stopped to look at a bullfrog resting by the water hydrant in the backyard. From the cockeyed way his truck was parked, half in front of the machine shed, half on the sidewalk to the house, the kids knew. They knew to quietly enter through the back screen door and not let it slam. They knew to rest their backpacks lightly on the edge of the kitchen table. They knew to gracefully scale the steep staircase to their bedrooms to hold their afternoon play sessions upstairs.

Ava lay on the floor of her room sorting tiny high-heeled Barbie shoes and hoping to find the other white one so that the blonde Barbie could wear it with the blue sparkly evening gown. The purple carpet on the floor of Ava's bedroom was well worn. It was older than the girl by two decades. In the spot she lay on, Ava could see the thin wooded slats of the floor underneath it. In the room around the corner, Eddy "vroomed" as he drove

Matchbox cars around on his own worn carpet. She laughed to herself, at the silliness of the boy and his fake car noises as she reached for a horse and did her best to jam Ken onto it so he would stay, thinking about how cool it would be to be picked up for a date by a guy riding a horse.

Far away, at the bottom of the stairs and through the kitchen, the back door opened and shut. It slammed. Heavy heeled footsteps clunked from one end of the house to the other. They stopped underneath Ava's bedroom in the center of the living room. The yelling started. The words were mostly incoherent, but the tone in her mother's voice was scarring enough to carry. Her father's voice was growly, almost as loud, but overshadowed and defeated.

Ava froze, half-dressed Barbie in her grasp, distracted by the emotional violence her parents were enacting on each other. Never raising a finger, the words they yelled, the things they did, were in ways worse than physical abuse. The end was near. She knew the amount of time her father spent drunk wasn't good and neither was the amount of time her mother wasn't home at night. At 10 years old, she understood what an alcoholic was. And she understood she didn't understand the look her mother gave Dean Howard when they passed him stocking shelves at the Flynn Country Grocers on Main Street.

"Av?" Eddy was standing in her bedroom doorway, holding a cracked gallon ice cream bucket full of Legos in one hand and a creation with wheels in the other. "Can I play in here?"

Ava nodded her head "yes." Her little brother tiptoed around the sprawl of Barbie clothes on the floor and sat in the corner. He was skinny, smaller than the other boys in his class. The faded blue jeans he wore were already too short for him, but loose enough he had to repeatedly pull them back up to his waist. Carefully, he dismantled the Lego automobile and laid the pieces out on the threadbare carpet. The kids resumed their play as their parents raged out of control downstairs. Finally, the back door slammed shut. Their father's truck backed away from the house and slowly swerved along the driveway and onto the dirt road in front without stopping. He would not come back to the farmhouse. Ever.

# 7

She was too tired to sleep. The hospital was too quiet to sleep in. Prior to her mother's death, Ava was a heavy sleeper. At six years old, when the tornado ripped through west of Flynn, destroying the barn and tossing the tin pig sheds half a mile into the pasture, she slept right through it. She woke only slightly when her father lifted her out of bed and carried her down the rickety wooden stairs to the spider-infested basement of the farmhouse. Curling up on Eddy's Hot Wheels sleeping bag beside her brother, Ava fell right back to sleep.

Noise was a comfort to her. The joints of the old house squeaking against the wind of the Kansas prairie as she slept. The chirping of the birds in the tree right outside the machine shed as she worked. The singing of the jukebox beneath crowd noise at Martha's as she sat at the bar. The growling of the worn engine in the Mustang as she drove through empty landscape.

There was nothing, not a single sound. She was alone in the ICU's waiting area. Ellis left to go on duty a few hours before. He offered to stay, to call someone to cover for him, but she refused to let him. His hand was on her knee and a look of great concern on his face. He told her to call if she needed anything, anything at all, then he squeezed her leg and walked away, but not without looking back a couple of times. Ava wasn't reassured by this. Instead she felt alarmed, nervous, in a way vaguely similar to the way the silence made her feel. He was assuming a role. Friend? Boyfriend? A new role, not

169

previously held. A role Ava was not quite at ease with yet.

Her boots were off and deserted underneath the thinly padded, wood armed loveseat. Knees underneath her chin, arms around them, Ava was half covered with a blanket Shannon brought her. It wasn't cold, but somehow the blanket seemed necessary to provide a false sense of comfort in the least comforting environment Ava knew. The wall in front of her was white with a row of windows overlooking a drive marked with red arrows and lines, instructions for ambulance drivers.

One ambulance arrived while Ava waited on sunrise. The body on the stretcher was little, wrapped tightly and unmoving. She thought the cover was pulled over their face, but she couldn't say for sure. She didn't get up, didn't want a better look, didn't want to know. Instead, in her mind Ava wished no more ambulances would ever come. She wished for a world where everyone stayed unsick, undiseased, uninjured, forever. Forever would be too long, though, she reasoned. Ninety. Ninety years would be plenty of time, an appropriate length for a life. She wished everyone in the world could be completely healthy until their ninetieth birthday, a time in which they would be given a day to tell their loved ones goodbye and then they would die peacefully while sleeping in their own bed at ninety years and one day old.

The public elevator around the corner from the ICU dinged faintly. Ava heard uneven footsteps grow quieter as they traveled the opposite direction from her. Then they stopped and grew louder again. She turned her head, interested to see who was behind the labored limp. A weak smile took over her drained face as Pode, freshly showered and shaved, appeared, looking in all directions, clearly lost.

"Av, hey." Pode crossed to her as quickly as his bum foot would allow. He took a seat on the loveseat beside her. "How's he doing?"

"Alright, actually." Ava repeated as much of what the doctor told her as she could remember. "He's burned pretty badly on the right side of his body. Mostly first degree and second degree burns, a third degree burn on his right arm, so they had to do skin grafting and he's on fluids and pain medication, but the doctor said his vitals are all good. The burning is mostly cosmetic. It didn't cause any more serious damage, I guess. They're watching him, close, but the doctor said she's really optimistic about the outcome."

"Ah, that's great. I couldn't sleep after you left, so as soon as the sun came up I got up and thought I'd head on over in case you needed anything." The relief on Pode's face made Ava feel better.

"I'm OK. I was ready for a lot worse."

"Did you get any sleep?"

"No. Hospitals are weird. I never could sleep in one. Even after all the time I spent with Mom." Ava trailed off. Tears crept into the corners of her eyes. She swallowed hard to try to hold them back, but it didn't work for the first time in weeks. They escaped and rolled down her face. She looked absolutely overwhelmed to Pode and he frowned, not knowing exactly what to do. "I'm sorry," Ava apologized, wiping her flannel sleeve across her face.

"No, no, Av. If anybody on this earth deserves a good cry, it's you." Pode stood and retrieved a box of Kleenex deserted on the side table. He offered it to her and took the seat beside her again. She took one and used it to wipe away a second wave of tears.

"Thank you," she said through a cough.

"Here." Pode took the blanket drooping onto the floor and clumsily wrapped it around her. He put his arm over her shoulders and pulled her closer to him. Ava let the tears fall. She sobbed into his chest until a damp spot

171

formed on his t-shirt. He was warm. He smelled practical like Old Spice and store brand bar soap.

"It's a lot to handle. A lot to handle. I don't know why some people get all the bad. I don't understand why life's so unfair, sometimes." Pode was talking, because he didn't know what else to do. Ava nodded her head slightly in answer and he went on. "I mean, I don't wish bad on anybody, but you'd think they could spread it around a little." He gave her a squeeze with the arm he had wrapped around her.

Outside the window the day was old enough for the first rays of sunlight to peek over the four-story office building across the street. They streamed through the crystal-clear glass of the windows and cast oblong triangles on the floor. Ava watched the shapes creep and grow as the minutes, then the hour, passed. She felt protected, distracted, from the events of the previous night. A piece of her believed that if she closed her eyes for a second and opened them, this would turn out to all be a bad dream. She would wake up having fallen asleep leaning against her best friend on his couch after a night of drinking beer and playing poker and laughing.

When she opened her eyes, though, after nodding off for a few minutes, it was to the sound of a raised voice. One she knew well.

"I don't give a fuck if it's not 'vising hours.' Fat fucking bitch can go to hell."

Ava sat up straight, Pode's hand falling off her shoulder. He had napped, too. Eddy Schaffer stormed into the waiting area. He wore an expensive-looking blazer over a button-down dress shirt and dark skinny jeans. His dark, almost black hair was sculpted. Trailing behind Eddy, a petite girl, Mindy, looked tired, bored by the event. They stopped as they reached Ava and Pode, the blonde girl flipping her processed hair back out of her face and over the shoulder of her pink sorority sweatshirt.

"Ava." It was a command for her attention not an expression of joy in seeing her. "They told me downstairs that I couldn't see him. Can you believe that? I drove eight hours after ten hours of class and six hours of internship to get here and they're barring the fucking door."

Ava cleared her throat, "Visiting hours don't start again until eight."

He had bypassed the greeting. The asking of if their father was OK. The asking of what happened. The asking of if Ava was OK. The acknowledgement of Pode in the room. The thanking of both of them both for being there. He had skipped straight to complaints. To his own selfish demands. To bragging about how hard his day had been. It was not surprising to Ava or Pode. It was expected.

"That's twenty fucking minutes from now." Eddy's tone was urgent, but ineffective toward the other three people in the room.

"Baby." Mindy's voice was so high it was jarring. "Just calm down. Sit. And stop cussing in a hospital. There's like kids and old people here."

"Yeah, Mitzie's right, man. Calm down. Have a seat," Pode added. Ava raised her hand to her mouth, trying not to laugh.

Eddy fired a look of death at Pode. "Mindy. Her name is Mindy. Why the hell are you even here, Wagner? You're not family."

Pode tilted his head to the side and stood up, not quite as tall, but twice as wide as Eddy as they stood face to face. "I'm here to support my best friend, cause that's the kind of person I am. I also greet people when I walk into a room and ask them how they are. Unless you plan to do that, now might be a good time for you to shut the hell up and wait patiently, because your sister's had enough stress to deal with lately. She don't need this shit coming at her from you."

Ava was flattered. Eddy opened his mouth, but decided against saying anything more, having twice received black eyes from Pode at different times in their youth. Once by accident, as Eddy was playing first base and missed a baseball thrown by Pode at shortstop. Once on purpose, when Eddy called Ava a bitch in front of a room full of people in Clay at a party. Both grown men now, Eddy was well aware of how a confrontation between a guy who threw hay bales for a living and a guy who sat at a desk studying law would end.

Taking a seat with Mindy in two chairs across the room, Eddy leaned forward, his elbows on his knees as if he were ready to jump to his feet at any moment. An awkwardly giant diamond on Mindy's left hand caught the sunlight and reflected on the wall across from her. Ava wondered how her brother could afford the huge ring. They sat in silence. Ava pulled the blanket tighter around herself and leaned her head back, resting it on the wooden trim on the top of the sofa.

Pode's truck slowed, the V-8 shifting smoothly into its lowest gear, as they crossed the cement railed river bridge at the edge of town. Ava's head was pointed out the passenger side window, but her sight wasn't focused on the sandbar poking up in the middle of the shallow water. The water was down the banks so far weeds with yellow flowers grew on the river bottom. The truck eased to a stop at the first of only two marked four way stops in Flynn. Pode looked both ways and kept going straight toward Main Street.

Ava raised her head, coming to as they missed turning off at Oak Street. "Wait, where are we going?"

"To the shop. To pick up your car." Pode studied her

face as she put the night before back together in her mind. "You left it there and walked to my house, Av."

"Oh, God." Ava shook her head. "Oh, God, what a long night."

"Are you going to be OK? You know you're welcome to stay at the house, grab a shower and a nap. I'll cook up lunch and you can eat before you head over to your dad's." Pode pulled his truck into an angled parking spot in front of Callahan's Auto Body & Repair. The Mustang was parked behind the shop. Only the corner of it and the driver's side headlight were visible at the edge of the white-washed building. It looked like it had inched out on its own to peer down the alley and watch for Ava to return.

"No, I'm fine. I want to sleep in my own bed. Thanks, Pode." He watched her walk away, entering through the front door, to the office of the repair shop. She had surrendered all feeling, again. She would be quickly wrapping herself up in her cocoon, again.

Three hours was not enough sleep to catch Ava up, but it was all her body would allow. Sun streamed in the window through the gap in the curtains, across the living room floor and across her face where she crashed on the couch in the living room. She had been unable to tackle the stairs. The gift quilt was wrapped around her, her boots and jeans and flannel shirt were strung along the floor. It took several minutes of staring at the water-stained ceiling before she realized where she was. And then several more for Ava to process the events of the former night and subsequent day. It was the same place she had slept, the same way she had felt, the day after her mother died. The first sleep after great exhaustion should be rejuvenating, a hard, heavy sleep. It wasn't. Once awake, with the facts sorted out, an arduous feeling took over. Thankfully, in this day after, she didn't have an appointment with Owens Funeral Home.

Ava showered and put on new clothes and drove to her father's house. After the divorce, on weekends they'd stayed with their father in the two-bedroom rental a mile west of town. As she and Eddy grew older, the increasing decline of the house made them want to spend less and less time there. Their father didn't blame them. He didn't want to live in the mess he had created either. He came to their school events and met them for supper at Martha's every Thursday night, but by the time Ava turned fourteen, they didn't stay with him anymore.

Ava turned the knob to the unlocked front door and pushed it open. A rank, horrid smell, worse than usual from the house being closed up for a few days, overpowered her. Taking a step inside, Ava shoved the door into the piles of trash, clothes, books, magazines, things. She traveled the tunnel that led through the living room to the kitchen and ended in the bedroom. Collecting a folded pair of jeans and a t-shirt and socks and underwear from the basket of clean laundry sitting on the armchair in the corner, Ava made a neat stack of the clothing. She escaped the precarious path between the junk, gagging from the smell of the trash and rotten food interwoven into the piles. The front door Ava had left half open swung wide and hit the stuff behind it. The stacks wobbled and looked for a moment like they might fall over and cause a domino effect, crashing into another stack and then another until they all caved in around her. Everything settled without disaster, though, only a few papers at the top fluttering to the ground in the open space of the doorway.

Eddy entered, the blonde close behind him with a hand flat on the back of his jacket. Ava's brother was speechless, in awe as he examined the state of the house.

Ava could see the blame rising in him before he said a word and she wished Eddy wasn't standing in the only path out of the mess so she could leave another way and not be forced to talk to him.

"Holy shit," Eddy whispered.

Mindy covered her mouth with the sleeve of her sweatshirt and inhaled heavily into it as she spoke. "It smells like something died in here."

"I'm sorry," Ava mumbled, the words barely audible.

Eddy disregarded her. He took a step further into the house. Ava brushed his shoulder as she ducked past him in the pathway that was not wide enough for two people to stand beside one another.

"He still lives here?" Eddy asked as he rotated in a complete circle, covering his mouth with both hands.

"Yes." Ava wasn't sure she could handle another violent outburst from her brother so she left without another word.

Shannon sipped black coffee from a fired clay coffee cup covered in bright flowers hand painted by Julia. Across the table, Ava broke a foldy-over potato chip in half and crunched a chunk between her back teeth. After finding out Ava hadn't eaten anything all day, Shannon forced her into the hospital cafeteria, almost physically. She picked at the chips, but the sandwich in front of her was untouched.

"Or maybe St. Joseph? I've heard good things about them, too." Shannon was trying to think of rehabilitation programs. She promised Ava a comprehensive list. Having heard the description of Ed Schaffer's home and absolutely agreeing with Ava that he could not return to it, they were brainstorming other ideas. Rehab, therapy, programs they could get him into so that Ava would not be solely responsible for his wellbeing. Shannon saw the potential of Ava caring for her alcoholic, depressive father as the last straw to finally break her friend's proverbial camel's back. Attending to and eventually losing Dora May had heaped on enough to fill a hay loft.

The chairs were uncomfortable, the top bar angled in an odd way that poked into Ava's spine. Shannon watched her friend's face light up as she raised her eyes to the double doors leading into the sea foam green accented room. Looking over her shoulder, Shannon smiled in greeting to Pode. He wore the same t-shirt and jeans from earlier in the day, but they were dusty from fieldwork he had slipped in during his daytime absence.

"Went up to the waiting area. Eddy's lady friend told me I'd find you here. How's everybody holding up?" Pode asked. He touched Ava's shoulder quickly as he took the seat beside her.

"Alright." Ava shrugged her shoulders.

"I'm making her eat." Shannon raised her eyebrows to the sandwich, "Unsuccessfully."

"Yeah," Pode responded as if Ava weren't sitting right beside him. "She doesn't do that anymore. I'm not sure what she lives on. Metal filings and paint fumes."

Ava sighed, knowing they were joking, but also slightly resentful, feeling as though they were treating her like a child who needed taken care of.

Shannon checked the petite gold watch on her arm, inherited from her grandmother. She wore it religiously and checked it often. "I need to get home. Movie night. Kale said the girls picked out Beauty and the Beast. I will be very disappointed if I miss "Be Our Guest." Lumiere was always my favorite." Shannon reached across the table and put her hand over Ava's. "If you need anything, have a question about anything they say or do, call me. I don't care if it's ten minutes from now or in the middle of the night. I will have my phone on and you will call it if you need anything."

"Thank you." Ava nodded her acceptance to the deal. Shannon called her a million times while Dora May was in and out of hospitals and clinics. Ava never called her back. She always pretended like she might, but the promise was hollow. Ava wasn't going to say false words and try to pretend this time.

"See you later, guys." Shannon rose from the table, dumping the end of her lukewarm coffee into a deep water fountain on the way out. The room was quiet, only the hum of a freezer of ice cream novelties beside them, the faint voices of two elderly folks as they ate at a table on the other side of the large dining area, and the beep of computer register buttons as a hospital employee in blue scrubs purchased a bottle of Coke from a cashier. Otherwise there was only lonely late afternoon in a hospital calm.

Pode stole a handful of potato chips off of Ava's plate. He tilted his head back and dropped them into his mouth, crumbs tumbling down his shirt. Brushing the chip flecks away, he pointed at the sandwich. "Looks like a good sandwich. Good tomatoes for this time of year."

"You want it?"

"No." He scratched his head. "I'm saying you should eat it. The last thing you need is to collapse in a hospital. They'll have you in here for observation for days. Pump shit into your arm. Question your mental stability. I know this is what you do. I know there's bigger things than eating a sandwich going on in your life right now, but we both know Eddy ain't capable of making any good decisions, and if you're half-starved, you aren't either."

She could not muster any appetite whatsoever. The sterile smell of the hospital made her nauseous, but a reluctant part of the back of her brain knew Pode was right. Picking up the sandwich, she took a bite and

179

chewed deliberately. Pode was satisfied with her little bit of effort. He got up and retrieved a couple of bottles of water from a cooler across the cafeteria. Ava took another bite and stared blankly at Pode as he paid the kid at the cash register.

"Does your mother keep her work keys somewhere we could steal them?"

A frown formed across Pode's face as he sat in Shannon's newly vacated space across from Ava. He opened his water, drank, pushed the other bottle across the table to her. "I want to know why you would ask me that question, but honestly, I am afraid to hear your answer."

Ava looked over both shoulders, scanned the room, and made sure everyone around them was out of ear shot as if she were about to impart government secrets in an epic movie scene. With an eye on the door she leaned flat against the table and talked barely above a whisper. "I need to get into Billy James' office."

Pode looked around the room in the same fashion Ava had. He was entertained by her suspicious transition into telling secrets, but also full of worry for his friend's sanity. "I'm sure she probably has the key to the front and back doors, but I doubt she has any for the offices." He stopped. "Wait, why am I telling you this? Why do you need to get into his office?"

Ava put her face in her hands. "If I tell you something, you cannot tell a soul. I mean not a hint of it to anyone, ever, for the rest of your life. Do you understand?"

"Sure. I mean, yes. Yes. Whatever secret you have is safe with me. I promise. You know that, Av."

As she told him, she wondered if she was making a mistake. Not with her trust in Pode, but with the questions in her mind. "Billy called me, last week, asked me to come in for a meeting. I thought it was probably more paperwork or something else I needed to sort out on Mom's estate, but it wasn't. Well, it kind of was. Billy told me," she looked over her right shoulder one more time, "That my mother had a life insurance policy she's been paying for the last twenty-whatever years. It's worth a half a million dollars and she only left it to me. Not Eddy."

Pode's mouth dropped open in a way that if someone had been watching them, they would have wondered what the discussion was about.

"I've thought about it constantly since I left his office. I searched through boxes and boxes of paperwork Mom had at her office and in the house. I can't find a single check, a single envelope, any proof of it existing. She could have shredded all the evidence for fear Eddy would find something, but I don't know how. I paid all of her bills the last few months. I took over everything and I know for sure I never wrote a check to a life insurance company."

Pode was in shock, calculating in his mind how much money half a million dollars really was. Ava paused, but when Pode didn't say anything, she continued, "Eddy was her favorite. That was perfectly clear to anybody who ever even met our family. Why would she not leave him half the money?"

"Maybe she felt guilty, you took care of her all that time," Pode offered.

"But the policy is from twenty years ago."

"She could have changed it to just your name at some point."

"Yeah. I don't know."

"You think something's fishy. That Billy James had more to do with it than telling you about it."

Ava shook her head to confirm his statement, "I think Billy James has been paying it all this time. I don't know if

Mom even knew about it."

"Why would he do that?"

"Because he thinks he's my father."

The congregation of the First United Methodist Church was standing, waiting to file down the burgundy carpet and out of the back of the row of maple wood pews, each set with a cushion the same color of red as the carpet. Though it was chilly outside, the sun was high in the sky and it seeped through the pastel blues and greens and pinks in the arched stained glass windows lining both walls of the sanctuary. The glow of the sun and the warmth from the cranked-up heater and the soothing sound of Pastor McEwing's voice as he read the scripture and preached the gospel left everyone feeling sleepy. So much so that several of the older men, sitting diligently next to their wives of 50 years, nodded off, heads lulling to the front or side, occasional snores startling them awake.

Kris escaped the sermon early and retreated to the basement of the church, where a small kitchen opened out onto a substantial gathering room packed with heavy banquet tables and scratched metal folding chairs. She was preparing for the noon meal. Mismatched Pyrex casseroles and Tupperware bowls and aluminum tins of varied sizes rested all along the counter tops and in the oven to reheat and on the top shelves of the refrigerator to keep cool. Lifting off pieces of tinfoil and plastic wrap, Kris carefully placed each dish on a bar counter that divided the kitchen from the larger room. Organizing each into the category of main dish and side dish and desert, she was still looking through drawers for proper serving utensils when she heard the first members of the congregation on the stairs.

"It smells wonderful in here," the preacher's wife's voice was not sincere. Kris sorted through an open drawer collecting wooden spoons and glaring at Sandy as the other woman rearranged a couple of the dishes. Her blouse was too low cut for church and tucked into high-waist slacks that were too tight. She looked good, after four kids, and she wasn't afraid to let everyone in town know she knew she did.

Kris bit her tongue. She fought everything inside of her not to tell the awful woman to get out of the kitchen. She never helped with anything, showed up just in time to get in the way and then be the first in line. Walking around Sandy, to the other side of the counter, Kris smiled warmly at the table of older couples nearest to the kitchen. They chatted and waited patiently for the potluck to be ready. Kris added spoons to dishes and returned the few the other woman had moved back to their original places.

"Did you hear about Ed Schaffer?" Sandy gasped, overdramatically leaning toward Kris over the food between them. Kris nodded vaguely. "I see his daughter at your son's house pretty often. If I were you, I'd put a stop to that. Strange girl."

Kris froze. Her brows furrowed at the woman as she stood up straight, a paring knife with bits of brownie on it clenched in her fist. "Ava is like a daughter to me. Don't ever let me hear you say anything bad about her, or Pode, or any of the rest of my family, again." Kris wanted to continue, but stopped herself. Her breath rose and fell in her chest. The realization that within months she would share a grandchild with the other woman kept her from saying everything she wanted to.

"I suppose it's hard," Sandy sighed, "To watch your son slip away from you. Alcoholism, like your father. You know if you ever need to talk . . ."

"Ahrrghh!" Kris let loose a frustrated sound as she drove the knife in her hand blade first in the nearest pound cake. "Listen, you, you, bitch! All you do is walk around this town and judge. Everyone. All of the time. But you have absolutely no right to pass judgment on any of us with your tight clothes and your flirting with all of our husbands and your children who are, well, your children are a mess! You and your daughter, Penny, you two especially need to have a long, long talk."

The room was silent, every member of the congregation's attention focused on the kitchen window where Kris Schaffer had finally lost it, had finally said to Sandy McEwing what they had all wished they could say to her for years. Kris left the knife sticking violently up from the cake, took a step back, wiped her hands on the nearest kitchen towel, and tossed it over her shoulder as she stormed across the room and disappeared up the stairs. Sandy watched her go, surprise of a fake sort on her face. With Kris gone, all of the attention turned back to the preacher's wife, who guffawed and crossed her arms across her chest, acting as if Kris had been the one out of line.

Smoothing her hair back, Sandy gathered herself. "Eat!" she insisted to the crowd. "Please. Everyone. Eat."

Looking at each other, the crowd slowly, cautiously, rose from their seats and formed a line and tried to pretend as if nothing had happened.

Ed was on a different floor. In a recovery room he shared with another man. The curtain was pulled between them and the stranger was fast asleep, snoring rhythmically. Propped up, watching the tiny television suspended in the corner of the room, Ed rested on top of a freshly made bed, wearing jeans and a t-shirt. He was ready to leave, but awaiting a signed release form from his doctor. Ava sat in a blue vinyl chair. It was like the ones in the cafeteria, with the pokey-outey backs. They were all over the hospital and she decided they must have been cheap because they were not purchased for comfort.

She picked at a loose piece of skin beside her thumbnail. Her hands were cracked from a mix of cold dryness in the air and the chemicals she plunged them into to clean her paint brushes. The more she picked, the more the piece of skin loosened and finally she raised her hand to her mouth and used her teeth to bite it off. The area began to bleed. Reaching for the box of Kleenex on the table beside her father's hospital bed, she pulled one out, tore the corner off, and used it to put pressure on the spot.

"Wonder where the hell she is," Ed grumbled, referring to the doctor they had been waiting on for a couple of hours.

"I'm sure she has a lot of other patients," Ava responded, mindlessly. She didn't want the time to go any faster. She had yet to tell Ed that she wouldn't be driving him home, but instead to St. Joseph's Rehab Facility. Mentioning it before it happened was ill advised. It would most likely lead to an outburst in the middle of the hospital. Ava decided to wait until the very last minute. Hopefully he wouldn't fight her too much in the car. Hopefully.

"Yes, ma'am, thank you." Ava heard Ellis's voice in the hallway. He walked into the room side by side with Ed's doctor. The pretty young woman in a long white lab coat and purple Crocs smiled ominously at Ava.

"Good afternoon, Mr. Schaffer." She was as professional as always. "I have your signed release paperwork here, so you are free to leave the hospital. However, Deputy Ellis is here to talk to you."

Ed frowned, but wasn't able to speak before Ellis stepped in front of the doctor with a quick plea for help glance at Ava. "Mr. Schaffer, I'm afraid I have to take you into custody."

"Why the hell would you do that? Is it illegal to wreck your truck?"

"Sir, you are being charged with D.U.I. and you did several thousand dollars with of property damage."

"Oh, to hell with you, boy." Ed stood and faced Ellis. His face set, tough, as if he had never smiled in his entire life. Ellis didn't move. He had seen far worse horrors than a belligerent old drunk.

"Now, there's two other deputies out in the hall who were ready to barge in here and throw handcuffs on you, but I talked them out of it with faith you'd walk out of here with me without any issue."

"What the fuck is this!" Eddy burst into the room, hands on his forehead as he yelled, disrupting the peace Ellis was desperately trying to keep.

"So," Ellis went on, ignoring Eddy entirely, "You can walk out of here like a man, with respect and I'll take you over to the station myself, or . . ."

Eddy grabbed the officer by the shoulder. "What the fuck is this? Are you arresting him? What did he fucking do?"

"This has absolutely nothing to do with you. This is between the state and your father. Please don't touch me again or I'll have to have one of the guys in the hallway arrest you, too, for impeding an arrest."

"Ava? What the fuck is this? You let our father waste away in that house, drink himself half to death, and now you're not saying a word when this asshole tries to arrest him. Goddamn fucking worthless . . ."

"Hey, whoa!" Ellis spun and lit into Eddy. "I will not stand here and let anybody talk to Ava like that, especially not her own family."

"I'll go." Ed stepped forward. "I don't really have a choice. It's fine, Eddy. It's fine."

Eddy's mouth hung open, stupidly. He watched as Ellis led Ed through the door, but not without screaming after them, "You know I'm a lawyer. I will sue the fuck out of you and the county and the state!"

The doctor barely touched Ava's arm and then exited the room, completely disregarding Eddy. Ava thought of a million things she wanted to say to her brother, but only made a single request. "Go back to Colorado, Eddy."

\* \* \*

The metal lockers were painted alternating blue and white. A line of them stretched the one long hallway of Flynn Junior High School. Ava sat on the ground, her legs crossed, a textbook open across her lap, a ragged spiral notebook in her hand held up in the air as she consulted the book. Shannon sat so close the girls' knees touched. Her skinny legs were stretched out in front of her, her book turned to the same page. She gnawed on the eraser end of an Eversharp.

"I don't knooow. Algebra's soooo haaaaard," Shannon groaned, tilting her head back into the locker behind her. "Where's Doug when we need him?"

"I think I got it," Ava whispered, scribbling the final step to the problem in her notebook. Shannon leaned close to Ava as she studied the work on the lined paper. Starting to speak, thinking she had found an error, and then reconsidering, Shannon sighed with relief.

"Yeah, I think you did. Can I copy it?"

"Sure." Ava handed her notebook to her best friend.

Down the hallway, in front of the double doors to the library, a gang of boys were gathered around something or someone. Ava and Shannon ignored them as they worked on their homework, but the noise coming from the circle of kids was rapidly growing louder. Finally looking up,

187

glaring in the group's direction, Ava could see her brother's bright blue winter coat in the thick of the crowd. He was the loudest, but also one of the smallest. Without saying a word to Shannon, Ava stood up and dropped her books and pencil on the ground. Something was wrong. She could feel it, and as she approached, she could see it.

There was a kid with his back to the wall beside the doorframe. He was new, a foster kid passing through a home. Ava didn't know his name. Her brother's hands were on the kid's neck, just above the neckline of his orange sweatshirt. Ava felt her heart beat faster as she watched from the edge of the crowd. It looked like Eddy was strangling the poor kid at first, but she quickly realized he was showing the kid how to do it himself. Pulling his hands away, the taller, skinner boy's hands were around his own neck, too. He pushed himself against the wall and closed his eyes. His chest rose and fell with shallow breaths.

"What's going on?"

Ava turned at the sound of Pode's voice. He and Baker were standing beside her, Baker finishing off a Honey Bun from the vending machine. A breakfast his mother wouldn't approve of.

"I don't know."

The kid's eyes rolled back into his head and his body sagged and fell, his head bouncing off the floor. The crowd gasped simultaneously and everyone took a step back. In complete silence, 30 kids watched, stunned, as the kid whose name nobody could remember convulsed and rolled into the center of the hallway.

"What's going on here?" Max Turner, the science teacher, a tall skinny balding man who was working out his last two years before retirement parted the crowd. He knelt beside the boy on the ground and looked up. "Well, somebody go get help." Pode took off at a sprint toward the office in the front of the building. Mr. Turner checked the kid's pulse at his wrist as he examined the newly forming softball sized welt on his forehead. "What happened here?"

The gathered kids looked around at each other, all terrified to admit to anything, terrified to be an accessory or a narc. Eddy had faded into the crowd, sneaking into the second row, his head bowed as he tried to pretend he was as innocent a bystander as everyone else around him.

"Eddy," Ava's voice carried in the echoey hallway. Her brother ignored her and took a step further back. All eyes, including Mr. Turner's, found him, though.

"Eddy Schaffer? Do you know what happened here?" Mr. Turner asked, standing and facing a faction that parted and left the sheepish boy singled out.

"No, I don't—I don't know." Eddy lied fairly convincingly.

"What were you doing?" Ava felt the kids around her move away from her, too, leaving the siblings standing face to face.

"Ava," Eddy hissed, glaring at her under his long dark bangs. Instantly turning from furious to sweet, Eddy again tried to lie. "He asked me if I would help him. He saw something on the internet about passing yourself out and he showed it to me and I said it was not a good idea but . . ."

"To the office. Right now, Schaffer. Sit down and wait for me there and do not move, do you understand?" Mr. Turner didn't let him finish the fabrication. He knew better. Thirty-five years of teaching kids just like Eddy had taught him how to read deceit like an FBI profiler.

"God!" Eddy marched past Ava stopping in front of her for an instant. "I can't believe you. My own sister? You bitch."

"Eddy Schaffer!" Mr. Turner roared at him, the yelling

189

like thunder in the brick building's hallway. Unexpected and deafening. "If you are not in the office in three seconds, you will be expelled from this school!"

Eddy didn't hesitate anymore. He marched toward the principal's office and out of sight. The bell signaling the start of the school day rang clear and loud. The kids who usually drug to class and barely made it on time, hurried, ran even, thankful to be out of the situation and to have an excuse to avoid looking at the unconscious boy on the ground.

"Come on, Av." Baker took her arm, hearing what Eddy had said and watching the affect it had on his friend. Shannon was on her other side, joining the crowd sometime after Mr. Turner got involved. She handed Ava her math textbook and notebook and pencil and together the three friends walked to class.

# 8

Catherine Ellis was an unnaturally tall woman. Thin without shape even after 52 years and giving birth to a son. A graying blonde bun rested at the nape of her neck, a long, beige cardigan wrapped over a white shirt and knit slacks. She was reaching for a box of rice on the top shelf, her slender fingers closing around it, as Ava hurried around the end of the last aisle of metal shelves in the back of the Flynn Country Grocers. The first urge Ava felt was to dive out of the way and barrel roll to safety then sprint from the store before the woman saw her. It was too late for dramatic evasion techniques, though, because when Ava froze, Catherine looked up at her and smiled. Maybe, Ava hoped, it would be a quick, painless small talk conversation about the weather. Or the high school football team. Or the package of Double Stuf Oreos in Ava's arms.

"Ava." The integrally beautiful woman flashed a row of the same big white teeth her son had inherited. "So nice to run into you." Catherine drawled her vowels. She was originally from somewhere else, Tennessee, Ava thought, but wasn't sure. She didn't know much about Ellis, except what she had heard around town and that type of information was unreliable at best. His father had died when he was young. He had been in the military. His mother was originally from the South. He had once been engaged to Corinne Yeards. That was it. That was all she could procure from the back of her mind.

"Hi!" The word Ava spoke was jarring, too loud and

191

possessed with nervous energy.

"How's your father doing? Lucas told me about the accident. That's just awful."

"Well." Ava smiled, relieved all she had to do was answer a question. Maybe it would all be questions, posed to her. She could give the stock answer and move on with her day. "He's doing well. The doctor said he'll make a full recovery. Some burn scarring, but that's it. He was very, very lucky."

"That's wonderful. I am so happy to hear that." She reached out and gently touched Ava's arm and left her hand on the worn cotton sleeve. "I don't know if Lucas has said anything to you or not, but when everything's all settled down I would love to have y'all over for supper."

Ava's answer took too long. "Sure."

"I would love to get to know my son's girlfriend better."

There it was. Girlfriend. Ava pressed her lips together as she wondered what exactly Ellis had said to his mother.

"We're . . ." Ava stopped, her honesty to her detriment yet again. How had she never learned to lie? Dora May built an entire life of lies. She lied to herself and to her husband and to her children and to her clients and to the people of Flynn. Eddy spent so much of his life telling lies, to hear the truth from him was miraculous. Ava should have learned from the best, but instead incessantly spewed truth as if she needed to be the balance for the lies all around her.

The middle-aged southern woman with echoes of Ellis's features gracefully awaited the rest of Ava's sentence. When it didn't come she pulled her warm hand off of Ava's arm and placed it on the steering bar of her shopping cart. She had always thought the girl was strange, but not unlikeable. "Well, I'd love to have you over for dinner. Have a good evening."

Ava responded with a nod and a duck past the woman. She ran her hand through her hair, brushing greasy blonde chunks out of her face. That could have gone better, Ava decided as she judged herself in her mind, immediately overthinking the entire interaction. She should learn how to lie.

Peering up at the cement block building, Ava only had a single memory of the inside of it. Each year the fourth graders in the Flynn County School District completed the D.A.R.E. program. On the last day of the program, they traveled to the jail in Clay, where they went through the steps of being fake booked and thrown in a jail for 20 minutes or so before raiding the lunch hour of the McDonalds next door. It was supposed to rile up fear, make the kids think twice about getting into trouble, but instead it became known as the Fourth Graders' McDonalds Fieldtrip.

Ava couldn't remember any feelings of terror, but she did remember making animals out of ink thumbprints with Shannon and helping Pode push Baker through the bars of one of the cells. They were convinced he was skinny enough to fit, only to find out fast that he wasn't. It took a whole bottle of dish soap and Sheriff Beatle and two of his deputies and a fair amount of shoving to get Baker unstuck. He ended up with vicious bruises that won him an astounding amount of attention mileage between showing them off and talking about his parents suing the sheriff's department. Even when they were nothing but yellow stains on white skin stretched across sharp rib bones, he would pull up his shirt and try to impress with his story about being injured by cops after being thrown in jail.

Several county cop cruisers were parked in a row in front of the building, but it was impossible for Ava to tell if one of them was Ellis's. She called him and left a message. She hoped he could meet her at the jail so she wouldn't have to trudge shamefully alone into the strange place. He didn't call her back. The first couple of days after her father's wreck it seemed like he called her once an hour, every hour, to check in. His calls lessened and dropped off as her interest in answering them waned, though, and she regretted not answering at least a couple of them if only for needing his help now.

As Ava reached for the door handle at the top of the wide set of marble steps, the door opened for her and she found Ellis immediately on the other side. He had been watching for her. He smiled, but formally. "Hi, Ava."

"Hey. Hi. Thank you so much for being here." She smiled back. "I wasn't sure where to go, or . . ."

"Sure, no problem." He led her into the large front room of the facility. "I had paperwork to drop off, anyway."

A series of empty desks spread across the room beyond a high, long booking counter and row of sturdy steel chairs. On the far wall, Sheriff Beatle shut the door to his office. He looked much the same as he had when Ava was in fourth grade. Short with a big round belly, the only real difference was his red hair, which had thinned and faded to a sandy gray. Divorced, four times, he had never had any children of his own. No one liked him, generally, but that was mostly because he had arrested them or their family members at one time or another and knew far too much about their lives. Nevertheless, they continued to vote him into office year after year, because no one else wanted the job.

"Miss Schaffer. How are you?" The sheriff smiled widely, a gap between his two front teeth. People joked that he was always in search of his next wife and from the way his eyes scanned Ava's body, she could see why that belief spread.

"Good, thank you," Ava answered quietly.

"Welp, I'm headed out, deputy. You kids have a good night."

Ellis nodded his head in answer. The sheriff waved his hand at the front desk crew and zipped up his polyester law insignia printed jacket and left the building. Ava watched as Ellis's expression relaxed and his smile faded into something more personal.

"I brought this stuff." Ava held up a plastic grocery sack. "Magazines, Oreos, clothes. Do you need to check it? I promise there's no pie with a file in it. I don't like pie and I have no idea how to make one. And I need my metal file for the project I'm working on right now."

The joke bombed, but Ellis politely chuckled as he took the bag from her. "I trust you."

Maybe she didn't know him well enough. Maybe his sense of humor was better than she had so far discovered, but what he laughed at and what he didn't worried her. Pode passed through her mind and so did the guilt she felt whenever she was with Ellis. How easy it was to laugh with her old friend. She took for granted how similar their humor was and had recently begun to worry Pode might be the only person she would ever meet in her life who would genuinely understand her and see things exactly the way she did.

"Please have a seat in here." Ellis opened a door to a small room beside them. It was windowless, empty, except for a plastic coated table and two folding chairs. "I'll go get him."

Ava felt anxious in the room. Another official place she could add to the list of places she never wanted to be in again. The list had grown much longer in the past couple of years: courtrooms, offices, hospitals, now jails.

Silence. She waited. She knew the situation probably

should be more humiliating, but Ava always guessed she would find her father in prison someday. And for Ellis, this was his job, to arrest people he knew. She liked the man in the inexplicable way initial physical attraction becomes fantasizing about a future together, even if she didn't mean to. With her world upside down, she had taken the path of indifference and stopped trying to impress anyone. The day on the roof of the feed and seed was a starting over point. A point at which she put herself on display for the whole town and didn't care that they were looking. For the first time. She was not her mother's child. Dora May would have been so disappointed, so concerned. Not for her daughter's wellbeing, but instead what others would think of Ava and more importantly Dora May herself. It was freeing, lovely, to live like no one was watching, and Ellis not only understood, but didn't seem to mind.

Ed led, Ellis followed, holding onto the incarcerated man's arm. Ava took a deep breath. Her father, his hands handcuffed in front of him, took a seat across from her. He looked good, the color of his face devoid of its usual pink tint. He was wearing a simple t-shirt and cotton pants of a grey-blue hue. Showered, shaved, as Ava studied him, she regretted her belief that Billy James, not this man, was her father. Maybe it wasn't too late, maybe she had given up too soon, maybe if the drinking stopped he could be a different man. The man she needed in her life, an example she could rebase her beliefs off of.

Ellis took a spot in the corner, standing, looking away at the other wall. He obviously felt bad about the rules that forced him stay in the room, about his listening in on their conversation. Ava wanted to tell him it was OK. It wasn't OK. This wasn't the way a father should get to know the man his daughter was dating. A ride home in a cop car, arrested at a hospital, the county jail. The list of their unions was progressing in the wrong direction.

"Hey, Dad." Ava smiled, her smile somehow still encouraging. He stared through her forehead as if it were a window. "I brought you this stuff. Magazines from your mailbox. An electronic solitaire game thingy. Thought you might be getting bored in here."

Still nothing. He seemed indifferent to the whole situation. It was as if Ava was not in the room at all. She went on. "I'm sorry I don't have money for your bail. I'm kind of broke right now. No consignment sales since last month."

"That's alright," he spoke finally. It wasn't much, but he spoke. And the words he said were positive. "I get showers. Three meals a day. And nobody wakes me up all night like they did in the hospital. It's not too bad here."

"Good. That's good." Ava picked at the cuticle of her thumb underneath the table. She wondered if it was better for a kid to have a father like hers or no father at all like Ellis. She pushed the awful thought out of her mind.

"Well." Ed stood, using the edge of the table to push himself up. Ellis took a step forward. "Thank you for the magazines and stuff."

"You're welcome." Ava stood, too, not surprised the conversation was already over. Ellis glanced at Ava, confirming she had nothing else to say and she pulled her lips into a straight line. He looked good. Her father looked good. That was her consolation. Ellis escorted him out of the room.

Ava collapsed backward against the chair. She listened to the sound of Ellis's boots reverberate in the hall away from her. She leaned forward and put her forehead flat on the table. The table was cool, smooth. Her eyes were so close to it, the flecks of blue and white and grey intermingled and blurred.

"Ava?" Ellis's voice was placid. She heard the chair across from her slide out. Quiet took over for a minute or two before Ellis broke it. "Huh, it looks like the ocean."

Intrigued, Ava rolled her head up and found Ellis sitting in the chair her father had vacated. His forehead was pressed on the table top exactly as hers had been. He looked absurd. Fantastically absurd.

"I've never seen the ocean," Ava whispered.

Ellis raised his eyes, then his head, from the table. The green in his eyes sparkled. "You should see it. I'll take you. What are you doing tomorrow night?"

"Tomorrow night? Kansas is a long ways from the ocean."

"Yeah. So, what about for now a high school football game? Do you want to go to the game? With me?"

If it had been any other time, she would have said no, but that he had mimicked her, pressed his head to the table, too, she nodded with the slightest excited smile.

The night was dark. Pitch black. Clouds hiding the stars and sliver of a moon. Main Street in Flynn was absolutely deserted. Not a single car parked in front of a single building. Not a sound, except a lone owl lazy hooting in a tree in a neighboring yard. Pode's truck crawled through the alley by the backdoors and dumpsters of the Flynn Country Grocers and Lois's Cut 'n' Color and eventually, the Flynn County Courthouse. He leaned forward in his seat, peering through the shadows in front of him. Headlights off at Ava's insistence, he drove only by the orangey glow of the street lamp light shining over the tops and around the sides of the buildings. The pace was painfully slow. Pode kept it in first gear, afraid to rev the engine.

The first plan included walking the six blocks from his house on Oak Street, but they were afraid they might run into someone who would pull over and offer them a ride. And then there was the escape. If, by some miracle, they were caught at 3 a.m. on a Friday morning in the uninhabited little town, they would need to be able to leave fast. So the plan changed to driving. Definitely not the Mustang. It was loud enough to cause a disruption in normal daytime traffic and the likelihood of it dying for good at this, the most inconvenient, time was extremely high. So it was the giant red truck they chose as the getaway car for the breaking and entering of the Flynn County Courthouse.

"Do you think one of these is for the back door?" Ava looked at the seat space between them at a ring with six keys and a chunky square keychain attached. She picked it up and examined it. Between layers of yellowed, scratched plastic, a photo of Pode and his brother and sister as children, in terrible early '90s outfits, sat at the picnic table in Henry and Kris's backyard, smiling up at her. Ava vividly remembered the floral jumper Wren was wearing in the photo, because she wore it three years later.

"I don't know. Hope so."

Ava slithered out of the truck, holding the door with both hands. She pushed it closed so carefully it didn't latch the first time and she had to push it harder a second. Pode, meanwhile, slammed his shut without thinking.

"Shhh!" Ava hurried around the front of the truck as she hushed him, cringing from the sound echoing off the buildings. She hissed, "What are you doing?"

"Sorry, sorry. I forgot. It's three in the morning. I'm sleepy."

"I don't want to get caught."

"Trust me. Me neither. But this town is d-e-a-d. I could strip naked and sing 'I'm a Little Teapot' in the middle of Main Street and nobody'd ever know." Pode pretended to be serious, but his eyes smiled.

Ava raised an eyebrow. "Except me."

"Hundred dollars?"

"You have no idea how tempting that bet is." Ava glared at Pode, actually considering owing her best friend a hundred dollars. "We don't have time."

She climbed up the cement stairs to the back of the courthouse and tried the first key, then the second. Neither worked, and the third was way too small, the key to a mailbox or a padlock. "Are you sure this is the right set?" she asked Pode, who stood at her shoulder watching as she tried a fourth then fifth key.

"Yep, these are all the keys Mom has, except for the ones to her car."

Ava tried the last key. It didn't fit in the lock. "Shit. Front door."

Pode and Ava scrambled along the side of the courthouse, Pode carrying a heavy flashlight, pointed toward the ground. At the corner, they stopped. Both leaned comically forward, peeking down the empty street. Without moonlight and devoid of sound, their hometown's main thoroughfare took on an eerie feel. Ava pulled her head back, ramming the top of it into Pode's nose.

"Ah, dammit!" Pode fell away sideways. Both of his hands went to his nose. The flashlight crashed onto the concrete sidewalk and went off as it rolled away from them.

"Oh, I'm sorry. I'm so sorry, Pode." Ava reached out to him, but he stumbled back another step. "Are you OK?"

"Yeah. Just eye watery." He sniffed and blinked hard a couple of times. "I am never robbing a bank with you."

"Deal," Ava agreed as she retrieved the flashlight and scrambled to replace the battery that had fallen out of the end of it and landed in the sorry patch of grass between the sidewalk and the courthouse.

They crept around the corner again. Ava led the way through the darkness, Pode a safe distance behind her, the stinging in his nose nearly gone. The midnight blue sweatshirt she wore with her jeans blended into the night. Handing Pode the flashlight, Ava carefully, quickly tried one key at a time in the deadbolt above the door knob in the front door. The fourth key slid in with ease, and she turned it until she felt it click. She started over with the lock in the knob. First key. They were in.

Pode gently pulled the door closed after them. It took a second for his sight to adjust to the new, deeper dark inside the front room. Ava was already out of sight, as quiet as a mouse on the linoleum. Pode passed his mother's desk and glanced at the shelves of picture frames full of pictures of his own smiling face. He wondered how often people who broke into places had to walk by a series of their own childhood smile. The whole thing felt wrong to him, but he justified his decision to help Ava with the fact that they weren't stealing. They were searching. They weren't causing any damage. They were, hopefully for Ava's sake, fixing something. He had tried to talk her into flat out asking Billy James, but he knew as well as Ava did, the lawyer lied for a living. Ava wanted—Ava needed—proof on paper.

"None of them," Ava sighed, defeated, as Pode caught up with her at the end of the hallway. She held the keys out in her hand and looked to Pode for help. Without a word, he took a drill and a handful of bits out of the deep pocket of his coat and passed off the flashlight. She shined it on the door lock as he examined it. In what seemed like only seconds, he had three of the four sides of the panel with the lock loose, the drill too noisy in the soundless void of the building.

"This last one's stripped. Can you go see if you can find a rubber band on Mom's desk?"

Ava nodded her head and disappeared. In the front room she slid behind the built-in desk and shined the flashlight around, instantly overwhelmed by the many, many drawers. Careful not to move anything out of place, it only took three drawers before a blue and white box of an assortment of rubber bands in different shapes and sizes presented itself. The fact that Pode needed one for a stripped screw made no sense to Ava, so she rifled through the box and took several of different shapes and sizes to be sure she had what he needed. She put the box back exactly where she had found it and eased the drawer shut.

"I didn't know . . ." Ava began to speak as she returned to Pode, but found the man at the end of the hallway, silent and waving his hands wildly. Ava froze where she was standing. Nothing. She heard nothing. She frowned at Pode. He pointed over his shoulder to the back of the building and the alley where his truck was parked.

She rolled her eyes around, scanned the darkness, waited. As she opened her mouth to talk, a car door slammed only a couple of yards away. Someone was in the alley. Heart exploding in her chest, Ava strained to hear anything else, but there was nothing. Was it someone else's car or was someone in Pode's truck? She couldn't tell. So she focused every bit of her energy on staying absolutely still.

Footsteps. Heavy, men's booted footsteps climbed up the concrete back steps. Someone tried the door knob, turning it back and forth. Ava closed her eyes. Twice, she thought. Twice the Flynn Country Courthouse been broken into in its entire 107 years of existence and both times would ironically be on the same night. What were the odds? They had to be worse than being hit by lightning.

Ava forced her eyes open and braced herself for being discovered. Pode was mouthing words in the semi-darkness, but they were lost to Ava. Pode's lips became more and more animated. She squinted at him, but didn't understand anything he was trying to tell her. Ava had never noticed how much expression Pode's face held and she was struck by how attractive she found him in his current bizarre state. The image in her head, an accumulation of all of the images in memories she held of him from childhood up until this single moment, was wrong. It was if she was seeing him for the first time. A stranger seated at a bar. A man crossing a parking lot. The person before her in a checkout line. He was not a boy, anymore, hadn't been for a long time. He was a man with a wide muscular body and cheeks littered with the beginnings of a beard and lines at the corners of kind, gray eyes. His face twitched desperately, trying to convey whatever message was in his brain and Ava found Pode's inability to speak, to use his most common defense mechanism, strangely humorous.

Static. The sound of static from a radio cut through the night and the knob stopped turning. Ava's breath caught. Pode's lips stayed in the exact position of the last word he was mouthing to her, an expression that made him look like he had taken a bite out of a lemon.

"Dispatch to Officer Ellis."

They had their answer. The only police officer in town was on the other side of the door. Ava felt crushing dread, followed immediately by immense relief. It would be easy to explain to Ellis. She would have to tell the truth about the insurance policy, the money. Letting another person in on the secret was not at all in her plan, but it would be fact, the logical explanation, and the easiest way to get them out of any breaking and entering charges. She would tell the truth. She knew how to do that. The presence of Pode probably wouldn't go over well with Ellis, but she could convince him Pode was simply the driver, an accessory to the crime. She would take all of the blame. Pode would be off the hook. Ellis, though maybe angry, would give in and let her go.

"This is Officer Ellis," his strong direct voice spoke on the other side of the door, inches from Pode's face. Pode closed his mouth and dropped his head forward. Ava thought he might be praying.

The footsteps retreated down the steps and into the alley. The radio conversation continued as a car door opened and shut. The engine of the police cruiser started, the only sound the sound of it driving away from them. Ava breathed again as she put her head in her hands and leaned a shoulder into the wall beside her.

"Holy shit," Pode said under his breath. Then he laughed. Ava looked up, surprised by his reaction, but sure enough he was laughing. "Oh my God. Holy shit, that was amazing."

Ava found herself laughing, too. Shaking her head, she stepped toward Pode and held her hand of rubber bands out toward him. He continued to laugh, a harrowing maniacal laugh, as he took a thick, stained newspaper rubber band from her hand and knelt beside the door knob.

"OK," Ava said quietly as she held the flashlight on his hands as he worked. "It wasn't that funny."

"No." Pode glanced up at her. "It was."

"I could have talked us out of it."

"You couldn't lie your way out of a wet paper sack, Ava Schaffer."

"I would have told him the truth. He would have believed me and let us go."

"Why would he let us go?" Pode spoke before he thought. He stopped laughing. He asked a question he didn't want the answer to. He slowly stood up, facing Ava, with the entire lock plate in his hand. The door to Billy James's office sagged open.

Something dissolved, something else transformed between the two friends as they stood face to face in the darkness. It was like summer air when the humidity level reaches 99 percent. There doesn't have to be a single cloud in the sky for it to rain on those few exceptionally humid days. The air itself is so full of water it explodes into droplets, bursts apart, and rains sideways. The world cools and every living thing feels the relief.

Pode dropped the drill and the plate on the ground, both of them landing with thuds. He pushed Ava up against the wall. His lips clumsily found hers, one hand on her waist, the other tangled in the hair above her ear. Captured by his intensity, she kissed back, Ava's hands wrapping around the back of Pode's neck. They fit together. They were perfect, anticipating the other's movements as if they had kissed each other a thousand times. Suddenly Ava realized what was happening and shoved Pode, her hands balled into fists as they violently struck his chest.

"What are you doing?" Ava gasped, out of breath. Her head cloudy. Her stomach on fire.

Pode looked as surprised as Ava felt. "I don't know. I don't—I don't know." He fled from her and vanished down the hall.

Ava reached for the wall behind her, laying both hands flat on it as she tried to stop her head from spinning long enough for her to remember where she was and what she was doing there. Time had passed, from trying keys, to searching for a rubber band, to waiting out Ellis, to—this. Ava didn't know how much time. They needed to get in and out before any of the farmers made their first rounds at 5:30. Ava pushed the door to the lawyer's office open, going immediately to the far left filing cabinet with the "Financial" label on the front of it.

In the front room of the courthouse, Pode sat heavily on the uncomfortable couch. A bead of sweat worked its way down his face and he pulled his jacket off with a struggle. Throwing it on the chair beside him, he leaned forward, elbows on his knees, hands folded together under his chin.

Why was this the night he had finally become caught up with emotion and chosen to kiss her? He had a lifetime of possibilities. Nights where they sat together on the riverbank with fishing poles. Nights where she had fallen asleep beside him in tents beside bonfires. Nights where they were both so drunk they couldn't see straight and used each other for support so they could walk out of Martha's together. It was Ellis. It was New York. It was the threat of losing her. The one person he loved more than the world.

Kate's curls bobbed about as she climbed over and under and through the metal supports of the splintered blue and white painted bleachers. She stopped, bending over the bars at an impossible angle, looking like she might fall at any moment, but she didn't. A monkey, her strong, skinny arms held on, swinging her to the lowest bar. Releasing her grip a foot above the ground, she landed like a feather and knelt straight into a squat to examine something lying on the ground at closer range.

Shannon watched her daughter, cringing as the little girl picked a filthy thing up off the ground. The abandoned object looked sharp. The woman had no idea what possessed a child to be fascinated with something like it, let alone pick it up and examine it. There was no use in telling Kate not to touch it, though. That would result in an increase in value in the piece. If she couldn't have it, she would want it. Have to have it. And some time in the future the mother would find it hidden in a dresser drawer or underneath a bed or in the pocket of a winter coat.

"Oww!" Shannon squealed as she felt a sharp pinch on the side of her butt that was raised as she tilted her body to watch her child. Turning quickly, she found a giggling husband standing beside her, holding out a bottle of Diet Coke. Shannon glared playfully and fake punched him in the gut. They were both unaware of the other people on the benches around them, smiling as they watched the couple flirt.

"Ooof!" Kale held his gut, overreacting. "Man, that's what I get for buying my girl a drink? Some people say 'thank you.'"

"Have you seen our daughter?"

"Julia? She's behind the concession stand with her friends. I lost track of Kate."

"Yeah, Jules. Kate's underneath us. Playing with trash."

"That's my girl," Kale joked, glancing through the gaps between the rows of seats.

The speakers, mounted on either side of the wooden shack that held a concession stand on the lower level and a crow's nest announcers booth on the top level, buzzed as someone flipped them on. The sky behind the visitors' side of the empty football field was deep indigo, with a hint of ochre at the horizon as the sun set early, earlier every day as the fall season moved closer to winter.

"Nice sunset tonight," Kale observed as he and his wife stared into it.

"Yeah, it is," she responded. Shannon's voice was soft, her attention captured by the brilliant shades of nature.

Leaning in close to her ear, he whispered, "Guess I should tell you I got a job today."

"What!?" Shannon jerked her head up to look at her husband, who had a mischievous grin on his face. "Kale! Why didn't you say something sooner? Did Lou hire you?"

"Yep. He did. Sorry, I forgot to say something earlier. I told him I can start Monday if your mom can take the girls."

Shannon stood and wrapped her arms around the back of his head and pulled him into a deep kiss that caused the big man's cheeks to flush. Letting go, the smile spread across Shannon's face was the type of smile Kale hadn't seen for years. He was instantly happier in the glow of her happiness and realized that he would gratefully sell used cars for the rest of his life if it meant his beautiful wife would continue to smile at him like that.

Pode jumped out of his truck. He reached in his back pocket for his scuffed leather wallet as he crossed the gravel parking lot to the open gate at the edge of the Flynn County High School's football field. Max Turner and Bud Cox, in VFW Post #7515 hats and vests, sat behind a card table, a green metal cash box of change in front of them.

"Mr. Pode Baker," Max greeted the younger man with a smile. "You look ready for winter."

It took Pode a second to catch on. The old man was referring to the now fairly heavy beard spread across his cheeks and chin. Thick and dark, like his hair, he hadn't thought about the fact that it was an apparent statement against the impending cold. Few men could grow such a fantastic beard. Pode understood this before he was out of high school, and so many of them were slightly envious and accusatory of anyone with such a beard being a show off. Pode wasn't, though. He just lazily hadn't shaved for a few days, found himself at an important shave-or-don't-shave juncture and decided to let the beard do its thing. And Ava had mentioned she liked the beard the winter before, as he was forcing a facial hair consultation on her. She joked that it made him look tough and caveman-y and laughed at him as he rubbed his chin and grunted and flexed.

Ava wouldn't leave his mind. She hadn't found anything in Billy James's office, despite two hours of searching. Neither of them spoke another word the rest of the night, or morning, Pode regretting the kiss, Ava discouraged by the lack of discovery. They both considered the night a failure, a complete failure.

Pode heard the grinding, awful sounds of an engine on its last leg as it struggled up the incline of the parking lot. The Mustang hadn't made it back to Callahan's yet, so Ava was limping it along. At the base of the hill the high school campus sat on, the dull red car groaned and growled as the engine throttled one last time and Ava eased it unevenly into a parking spot. It gave up and died before she turned the key off.

Ava fled from the car, embarrassed by it and trying to ignore it and its problems as she turned her back on it. Her hair was extra shiny and extra blonde. She had on a tight pair of jeans and a lacy white blouse she hadn't worn for years. As she drew closer to Pode, he noticed her eyes first, because they were highlighted by dark, heavy makeup. She didn't look up until she was standing right in front of him, the crowd of fans flooding through the gate on either side of them.

"Av?" Pode called to her.

Ava flinched, her thoughts disrupted by his voice and her expression full of guilt.

"That doesn't sound good." He pointed toward the

Mustang.

"Oh, yeah. I think it might be done for."

"I can give you ride home later or you can stay with . . ."

"No, I'm . . ." Ava stopped and glanced back toward the parking lot. Ellis, making a rare appearance in normal people clothing, waved to her. He was a few inches taller than the crowd of folks walking up the drive around him. His jeans were new, a short sleeved western shirt stretched across his chest, not too tight, but showcasing his flat stomach. Pode self-consciously crossed his arms across his loose blue t-shirt, trying to conceal his recently established beer belly.

"Ava." Ellis smiled and she smiled back. He regarded Pode, the smile fading. "Pode."

"Lucas." There was a cool tone in Pode's voice.

"Well, shall we go stake out a good spot." Ellis took a step closer to Ava and placed his hand flat on the small of her back.

"Sure." Ava continued on with him, through the gate and toward the bleachers. Pode rubbed his beard as he watched them walk away together.

"Waggy-Waaggy-Wagner!"

The overwhelming smell of alcohol filled the space around Pode as Baker laughed and sucker punched Pode in his back and side.

"Dammit, Dougie. You drunk already?"

"Uh." Baker faked offense to the question. "I can't believe you would ask me that. Of course I am! Let's go watch some foos-ball."

Pode laughed as he walked with his friend to the congregate of overzealous male spectators on the home team's sidelines, thankful for a distraction in the form of Baker. Kale shook his head at Pode and Baker as they joined him. On the far side of the field, the Flynn Blue

Jays were lining up to receive the kick off from the Harrier Eagles.

"Goddammit," Kale laughed. "Are you two tore up?"

"Yes, sir!" Baker tried to line up beside Kale, but weaved to the right and man-giggled. A few of the men standing in the row shot him looks from the corners of their eyes.

"Alright." Pode grabbed Baker's arm and steadied the man between himself and Kale, "You're going have to keep your mouth shut so they don't kick you out, buddy."

Baker understood and did shut-up at the same time the crowd went wild. Penny's little brother, Pastor and Sandy McEwing's son, Craig McEwing, caught the kickoff and ran it back 40 yards before finally being brought down midfield.

"McEwing a junior, yet?" Kale asked as he gestured toward the field.

"Sophomore," Pode answered.

"Damn good football player. Gain weight, he'll get a nice scholarship. Maybe even Division I."

"Yeah, Penny said he's already got several colleges interested in him. I think she said Washburn. Maybe Butler."

"Butler'll get him bulked up. Love to see another hometown boy on the team."

"Yep," Pode answered.

Baker burped loudly, but managed to hold himself together otherwise.


Ava spotted a waving Shannon near the top of the bleachers. She led Ellis through the crowd and up the steps, no fewer than a hundred people covertly watching what appeared to be a couple. Most smiled, or looked away. Ava imagined what the rumors around town might be the next day, but only from the angle of curiosity, not because she cared at all. A new beautiful freedom overtook her mind, instead.

"Ava, Lucas, good to see you guys!" Shannon's smile was wide, genuine. She patted the seat beside her. Ava gladly took it and Ellis sat close to her, stretching his arm across the next row of seats. Ava leaned back into it, her shoulder against his chest, feeling as though she owed him a good public appearance in front of the crowd after previously humiliating him at Martha's.

"Hey, Shan. The girls with you?" Ava asked.

"Yeah. Julia and Kate. Grace is at Mom's." Shannon pointed to the ground and Ava spotted Kate underneath the stands. She waved and the girl returned her wave.

"Hi, Aunt Ava!" Kate's shrill voice yelled.

"Wow, *Aunt* Ava?" Ellis smiled, impressed. "You're aunt status, huh?"

"And don't you forget it," Ava joked.

"What a cutie." Ellis's eyes were far away as he watched the child, then they focused as he smiled again at Ava. It made her uncomfortable and she crossed and uncrossed her legs. Ellis liked kids. Ava guessed he probably wanted a family. He was older than she, maybe a decade older. She didn't know for sure.

Everyone cheered. Ava, Ellis, Shannon, even Kate and the other kids on the ground shouted and applauded. Their attention was on the game as Craig McEwing ran the ball in for the first touchdown for the Blue Jays. The cheerleaders gathered on the lanes of rubberized track in front of the grandstands. The smallest two girls climbed up onto the shoulders of their counterparts and prepared to flip backward. They looked so young to Ava, who hadn't been to a high school football game since before her mother's diagnosis. At some point in those few years, she had crossed the early twenties age gap to a place where teenagers blurred with younger children into a total group she referred to simply as "kids."

"Is the side of your face burning?" Shannon whispered to Ava, unscrewing the cap on her bottle of pop and taking a sip.

"What?" Ava asked, following her friend's eyes to the ground. Beside the concession stand, Corrine, hand on a jutted out hip, glared at Ava as if she might bore a hole through her cheek. Caught, Corrine quickly looked away and back toward the football field, nervously straightening her jacket. Shannon laughed as Ava shook her head. She considered mentioning something to Ellis, but he hadn't noticed. His concentration entirely on the football game.

Ellis and Ava's hands had been intertwined since the end of the third quarter, but Shannon pretended not to see it. The women talked about everything except the game, rooting for the home team when necessary to fit in. Ellis interjected in their conversation now and then, but was mostly sidetracked by the game. A big football fan, if not for Ava, he would have been standing on the side lines pretend coaching with the other men from town. Everyone began clearing out early, with the home team up 28 points and only a few minutes left on the clock. Ava and Ellis, their hands staying connected, and Shannon, stood at the same time to file down the steps with the departing crowd.

Kale, a dirty, sleeping Kate flopped over his shoulder, stood at the edge of the field. Julia and a little blonde friend pleaded with him, making the case for something with sweet smiles and dramatic hand gestures. As Ava and Ellis and Shannon approached, Kale shot a look of request for support to his wife.

"Mom! Mom. Mom. Can I stay the night with Mari?" Julia's face was full of excitement, optimism. After having not received the right answer from her father, she saw her mother as a whole new possibility. The parents were way ahead of their daughter, though, accustomed to the tag team effort it takes to raise children. Ava couldn't help but see herself and Shannon standing there in front of Shannon's mother 20 years before. Maybe children weren't so scary. Maybe motherhood wasn't a bad thing, an inconvenience, a method of life ruination as Dora May had made it seem. Shannon didn't think that at all, but she was a natural, possessing the perfect balance of nurturer and enforcer mixed with a sizable sense of humor.

"I don't know," Shannon sighed. "You don't have any of your stuff."

"Mari says I can borrow her pajamas and I can brush my teeth twice when I get home tomorrow to make up for not brushing them tonight." Julia had it all figured out. "I bet if Aunt Ava had kids, she would let them go to sleepovers."

"Whoa," Ava laughed and took a step back. "Nope, I'm not getting into this. Good luck, Team Parent." Ava pulled Ellis away, with a wink at her friends. As they walked toward the emptying parking lot, Ava could still hear the girls negotiating.

"Oh, man. Kids," Ellis chuckled.

"Those girls are so good, but so smart. Shannon and Kale have a long life ahead of them."

"Do you want kids?"

Ava shrugged her shoulders, trying not to act too alarmed. "Maybe. I don't know. I used to say no. No kids, nothing to tie me down. I want to create art. Travel the world. Eccentrically sock away money. When Mom died, though, I don't know. I miss a connection with her, as flawed as it was. I've wondered if I had a daughter who she would be."

"What about getting married?" He snuck it in, in a way

that made it not as awkward as it should have been.

"I—I don't know."

"You look good in white."

Ava wished she was wearing her oversized flannel mess. What did he mean? She didn't know his birthday, his middle name, surely he didn't mean "white" in the sense of a wedding dress. Plus all he had ever seen from her was crazy. The roof, the bar, the bonfire, the hospital, the jail. This was the first normal night of interaction they had had. She knew he must be incredibly fond of her to have persisted this far, but this was a whole new level. His hand was warm in hers, strong and reassuring. They were stopped at the end of the parking lot beside Ava's car. She welcomed the excuse of it being broken to change the subject.

"Oh, actually, my car died as I pulled in. Not died, like it does on cold mornings, but dead died. Never to start again. I guess Callahan's will probably have to tow it out of here in the morning. Is there anyway, or, would you be able to give me a ride home?"

"Oh, sure. Absolutely, Ava." Ellis paused, deliberately. "Or you're welcome to stay with me." He quickly corrected, "On my couch. I can give you a ride home, or back here, in the morning."

Ava enjoyed his forwardness. His game was improving, slowly. "That would be great. Thank you."

They left the Mustang and strolled to the grass field of overflow parking beside a windbreak of evergreen trees. The trees split the school's property line and a hundred acres of recently harvested cornfield that had been in Pode's family for four generations. The only car left was a 1966 Corvette. The body of the black beauty was in perfect shape, but a patch in the back was primer gray. Ava vaguely remembered seeing Ellis's father in the classic machine a couple of times in her early childhood, but had no idea the car had been kept.

"Wow, nice car." Ava smiled at Ellis, admiring the classic Detroit design of the vehicle.

"Needs a coat of paint," Ellis admitted as they climbed inside. "And a transmission overhaul."

"I don't know. It looks good to me. I've always liked things that are a little . . . worn-in."

"Not afraid of scars?" Ellis asked as they climbed into the car at the same time.

"Not at all. Have a few of my own."

Ellis had a perplexed look on his face. The same look he had in the shed the night of the bonfire, like he wasn't sure what to make of her. She wasn't like anyone else and he didn't think that was a bad thing. In the darkness, in the lonely parking lot, Ava studied his thoughtful expression. She put her hand firmly on his thigh and pulled herself up to kiss his lips. They parted for a moment and Ellis seemed stunned. He started to say something, but changed his mind and leaned in to kiss her again.


Pode waved as he passed Kale and Shannon, losing track of Baker in the mob of fans exiting the game. Standing up straight and peering over the crowd, he spotted Baker, a head taller than the people around him. Sneaking through with several "excuse me's," Pode caught up with his friend as they stepped onto the asphalt of the parking lot.

"Baker! Bake! Doug!" Pode shouted over the noise, catching Baker by the shoulder as the taller, skinnier man stopped and gazed across the nearest row of cars. Audie was easy to recognize from the back as she walked with a familiar guy Pode thought might be from Clay. The guy's arm was around her waist and as they walked, it moved and playfully grabbed her butt. Audie took a swat at his side, only making contact with his jacket. The guy wrapped his arm around her shoulders and pulled her close to him, his face buried deep in her hair.

Pode left his hand on his friend's shoulder as he paced around Baker until they were face to face. "You alright?"

Behind Baker, headed for the overflow parking in the grass yard along the side of the brick high school building, Pode's heart sank as he spotted Ava and Ellis. They were in Ellis's Corvette, leaving together.

"Hey, let's go to Martha's!" Pode jabbed Baker in the side. "See what kind of trouble we can get into."

"Naw." Baker backed away, Pode's hand falling off his shoulder. "No, I'm headed home."

"You alright to drive?"

"Fine. I'm fine." Baker wove away, almost crashing into a trio dressed in the crimson and gold of the visiting school.

"Baker," Pode spoke his friend's name one last time, then let him go.

Everyone cleared out fast. The last remaining cars belonged to the kids on the football team and the high school coaching staff. Pode sat in his truck for a long time, tried to decide if he wanted to go to Martha's and help his fellow Flynnians celebrate their win, or run by the Quick Stop and grab a twelve of Bud Light and go home.

They sat across from each other at the temporary plastic table in Ellis's kitchen. All around the room, the cabinets were pulled out from the walls, a shiny new white refrigerator displaced to the center of the room and no oven to be found. He was remodeling. The first of two bathrooms was already done. For what he claimed was limited experience with carpentry or tile work or electric or plumbing, Ava thought the bathroom looked professionally finished.

"You just follow the directions. Don't take shortcuts," Ellis said sternly, tilting forward in his chair as he took another sip of wine from a green plastic cup with the Flynn County Fair's logo on it. His eyes were glazed over. Two empty bottles and one almost drained decorated the center of the table between them, the wine leftover from a benefit auction the police department had hosted a few months before. They insisted he take a whole case, for volunteering to be the auctioneer. At the time he could not dream up a possible situation in which he would need so much cheap wine.

"Can't blame the Army. I've always been a rule follower."

Ava wanted to know more. She hadn't thought about Ellis in the context of a war a million miles away from Kansas. It was almost not comprehendible. "How long were you in the military?"

"Four tours. About six years."

"What . . ." She didn't know how to phrase her next question. "What was it like?"

Ellis laughed, ironically. "A lot of standing around in a desert."

He guzzled the end of his wine, picked up the bottle with a half a glass left in it and slopped some into his cup, some into Ava's Callahan's Auto Body & Repair stamped coffee cup, and the rest onto the table between them.

Ellis frowned at the spilled wine and Ava pretended to be disappointed as she shook her head at him. "You spilled. Everywhere."

"Wasteful," Ellis agreed, trying to be firm, trying not to smile. He didn't drink much, Ava realized at the end of their first bottle. He was drunk before she felt a buzz from the sweet table red.

"It's not like you think," he went on. Ava was confused

in her drunkenness for a second before she understood he was still answering her question. He looked past her, remembering in a way that was not dramatic, but painful. "It's not a bunch of shooting guns at each other. It's sitting in a desert, waiting. It's an old car or an old woman or a kid with bombs strapped onto them that blow up a bunch of your friends at a checkpoint or a school or in the middle of a field. It's not knowing who to trust and not trusting anybody. It's frustration in trying to help people who clearly don't want you there. They accept crayons for their kid one day and try to kill you the next."

Tears streamed down his face. Ava didn't know what to do. She felt her mouth hanging open and closed it. This wasn't the result she intended from the question, but mixed with too much emotion and too much alcohol, conversations often took unexpected turns.

"It wasn't so much there, then, but here, after. You come back—different. I came back—different." Ellis cleared his throat and his tears dried up.

Ava hadn't caused the trauma, but whatever horror Ellis drug up in his mind, she felt responsible for. Pushing her chair back, she took a step around the edge of the table and wrapped her arms around Ellis's neck. He nuzzled his head into her chest, his long, strong arms wrapped tightly around her body, taking up the whole space of her back. Ava straddled his knees. It wasn't the most comfortable spot, but they stayed in it for a long time. Finally, she leaned her head back and their eyes met for a moment before their lips did.

\* \* \*

Dora May stared at a shelf of canned goods. Reaching for two cans of golden whole kernel sweet corn, she held the cans and a package of chicken breasts against the front of her beige silk blouse. Dean Howard, lanky and mostly bald, stopped at the end of the aisle at the sight of her. Pretending not to see him, but fully aware of his presence, the woman took a side step and spent far too long considering a metal cylinder of grape Juicy Juice.

Dean knelt beside a new cardboard case of Cheerios left in the aisle earlier in the day. He scratched his nose nervously, then went to work skillfully opening it with the box cutter in the back pocket of his jeans. Like a dance, a strange tango, the woman slowly moved closer, taking a step each time the man reached for a box of cereal and placed it on the shelf in front of him. Once they were only a foot from each other, Dora May studied the instant oatmeal section with a wicked smile as Dean stood, flipped the newly emptied carton over and flattened it with three quick movements.

"Big fan of the apple cinnamon, myself," Dean gestured with his shoulder toward the product.

Dora May nodded, still not looking at him. "I never cared for oatmeal. Too bland for my taste."

"That doesn't surprise me," Dean chuckled. "How's tonight?"

Dora May raised her left hand to her rub her forehead, a gold band on her ring finger. "Tonight's good. Are you off at seven?"

"Yes, ma'am."

From the next aisle over, where slanted open shelves held produce sprinkled with water from veins with holes above the lettuce and peppers and asparagus, Ava skipped on one leg, like kids do. She could hear her mother's solid voice speaking nearby and hopped toward the sound. Looking from her mother to Dean Howard to her mother again, the girl sensed a feeling between the adults that she did not know how to process.

"Hi, Ava," Dean spoke cheerfully, recovering faster

than Dora May.

"Hi, Dean," the girl echoed.

"Well, lovely to see you, Dean." Dora May's face was solemn. She grabbed Ava by the forearm and steered her toward the checkout lane in the front of the store. Neither the girl nor her mother said a word, Ava knowing better than to ask questions in front of other people. Dora May paid cash with correct change for the food that was to be their supper and swept out the glass double doors in the front of the store, Ava running after her to keep up.

Safely within the confines of her mother's newish Mustang, Ava buckled her seat belt around her tiny body as she spoke. "Do you have to work late again tonight?"

Dora May was turned in her seat, her hand on Ava's headrest. She had begun to steer the car out of its angled spot in front of the Main Street store, but with the question she hit the brakes and met her daughter's curious brown eyes. Dora May reached for the shifter and put the car into park. The woman pursed her lips, causing creases to form on either side, as she tried to decide how to answer Ava's question.

"Ava," Dora May sighed. Guilt filled her as an invisible list of all of her mistakes, her weakness, her hypocrisies, materialized in front of her. The mother was too selfish, though. She wouldn't own up to any of it, even for her daughter's sake. "You're too young for this discussion, but we may as well have it now before it's too late. Men, boys, are not interested in anything but using you. They're horrible creatures. You can use that to your advantage or you can be taken advantage of. I'd rather have a daughter who did the first." Dora May stopped, thought about her next set of words. "If there's anything you take away from what I'm telling you right now, remember there is no such thing as a good man."

# 9

The steady sound of rain plinking against the metal drain from the eaves trough lining the outside of Ellis's bedroom window soothingly ushered Ava out of sleep. The feeling of calm was replaced by an intense feeling of fear, though, as she tried to figure out where she was. Tangled up in Ellis' long arms and legs, they were both clothed in everything, even their boots. She rolled her head to the side, the only part of her body she could move without disturbing the snoring man. She recalled the events of the night before through a fierce pain surging behind her eyes.

Ellis's face was covered with thick blonde whiskers. Ava wondered if he had ever grown a beard. Mouth partially open, drool puddle forming on the dark green cotton sheets beside the pillow his head had slipped off of sometime in the night, she simply watched him breath. It was not his most attractive look, but it was human. It wasn't the tall, good posture, perfectly pressed uniform, shined boots, sparkling white smile she was used to. It was imperfection. It was intriguing.

There was crying. And kissing at the kitchen table. And moving to the bedroom. And more kissing. Sloppy, drunken kissing. And Ellis passing out. He passed out upon hitting the mattress, before they even had the opportunity to do anything stupid, though Ava was fairly certain that no matter how intoxicated Ellis became, the man's inability to do something stupid was stronger. It could be her life. A life without stupid. A life of making good choices and following rules and remodeling houses and wearing a white lace wedding dress and raising blonde children with big teeth and good posture.

"Aspirin," Ava gasped as she squirmed out from under Ellis's heavy arms and legs. She tried to be gentle at first and then struggled. Then fought. Fought for her life. Not the projected life she was imagining, the life she was currently living.

Ellis squinted at her, as foggy as she had first been. He slowly began to put everything together as Ava had a few minutes before. Twisting her foot, only half in her boot, as she stepped on the floor, she fell forward and clumsily grabbed the door to steady herself. Three deep breaths later, she kicked her boots off into the corner of the room and ran her hand along the wall as she left the bedroom and found her way to the bathroom.

Ellis's house was so clean. Ava sat on the sparkling white toilet long after she was done using it and studied the perfectly white tile around the bathtub. She wondered if Ellis would be horrified by the cobwebs in the corners of the rooms of the farmhouse. The stained, yellowed sink in the only bathroom on the back porch. The flecks of dirt and dust on the wood floors. It wasn't her house, it was her mother's. She only lived there because she had nowhere else to go. Most nights she fell asleep on the buckled leather sofa in her shop, still wearing all of her clothes, traces of paint up and down her arms.

Ava stood gingerly, pulling her jeans back on and flushing with the shiny chrome handle. Stumbling to the sink, she looked in the mirror. Really, really looked in the mirror. Her shirt was wrinkled unevenly on one side, her hair greasy, straggly. The skin of her face muted, hollow half-moons under her eyes. She thought she looked older than 24. Haggard and tired and worn, she could hold it all inside, pretend to be fine, but anybody who looked at her had to see the stress in her physicality.

Jerked out of thought by her hangover headache, Ava rubbed her eyes with the backs of her hands, streaking them with black eyeliner. She pulled on the handle of the mirrored medicine cabinet in front of her. There was almost nothing in it. A razor. A tube of deodorant. The end of an unlabeled container of greenish tinted cologne. An ancient bottle of store brand aspirin tablets. Ava seized the bottle and struggled with it for a bit before it popped open. Dumping a handful of the pills into her hand she shoved them in her mouth and filled the plastic cup by the faucet three times and drank so fast she nearly gagged on the third glassful.

Ava carried the cup, refilled again, and the lidless bottle of aspirin back to the bedroom. Ellis sprawled on his back across the entire bed. His arms and legs seemed grotesquely too long for his torso. His eyes were tightly closed. The rain had all but stopped, the drips reduced to one every few seconds or so.

"Here." Ava collapsed on the bed and held the medicine and cup out to him.

Ellis groaned and took the pills and water from her. "Thank you." His voice was lower, a rough edge to it. Ava curled up beside him. She listened as he rattled the bottle and gulped the water, the sounds grating on the ache in her brain.

"Uhgrghh." The noise Ellis made reflected perfectly how Ava felt. He frowned at the glowing alarm clock on the bedside table. "I go on duty in two hours."

Ava didn't respond. Her eyes were closed, and she was already falling back into broken recovery sleep. She had hauled the sheet and the blanket up under her chin. She looked so peaceful, so comfortable, so beautiful to Ellis. Already knowing he would regret not having enough time to get ready later, he pulled off his boots and belt and scooted back down into the bed. Slipping an arm under Ava and an arm over her, he held her close, his chin against the top of her head, his body curled around hers as they both dozed.

The air was cold. Not chilly like it had been the previous couple of weeks, but cold with impending winter on it. Flynn was quiet for a Saturday morning. The cold keeping kids and dog walkers and runners indoors until later in the day, when the sun was expected to come out and warm the world. In patches where the clouds parted, the sky was raw blue and so close Ava felt like she could reach out and tear it open with her fingernails.

She wore a sweatshirt Ellis tossed onto the bed for her as he retrieved a uniform shirt from the bedroom closet. It was blue, a deep, dark indigo with Flynn County Sherriff's Department printed in bold white letters across the front. He had then turned from her and pulled off his plaid western shirt and white undershirt to reveal a bunch of oddly shaped, oddly spaced scars the entire width of his back between his shoulder blades. She was fascinated by the marks. They were without a doubt shrapnel wounds and she wanted to ask about them, but her thinking was blurry. Her attention strayed to the strength of the muscles in his chest and arms as he bent over the bed to kiss her one last time, then left the room in search of a sobering shower.

Ava walked through town alone, opting to stay in Ellis's bed and sleep longer when he offered her a ride. She was in the same clothes from the night before, except for the sweatshirt. Smeared makeup, a strange sweatshirt. Ava didn't think it could be called a walk of shame, since she hadn't done anything to be ashamed of. She would have, she admitted to herself, if the opportunity had presented itself, so she decided she would refer to it as her walk of *semi-*shame.

As she rounded the corner of 6th and Washington, she stopped. At the end of the street, in the parking lot in front of the high school, the only cars were the abandoned Mustang, its hood up, and Pode's red truck parked the wrong direction. A turquoise sedan stopped at the corner of 7th Street and Martha, in the driver's seat, waved at Ava as she cruised by. Ava waved back, then nestled both of her arms inside the front pouch pocket of Ellis's sweatshirt.

Pode's feet were sticking out from under the front of the Mustang. A clanging sound as he dropped a wrench on the ground made Ava blink hard. She stopped beside the car, eyeing her friend's muddy boots. Scooting on his elbows, either done with the work or having heard her as she approached, Pode climbed out from underneath the car. He sat up, the wrench in his hand, grease from his arm smeared across his forehead.

"Alternator." Pode used the front bumper of the car to drag himself up and stand. His face was squinty, full of pain. He was as hung over as Ava.

"You fixed it?"

"Yeah, took the one off of Grandma's Crown Vic. It'll last a while, but you probably ought to have Callahan get you something the right size."

"Why did you do that?"

"Well, the Crown Vic's just sitting in a field behind Dad's. Might as well part it out."

"No." Ava pulled one of her arms out of the sweatshirt pocket and used it to tuck her hair behind her ear. "Why did you fix it for me?"

"When you drove in last night, it sounded like it might be electrical and that's a pretty easy fix, so . . ."

"No." Ava's voice was hoarse. She was aggravated. "Why?" She paced away from him and back, her hand still in her blowing hair.

Pode's face scrunched, like he was trying to figure out what she meant. They were at a standoff, scowling at each other, neither of them fully functioning. Ava had drawn the line years ago in high school. They were friends. That was it. It never seemed like Pode believed it completely. Ava ignored this about him, but every single person who knew them saw that he was holding out hope for something else. They both dated other people off and on, but neither of them ever approached anything serious. Now they were older. Pode knew Ellis was a good man. He could throw a kink into the whole thing. Even leaving town, going to New York was a better option. If she met someone there, Pode wouldn't know him. He would never have to see them together. He and Ava would drift apart, and they would both be forced to find other people. If Ava didn't leave, though, if she ended up with Ellis in Flynn, Pode wasn't sure he could handle it.

"I don't know," Pode mumbled. "Trying to be helpful. Sorry."

"Well." Ava couldn't put words together appropriately and gave up. "Well, fuck you!"

"Yeah." Pode took a step away, toward his truck and yelled, "Fuck you, too!"

As he opened the door to climb inside, his phone rang the annoying digital tone of an ancient Nokia. He picked it up, hit a button and held the technological brick up to his ear. Ava reached for the driver's side door handle of the Mustang, wanting more than anything to hide somewhere and sort out her feelings. Something wasn't right, though. She watched Pode's face go from slight anger to silent shock. He was listening, just listening, to whoever was on the other end, and he was not responding. Pode wasn't talking. Something was horribly wrong.

Crossing the lot, Ava stood in the space between Pode and the truck's open door. She felt her heart beating in her throat. Her expression demanded an answer from him.

Pode's words were heavy. "Av's here with me. We'll be right over."

"What?"

"Uh." He went white and raised his free hand and gripped the steering wheel in front of him tightly, the other falling to the seat as it continued to clutch the phone. "Baker's dead. He's gone. Shot himself. In the head. Sometime last night. This morning. Jack found him on the couch in his trailer."

"What?"

"He's dead, Av."

"What?" Ava reached for the arm rest in the interior molding of the door to steady herself. They both stared off, letting the truth sink in. Pode coughed, causing Ava to look up at him. He was choking, sobbing, on tears and snot. Wiping his face with his sleeve, he placed his other hand on top of the steering wheel, as well, and leaned his forehead against them.

"Pode," Ava whispered, her hand on his knee.

He suddenly sat back, violently, his hands on the top of his head. "No. No. He went home last night. I saw him like twelve hours ago. I don't—he didn't. No."

Ava felt helpless, again watching a strong man before her cry. "Who was that? On the phone?"

"Mom." Pode struggled for breath. "They're headed over to Deanna and John's."

Ava wiped away tears. "Scoot."

Without any hesitation, he slid across the bench seat. Ava climbed in and turned the key. The truck started flawlessly. Turning to look out the back window, her eyes fell instead on Pode, whose arms were crossed across his body, head and shoulders sagging forward. The big man was a helpless ball in the seat beside her. Ava turned the engine of the truck off. She swallowed hard and joined him on his side of the truck, wrapping her arms around his waist and leaning her head on his shoulder. She held him while he cried.

\* \* \*

A beep. Then the mechanical sound of a pump. The pattern continued over and over and over. The noises reminded Ava of Girl Scout Camp in grade school, of the device they plugged into the cigarette lighter in Shannon's mom's minivan to blow up their flimsy air mattresses. They would all be empty by morning. Each girl would be lying on her own pile of plastic and blankets, yet every night they filled them up and tried again.

Her mind was in a phase of odd association. A distraction technique to keep her from focusing on reality. Eddy was lying on the couch in the waiting room, staring straight up at the ceiling. Catatonic. Useless. It should be a joint decision. It should be a long discussion, but he refused to talk and Ava did not have the motivation to make him.

Holding her mother's hand, Ava didn't know why. The logical part of her did not believe Dora May could feel it anymore. It was cold and dry and a piece of her already dying. Yet she held it, if not for her mother, for herself. Days before, when Dora May was still harassing nurses and complaining about hospital food, the hand was swollen. The medicine that made her retain water so drastically had been taken away. It served no purpose now. Dora May's body looked normal for an hour or two, as the swelling went down, but now, without any inflammation, Ava thought her mother looked like a skeleton. Never heavy, but always built like a woman, strength with curves, the cancer and the treatment of it took every single ounce of excess fat from her.

A nurse entered as quietly as she possibly could through the sliding glass door of the private ICU room. She intended to quickly be in and out, but Ava stopped her.

"Excuse me," Ava's voice wasn't her own. It was shallow and high.

"Yes, ma'am." She was middle-aged and lovely with a striking dark complexion. She gave Ava the same smile all of the nurses gave her when they entered the room or passed her in the hall.

"Do you know if Mom's doctor is still here?"

"He is. Would you like me to call him for you?"

Ava studied her mother's face. Two-thirds of it was covered by a contraption that held the tube that went into her throat in place. Dora May would never want to be seen like this. She would never want to live like this. It was the only moment in Ava's entire life that she saw an advantage in her mother's obscene selfishness.

"Yes. Yes, please."

# 10

News travels fast in a small town. Almost as if it passes from person to person by osmosis. Travels on the air like a scent. First comes the food. Cakes and pies. Casseroles and crockpots. Next groceries and necessities. Toilet paper. Kleenex by the case. Books of stamps. Bearing the things, the people. Neighbors and friends and their whole families stop by. They offer to help with serving the food. With things around the house. With the farming.

By the time Ava and Pode pulled up, the First United Methodist Church had put together quite a collection of items and Pastor McEwing's SUV was backed up into Baker's parents' driveway. Pastor McEwing and his children carried bags of groceries into the picturesque brick home. Cars and trucks lined the road that led to the river and the old homestead and the bank where another bonfire had been planned for the same evening. Driving past the rows of cars and turning around in a drive to a muddy field of crushed corn stubble, Ava parked Pode's truck in a recently vacated spot. Glancing sideways at him, he met her eyes. He had collected himself. His face was puffy and red under his thick beard, but his expression set and ready. Ava mirrored his solemnity. They took matching deep breaths. They had to do the next worst thing to receiving the news that their best friend was gone—hug his mother with the knowledge that she would never hug her son again.

The house was so full of folks the crowd spilled out onto the porch. Ava couldn't remember all of the faces she had seen in the first couple of days after her mother died. There were even a few she didn't recognize. They brought her the requisite food and kind words and she thanked them. Or Eddy thanked them. He was much better at taking free things. Ava's arms felt empty, she should have something for Deanna and John. They had brought her and Eddy a roast and a lovely card. There would be time, she decided. She would come back and visit them. Always.

Ava had been inside the house only a handful of times. Baker's parents built the handsome home and moved from their house in town on Oak Street the summer Baker and Pode and Ava and Shannon graduated high school. It seemed like the whole town of Flynn was in the living room, as Pode led the way through the front door, shaking hands with Max Turner and his wife as they exited the house. Sandy carried boxes up the porch steps behind them, a disinterested look on her face. Penny followed her mother, her face vacant, the slightest beginning of a bump under her tight t-shirt. Dropping the bag where she stood, Penny ran to Pode and Ava's arms. They all sobbed together in the middle of the crowded room, guests looking away, giving them privacy.

Ava held Penny's hand and walked close to Pode, afraid to lose him in the crowd and not wishing to make small talk with anyone. Wren stood in the arched opening to the kitchen in front of them. She threw her arms around her brother and he hugged her back as tightly as he could over her enormous pregnant belly. Letting go of Pode, Wren hugged Ava, and Ava felt a wave of tears coming. Why Baker would time things so that he would never meet Wren and Jack's child, his first nephew, didn't make any sense to her. He would have been the best uncle. Then again, none of it made any sense. Ava, and she was certain everyone else in the room, could come up with a million reasons why Baker should still be in the world, but Baker had come up with at least one that made him think he should remove himself from it.

"Where's Jack?" Pode cleared his throat. He was trying not to break.

"He and John went for a walk," Wren whispered, letting go of Ava. "They needed to get away."

Pode understood. He felt claustrophobic in the packed house and wished he could go to wherever John and Jack were. The kitchen was mostly full of women, their husbands deserted in other parts of the house. Taking a step further, Pode scanned the room and found Deanna Baker sitting at the kitchen table. Defeated, a plate of untouched food on the table in front of her, the woman bowed her head of short blonde hair forward. Crossing to her, Pode cut through a hushed conversation between his mother, who briefly grabbed his arm, and Corrine Yeards. He knelt at Deanna's shoulder and took her hand. The woman was numb to his touch for some time before she realized Pode was in front of her.

"Oh. Pode." The woman draped her arms around his shoulders. Pode held her and they sobbed together.

It was too much. Ava felt like a string was around her throat. Gagging for air, she turned from the kitchen, sprinted through the living room and out the front door, nearly crashing into a newly arrived Shannon and Kale who called after her. She didn't stop for them, though, she came to a halt only when she reached the end of the sidewalk. Ava folded her arms tight across her chest. She studied what remained of a slightly crooked free throw lane painted on with blue automotive paint. She had been standing in almost the exact same spot the day Baker and Jack and Pode carefully measured and painted the lines on the newly poured concrete.

"Av, you alright, dear?" Ava felt Henry's hand on her

shoulder as he asked. He must have been in the living room or on the front porch. She missed him in the crowd when they walked in.

"Yeah, I, I saw Deanna and I couldn't . . ."

"I know."

"He's really gone?" Ava's voice gave out at the end of her question. The expression on Henry's face was enough; she didn't need a verbal answer.

They stayed in the truck for forever, staring out at the sun as it set. Neither of them attempted to say anything. It was a bad dream, a nightmare. They were having it concurrently and wishing desperately to wake from it. Days, months, years would pass, but the events of the late fall day would never fully sink in. They would live into old age, but never completely grasp the extent of how their lives changed in the instant their friend ended his. Such intense, unreasonable pain spreads itself out over a lifetime, because the human mind can only process so much at once. Decades would go by and they would still find idle thoughts wandering back to the whys. Theories and excuses would be presented. They would even invent them for themselves, but they would never discover any exact reason. They would have to accept that there was no definitive why and they would have to move on and they would move on, but an irreplaceable piece would always be missing.

Pode was the first to come to. The cab of the truck was beginning to grow cold from the night air seeping in and he was the first to register the frigid temperature. He took Ava's hand, where it lay on the passenger seat beside her. She jumped in response to his touch, deep in an exhaustive trance.

Ava trudged up the steps behind Pode and followed him into his house. He went straight to the kitchen.

When he offered her the bottle of Jack from the shelf above the sink, she denied it. He drank it as if it were water. Replacing the lid, he took the bottle with him as he staggered away, again Ava close behind. In Pode's bedroom in the back of the house, she yanked her boots off and crawled into his bed as he worked on removing his own boots and downed another swig of the whiskey.

Joining her under the covers, he tucked them both in tight. The alcohol sloshed around in his empty stomach and Pode coughed. He found Ava in the bed and pulled her body close to him and wrapped her up like a ragdoll in his arms. She felt his tears dripping onto her forehead and cheek as she began to soak the arm of Ellis's sweatshirt with crying of her own. Pode's hand moved along the side of her body, over the waist of her jeans and underneath layers of clothing to rest on the bare skin of her stomach. She raised her hand. She wiped the man's face. Pode touched his forehead to Ava's, so close to each other their eyes couldn't focus. Ava felt Pode's beard tickling her chin. Pode buried his face into her neck, the smell of her skin hinted at lavender.

It was hard to tell and in the end unimportant who kissed who first, but the kiss was long, deep, leading to another kiss and to Ava pulling Pode's shirt off over his head. They stripped each other's clothes methodically. The iron bedframe groaned as Ava changed positions. Her hair fell over her shoulders and into Pode's face as she bent her body in half to kiss his lips and his cheek and his neck and his chest. He tasted like whiskey. His labor calloused hands were rough on the soft skin of her breasts as he felt the fullness of them and then on the small of her back. Goosebumps sprang up all over Ava's body as the hair on Pode's stomach brushed the surface of her own at the raising of her hips and the lowering of them into him.

The only sounds in the room were of their rhythmic breathing and the creaking of the bed. They didn't need sight to find each other in the dark. Like during the illicit hallway kiss, they fit together. It was as if they had made love to each other a thousand times. The intimacy of sharing so many thoughts, so many moments, for the vast majority of their lives created an impossibly strong connection. Ava didn't think about Ellis, and neither of them thought about Baker. They cleared their minds and held on with the intense need to comfort each other and themselves in the way only skin against skin can.

The world was dull. Shades of brown. All of the remaining tree leaves mangled and black. The fields flat and boring, dirt concealing brand new seed or dirt overturned waiting to be sown. Even the sky was devoid of any color, painted an ominous dusty gray. It was as if nature was grieving in reflection.

Ava revved the Mustang up a hill in the northwest corner of the county. It was a no man's land containing only an offshoot from the river, a couple of deserted homesteads and thousands of acres of fields and pastures. The Wagners owned a couple of the smaller fields, 100, 200 acres each. The week before, Ed mentioned to his son, in Ava's presence, that this ground still needed attention. Pode's truck was parked beside the machine shed in his parents' backyard, so she made an educated guess about where she would find him. He would be in a tractor, working the ground as he worked out the problems in his mind.

Bumping roughly over the washed-out road desperately in need of a good grading and a coat of gravel, Ava parked her car in the middle, confident no one else would need by. At the far end of the tract of land, a Farmall Series with a disc attached behind slowly toured the landscape. The glossy red metal contrasted wildly with the gloominess of the earth and sky. Climbing out of the car, Ava shut the door and leaned back against it, her arms folded over her flannel shirt. She shivered in an icy gust that tossed her damp hair across her face. Everything had frosted overnight for the first time in the season, while they slept restlessly, clinging to each other in Pode's bed.

Pode turned the corner at the edge of the field and Ava thought for a second he might not stop for her. The tractor paused, though. The latch on the bubbly glass door of the cab popped and Pode held the door open. It was funny to Ava that even tractor manufacturers tried to make their vehicles look stylish, futuristic, as if a machine meant to never travel faster than 40 miles an hour, mostly through soil, needed to be wind resistant and attractive. Mounting the metal steps, Ava hoisted herself into the cab. She expected, like in her father's ancient tractors, to have to sit on a vinyl seat cushion propped on a hand-built wooden toolbox, but instead found she had a passenger seat with an adjustable headrest and seatbelt all to herself. The fancy CASE IH was littered with computer screens and Pode's heated, lumbar support driver's seat looked like it belonged in a Mercedes.

"Wow," Ava scanned the whole package of the tractor cab before sitting. "Nice."

"Yeah." Pode stood as he reached across her and strongly slammed the door closed. He smelled like beer. "Not sure why they put passenger seats in these when you barely even need a driver anymore."

Ava looked up at the largest screen in the top corner of the space. Pode reached for it and hit several buttons on a touch screen GPS system that told him where he was in the field, how much ground was left to work, if the disc blades were up or down and a menu of a thousand other options he wasn't currently using.

"It's been a long time since I rode in a tractor." Ava watched him zoom in on the map of the field with the tap of his finger.

"Dad doesn't like it. But we had to have a new tractor and it's already hard enough to keep up with all the big time farmers. The Johnsons. Goodmans. Technology's the way of the world. You can't beat them. You have to join them." Pode was talking, talking and avoiding a serious conversation.

"You're not answering your phone." Ava's voice was low, which was completely effective in the zero cabin noise feature of the space.

Pode gazed straight out the front window, taking in the view of the miles and miles of fields on all sides of them. "I'm sorry, Av."

"It's OK. I was just worried about you."

"No." Pode scratched his beard. "No, I—I mean I'm really sorry. I screwed everything up, didn't I?"

"I'm not sure what you're including in 'everything' but no, I—I don't think so?"

"I mean, I know you and Ellis . . ." he trailed off.

"Pode." Ava reached her arm through the gap between his body and his arm and took his hand where it lay on his armrest. A head against his shoulder, she could hear his breath grow irregular. "No, Pode. You didn't screw anything up. You saved me. Again. I promise."

He stopped the tractor in the exact center of the field. It wasn't that the town or the immediate area around Flynn was overly populated, but the place they were in was so desolate it made every word, every movement, every thought agonizingly raw and heartbreaking.

"I should have made him stay with me."

"No."

Ava knew it was the next step in the processing and it

was the reason she came to find Pode when he wouldn't answer his phone. It was the same type of guilt, blame, she dealt with immediately following her mother's death. He was the last person to see their friend alive and Ava knew it would shake him. She hated that she knew him so well.

"It would have been a lot harder for him to shoot himself in the face if he'd been on my couch. Or if I'd taken that goddamned gun from him the night he tried to give it to me."

"Do not blame yourself for this."

"Well, I don't get it." Pode's voice grew louder with each word, almost a violent tone in it. He leaned back in his seat, pulling away from Ava. "Why did he do it? Give me a single reason why he would do something like this. He didn't leave any sort of fucking note. Do they even know for sure it wasn't an accident or that somebody didn't shoot him or . . ."

"Yes, they know. Why would somebody shoot Baker?"

"Then why the hell did he do it?"

Ava was at a loss. She was sideways in her seat, her right leg tucked under her, tears in her eyes. She stared at the side of Pode's angry face. He cried, too, devastated. They were both silent. They were together and alone. Found and lost. In love and not.

"He talked about death all the time. I didn't think he ever really meant it."

"Nobody did."

Thinking for a second before he spoke again, Pode calmed himself. "He would of told us—if—wouldn't he?"

"Maybe." Ava shrugged her shoulders. "Maybe not."

"Why not?" Pode faced her. "Why wouldn't he tell us? Of all the people in this goddamned backward country, he should have known he could trust us."

"I think he did trust us. I'm sure he trusted us, but I don't know if it's that easy."

Pode rubbed his face with the palms of his hands. "Goddammit." He sucked in difficult breaths. "Just one phone call. I wish he would have made one phone call. To me or you or anybody. So we could tell him . . ." Pode stuttered, losing it. "Tell him how much we loved him."

Snow began falling during the early hours of the morning and left a dusting over every surface in the town of Flynn. A gentle, cleansing snow, without the vicious ice storm preceding it as so often happened in Kansas. Business continued as usual for a Monday morning. Mothers and their children shopped the grocery store to retrieve food for the week ahead. Ladies sat underneath the orange Plexiglas domes at Lois's as their new perms set. Farmers lined up at the pipe beside the waterworks building at the edge of town, filling giant aqua-colored tanks strapped to the backs of their trucks to take water to the cattle in the pastures with frozen ponds.

Stretching her arm out in front of her, Ava watched as several snowflakes rested on the green fabric of her jacket. She examined them at close range. Pure white and exceptionally fragile, each crystalized arm of microscopic branches was different from the next. How there could be so many patterns was baffling. Why did such a tiny thing need to be so complex when it would only exist for an instant and then melt away? It felt like every single thing she encountered in the days after Baker's death was in some way a subtle reminder of how amazing and fleeting life could be.

The First United Methodist Church was covered with the snow. Dora May was not a religious woman and so as Ava stood on the front steps, she realized she had never actually attended a normal Sunday church service in this building or any other. Only weddings and funerals. When her mother died, Ava scheduled Dora May's service in the large gathering room of Owens Funeral Home, per a request in her will. Not certain what faith her mother considered herself; the lack of religious influence throughout her childhood was something Ava saw as a benefit and a disadvantage. Any path, any belief, was open to her. No one would judge her should she decide to be Methodist, or Catholic, or Buddhist. However, she was jealous of the kids who believed in God steadfastly and had him to turn to in hard times. The more experience she had with life, the less confident she was any sort of God existed at all.

Pode pressed through the crowd the wrong direction like a salmon swimming upstream. He held Ava's phone in his hand. Her shoulders relaxed as she spotted him and she stepped out of the moving line she was in. As he hurried toward her, she took in the entire picture of her friend. The beard was gone. His face was cleanly shaven, and he looked older than he had even the previous week. Pode wore a black suit with a dark shirt and black tie. The material across the back was tight, the jacket only able to be buttoned when he was standing, the sleeves a hair too long. The outfit borrowed from a taller, skinnier Cort or Kale.

Throwing his arms around her, Ava gladly accepted a hug and a kiss from Pode that drew a few wandering eyes. She had left him in the field the day before to finish his work only to reappear at his house with takeout supper from Martha's. They ate the food and left the TV off as they talked and cried, crashing in Pode's bed, together, for the second night in a row. Ava had forgotten her phone on his coffee table when she left him early in the morning to return to the farmhouse to change into the same black dress she had worn to her mother's funeral. Pode let go of Ava and she slipped her phone into her coat pocket. She saw Ellis at the same time the man noticed her. He froze halfway up the sidewalk on the far side of building. Ava disregarded the officer and wrapped her hand around Pode's arm above his elbow.

"We're sitting over here," Pode whispered as he led her into the church. Most of the seats were already full. Several people stood, many of them gathered at the back of the sanctuary around a casket of dark polished wood. Corinne bowed her head and sobbed with her mother. They were cousins, the Bakers and the Yeards. Ava couldn't remember which of Baker's parents was the sibling to which of Corrine's. The top of the casket was completely closed. A large arrangement of stark white lilies took up half of the top and a gold gilt framed picture of Baker, decked out in camo, goofy smile spread across his face, standing beside his truck, was displayed on the other half. Ava stopped beside the wooden box that held their friend's body. Pode didn't realize that she had until their arms were extended to the fullest. He returned for her and took a visibly deep breath, his wide chest extending so that it looked like he might pop the top button on the suit jacket.

"He's not in that box." Ava leaned in closer to Pode. He was unsure of what she meant. Sensing the confusion caused by her comment, Ava continued. "He's dead. I know he's dead, but it's just his body in there, not his soul. Can you imagine Baker spending eternity in a box? He's in a deer stand right now."

Pode grinned and added to her revelation. "Flask of Jim Beam stashed in his pocket. Fourteen-point buck entering his sights."

"And he's wearing camo."

Ava and Pode both burst out laughing. Corinne and

several other folks standing nearby acted horribly offended.

The first two pews held the Baker family, the third the Wagners. Sliding in beside Cort and Penny and Kris and Henry, Pode put his arm around Penny. She clutched a wad of spent Kleenex in her hand and pressed her red puffy face into his chest. Once she finally managed to calm her sobs, she leaned back and used the tissue to wipe rivers of black eye makeup from her cheeks. Ava bent forward and Penny reached for her hand over Pode's lap. Cort, on the far side of Penny, and Pode added their hands to the stack.

Ava felt tight arms around her before she had a chance to turn to see who they belonged to. Shannon, Kale and Audie behind her, loosened her grip on Ava long enough to allow her to stand and deliver a proper hug. Ava hugged Kale and a crying Audie, who looked so distressed Ava believed their drama queen friend really was incredibly upset. Pode was close behind her. He greeted their friends in the narrow space between the pews with hugs of his own.

"Are we supposed to sit someplace special?" Kale asked Pode. He was also dressed in a black suit, but one that fit him well. They were two of six pallbearers.

"No." Pode shook his head as he waved to someone in the back of the chapel. "They said we're welcome to sit with our families. We need to meet in the back, now, though. Steve from the funeral home is waving at us."

Kale bent his head and kissed Shannon sweetly. "We'll be right back."

Shannon nodded as her husband followed Pode and Cort to the back of the church. The women sat close to one another, each staring straight ahead. Audie's wide face was partially hidden by her newly shortened and styled hair. She wore a black and white polka dot wrap dress that was too tight and low cut for a funeral. Shannon's thin white face was framed by long ringlets of black hair. She had put on a simple black blouse and black knit skirt over thick tights. Ava's blonde hair hung lifelessly straight. Her black shift dress draped off her shoulders, two sizes too big because of all of the weight she had lost in the months since her mother's death. Shannon reached out and held the hand of her girlfriend on either side.

The organ, hidden away behind a walled in box with decorative squiggly holes lining the front of it, began to play. No one could see her, but everyone knew Catherine Ellis sat on the other side providing the resonant sound. The last few milling about took their seats and the room was hushed except for the music and a muffled sob from the front row. Deanna lowered her head and John bent his body over hers as he held his wife of 29 years.

Pode and Kale and Cort and Jack and two out of town cousins Ava remembered meeting a couple of times, dutifully brought the mahogany casket up the center aisle of the church. They placed it upon a silver stand in front of the lectern as if it were so fragile it was made of eggshell. Jack coughed, trying to catch his breath. His eyes shined. He fought tears. Pode put his arm around Jack's shoulders, helping him to his seat in the front between Deanna and Wren, his own mother and the future mother of his child.

Ava wondered what it was like to bury a brother. She understood what it was to bury a mother and now to bury a good friend, but brother would be different, still. Eddy was no longer only the responsibility of her and their father. He was Mindy's, too, and any children they might have would help care for him, have to bury him, someday. Her brother a father was a thought she had not yet entertained. It perplexed her and slightly frightened her. Deep into imagining Eddy's future, Ava was interrupted by the need to shift her knees to let Pode and Cort take their seats.

Pastor McEwing entered from a side door, dressed in a floor length dark red robe, his hair grayer than Ava remembered, though she'd watched the back of his head move up and down the sidelines during the football game Friday night. The organ music stopped and the preacher opened the Bible he held against his chest, laying it on the platform in front of him. It took a long time, or at least it seemed like a long time, for the preacher to start. When he did, he cleared his throat roughly and Ava thought she could see tears on his face. The man had, after all, watched Doug Baker grow up in the yard next door.

"Let us bow our heads and pray," the preacher spoke softly, but clearly. His voice was broadcast over the speaker system so that the attendees in the back and up above in the choir loft jammed with folding chairs could hear him.

Ava bowed her head. She heard the preacher's voice, but she found it hard to listen to the actual message he was conveying. It seemed too generic. Closing her eyes, Ava tilted her body until her head was under Pode's chin. Wrapping his arm around her shoulders, he held her tight. He rested his cheek against her soft hair, bent his head to pray at the appropriate times, but did not let go of Ava until the last sentence was spoken. At the completion of the service, he and his brother and his brother-in-law and his friend rose from their seats and helped carry Baker's body out of the church under the respectful gaze of friends and family and carefully put it in the open back of the waiting hearse.

Shannon held Kate high on her hip, propping the curious little girl up so she could see her father standing beside

Pastor McEwing at the front of the green canopy tent. Shannon's mother and father stood on one side of her, Grandpa holding Grace and Grandma holding the hand of Julia, who was on her tiptoes as she peeked through the crowd. Ava stood on the other side of Shannon, and Audie one more spot over, close enough their shoulders touched. Ava wondered if she was the only one who noticed Pode's absence from the row of pallbearers. He had helped carry the casket then promptly disappeared. Ava was worried that he had left because he was breaking, unable to accept the physical burial of their friend.

The preacher began the graveside service. He said only a single prayer, a common prayer that was even familiar to Ava. It was growing colder as the day went on. Underneath the shelter, pressed close together, were 50 people brave enough to weather standing outside. The warmth of the close bodies could not counteract the north wind. Blessing the box that held Baker's body a final time, Pastor McEwing dismissed the crowd and asked them to join the Baker family for late lunch at the VFW Club. As the crowd parted, the sound of Baker's truck revving down the rocky road that ran through the middle of the cemetery, caused every head to turn. It came to a stop at the edge of the line of parked cars. Ludacris boomed out of the 600 watt speakers and half of the crowd was as horrified as the other half of the crowd was overjoyed.

"What on earth is he doing?" Ava heard Shannon's mother gasp.

Pode climbed out of the Silverado and left it running. The crowd, with the exception of Deanna, was paralyzed. Baker's mother met Pode midway between the tent and her late son's truck. She smiled and embraced him in a sign of thank you. The family and friends looked at one another and though quite a few of them were still full of judgment over the disruption, they all decided that if

Deanna approved, they did, too. It was hard to be sad as the next song started and everyone could hear in their heads Baker's monotone warbling over Willie Nelson's voice as he stood beside a pool table at Martha's and belted out, "Mama's don't let your babies grow up to be cowboys . . ."

Martha held a cloudy plastic pitcher under the Bud Light tap at an angle, a bright red apron tied around her black dress. The group pulled two round tables side by side, not wanting to be split up, and loudly told stories about their friend. They escaped the VFW's banquet hall soon after lunch was served, but not without another round of hugs for Deanna and John. Martha watched the kids from behind the bar. She felt like their adoptive mother, having seen them grow up before her eyes. They were adults now, but she thought of them in a way not unlike the way she thought of the three children she'd given birth to. They were drinking for free on this day, because it was the least Martha felt she could do, the only thing she had to offer to ease the pain they were feeling from losing one of their own.

"Do you remember freshman year?" Pode spoke over remaining laughter from the preceding story. "Football camp. First day. They didn't have pants small enough to fit his skinny ass, so Coach Kent used like a whole roll of tape, wrapped it around his waist a hundred times? First drill, the tape breaks and he's standing there bare-assed. Nothing on but a jock strap."

The table erupted. They had heard the story a thousand times, but laughed again anyway. The laughter wouldn't heal the pain, but it would at least distract from it for a while. Kale, his arm around Shannon, leaned forward to take the new pitcher of beer from Martha and refill everyone's mug.

247

"Then he grew like two fucking feet the next summer." Kale slopped beer onto the plastic table cloth beside Ava's glass. "Put him on the basketball team just so it looked good to have a six foot five kid on the roster. Never played more than two or three minutes a game."

"I remember that block, though, against Washington. Do you guys remember that block he had at the end of the game?" Cort's elbows were on the table, suit jacket and tie long gone, sleeves of his dress shirt rolled up. Penny sat close to him, slouching, with a hand on his leg.

Everybody at the table nodded their heads and grew quiet as they remembered. It was their friend's NBA moment, the last second block that got them into sub-state play over their arch rival. Ava ran her hand through her hair as she took a sip of beer. Her throat was raw from so much crying and each time the alcohol and fizz hit her throat it burned.

"Bathroom," Ava mouthed to Shannon, pulling herself up with the back of Shannon's chair. She swerved as she crossed the bar, the amount of food in her system minimal compared to the amount of alcohol. The back hallway led to a storage room and a single unisex bathroom. Ava smiled at Martha as she passed the town's matriarch.

Ava reached for the door knob on the bathroom door as the back door of the bar opened. A flood of wintery air hit her in the face. Ellis stomped the snow off his boots onto the black plastic rug inside the door. Ava stared through his chest and waited. There was no way to avoid him. The man stiffened, surprised to find her right in front of him. She was the reason he had come, but he hadn't expected to run straight into with his first step inside. Slowly closing the door behind him, it took a shove with his shoulder to catch the bent latch.

"I thought I'd find you here," Ellis's voice was somber.

"I saw Pode's truck parked out front."

Ava heart beat faster. "You're welcome to join us."

Ellis shook his head, took off his flat brimmed hat and held it at his waist. "Us? You and Pode? No thanks."

"I meant join the group. There's a big group up front. You're welcome to sit with us."

"It'll always be you and Pode, won't it, Ava? I fooled myself into thinking you and I had something good going, but he'll always be around, won't he?" Ellis's face was red, not entirely from the cold.

"Yes. And we've had this discussion before. I told you he's my best friend." Ava didn't feel like she should have to justify anything to anyone, especially Ellis. It wasn't her fault he had already planned her into his happy family man future. She never promised him anything, had no expectations of him. Why should he be allowed to have expectations of her?

"I don't kiss my friends like that. Look, this is your choice, Ava, and I hate to make you make it, but it's me or Pode?"

"Pode," Ava answered decisively. "If you ask my something like that, my choice will always be Pode."

"Av, did you fall in . . ." Shannon yelled. She stopped in the doorway, "Oh." Looking at Ava, then Ellis, then Ava again, Shannon retreated behind the bathroom door without another word.

Ellis's face was cast with disappointment. He jerked the backdoor open and returned to the cold. Ava took a deep breath and looked up. Above her, names and initials and drawings and quotes were scratched into the wood paneling on the walls and ceiling. As a kid, she had noticed the heart in the top corner. It stood out from the other things, this specific act of vandalism took extra time, care, to make sure it would remain prominent 30 years later. *DML + EJS.* They were her parents' initials. She assumed they had done it as young kids in a love that would only grow more destructive with time. A love that Billy James and Dean Howard and jealousy and alcohol and selfishness would eventually destroy. They never left. They lived big lives for such a small town.

Ava sat on a bench in the hospital. She didn't like it, but at least it was a happy reason this time. Wren went into labor as she and Jack drove home late in the afternoon, after the meal. Everyone was still in their funeral clothes, heading straight to the hospital with a round of alert calls. They created a dismal black and gray scene in the waiting room nearest the maternity ward. Fatigue set in across the friends and family, and most of them were asleep four hours into waiting.

Ava predictably couldn't sleep, despite Pode's warm arm around her. She stood and crossed the room, twice filling a cone with water from a bubbling blue vessel of purified water. Henry couldn't sleep either and stepped outside, mumbling something about fresh air. He returned a few minutes later as Ava filled the cone a third time. He watched the cartoonish bubbles float to the top of the water bottle.

"I'm going to be a grandpa, Av."

"I know."

"Do you suppose I'll know what to do?"

Ava mustered a smile. "Well, you're going to have to learn fast, because you'll be grandpa twice before this summer's over."

"Huh, yeah, I guess so. Life's a strange thing."

"Yes, it is."

Behind Henry, Jack, in a bright yellow isolation gown and rubber gloves and a filmy mask and hat beamed as he shouted, "He's here! And he's perfect!"

Instantly the room was awake, everyone smiling and

laughing and climbing to their feet with the surge of excitement. Henry slapped Jack on the back as Deanna ran to her oldest son and grabbed him up in her arms, bursting into happy tears for a change.

Henry looked sideways at Ava. His smile was overcast with sadness as he repeated, "Life's a strange thing," and added, "One leaves it. One enters it."

Ava slammed the Mustang's door closed. The sound echoed over the open space of the cemetery on the outskirts of Flynn. She walked between gray stones of different shapes and sizes, resting a hand upon the top of her mother's polished perfectly square monument. Dora May picked it out before she died, but it was simple and nondescript, looking as if a family member who didn't know her well was forced to select something. No pictures, no verses, simply her name and birthdate and a line that read "Mother of Ava and Edward."

Three rows away, a high mound coated with a layer of frost, enclosed the place Baker's body lay. At the top of the plot, a round metal marker read simply "Douglas Grayson Baker, b. 7/23/1987 d. 10/22/2011." The arrangement of stark white lilies from the top of the casket lingered in the center of the grave. The petals of the flowers hadn't fared well in the bitterness, their edges brown and crisp, some of them scattered down the row of other graves.

Ava put her hands in her jean pockets and looked at the dirt. She didn't know what to say, where to start, but a force she couldn't describe told her she needed to visit. Kneeling beside the grave, she reached out and picked up one of the escaped flowers, turning it by its stem between her fingers as she spoke. "Hey, Baker."

She paused for a long time. He wasn't here. It was the same thing she felt at the funeral, that there was no way such an enormous personality, such an effervescent soul, could be captured in a box and buried in the ground. She wanted to talk to her friend, though, and this was the best she could do.

"I held your nephew. John Douglas. They're calling him JD. Pode made a joke about it standing for John Deere and Wren didn't think that was funny. Apparently she and Jack hadn't thought that angle through. I'm not really a baby person, but he is pretty cute. Super chubby. Pode already bought him a BB gun and promised him he'll tell him all kinds of embarrassing stories about you when he's old enough."

"Pode and I hooked up. If you were alive and I told you that you'd probably say something like 'About fucking time.'" Ava laughed, hearing Baker's voice in her head. She wiped tears from her eyes.

"I'm moving to New York. I've got an apartment and an interview. At a gallery. I haven't told anybody else yet. I'll come back and visit you. I promise. And your mom. Whenever I'm back I'll visit her, too. I'm worried about your mom. If you can hear me, you should probably check on her. She's taking this really bad."

Ava was now sitting in the wet dead grass, her knees pulled up under her chin and her arms around them. "We're all taking this bad. I kind of hate you. Or maybe I don't hate you, but I am really mad at you. I love you, Baker, but right now I feel like you're a fucking selfish asshole."

Ava sniffed. "Sorry. Sorry. I wish I had known whatever you knew that made you do this. I wish you'd said something. I'm sorry I didn't know."

A gust picked up the loose flowers scattered around the grave and held them in the air in a tiny whirlwind for a split second before blowing them Ava's direction. Falling over her, the white remnants of petals landed in her hair and on her lap and on the grass in a perfect circle around her. Looking up at the cloudy sky, Ava smiled and sighed and missed her friend.

Kale's suit was cheesy. A shade of blue that screamed used car salesman. That's what he was, in actuality, and he seemed proud to be employed again, so Ava didn't make fun of it. Instead, she intently listened to his pitch about the safety features of the black SUV she sat in the driver's seat of. It was a nicer car than she needed, but it was the only one on the lot she could see loading and moving across the country in. She could sell it, she decided, if it was too cumbersome for the city. It would do for now.

"What do you think?" Kale managed only an anxious grin.

"I'll take it." Ava shrugged her shoulders.

"No, I mean, did I sell you, though?"

"Sure. I was definitely going to buy something today. And I've known you for forever. And you're married to my best friend. So I'm probably not a great judge of that."

Kale unbuttoned his jacket. "I don't know, Av. I don't know if I can do this."

"Well, it's a job. And you can still look for something else while you're here."

"Yeah." There was no doubt in her mind that she was his first sale. He snapped himself out of the pessimism. "Hey, I'm sorry. Let's go do paperwork. We should both be happy. I got a sale. You got a fancy new ride. No more Mustang."

"No more Mustang," Ava reaffirmed.

She followed Kale through rows of used cars with giant yellow price tag stickers on the windshields and into a building with a showroom of sparkling new cars parked at different angles in front of 20-foot windows so they could easily be seen from the highway.

"Did you want to trade it in? We could maybe give you a few hundred bucks for it."

Ava stopped before taking the seat across from Kale in his own personal cubicle at the back of the building, beside the service entry bays. She thought about his offer, and then thought better. "No, I think I'll keep her. Could you have somebody deliver the Escape to the farmhouse?"

"Sure," Kale agreed, watching Ava's face as she plotted. "OK, so the price we have on the Escape is twenty-one thousand. . ."

Ava sat in a plastic chair that she pulled close to the front of Kale's laminate desk. He sorted a stack of paperwork in front of him.

"Would you take seventeen?"

"Whoa." Kale dropped the papers and rolled backward in his chair. "I'm all about working with you Av, but that's a huge difference. I don't know if Lou will go for that."

"What if it is all in cash upfront?"

Kale frowned at Ava. "You're not making meth out in that shed, are you?"

"No, I'm not making meth," Ava lowered her voice, "Please, don't tell anyone, but Mom had a life insurance policy I didn't know about until a couple of weeks ago. I promise it's all on the level."

She knew he would run home and tell Shannon, even if she specifically told him not to. It didn't matter to her if people knew, though. What really mattered to her was who paid for it all those years and why and those were questions Ava doubted she would ever have the answers to.

"Oh." Kale accepted her answer. "That's great. Not, I mean not the reason for the money, but it's nice she left you something like that." He rose from his seat. "Let me go talk to Lou. I'll be right back."

The door to Billy James' office stood ajar, light pouring out into the shadowy hallway. Kris had the day off, so he had placed a sign on her desk directing folks to his office, as if anyone who stopped by wouldn't already know how to get there. Ava's boot heals clunked hard, determined, on the worn floors. Billy raised his head, awaiting the person behind the sound of the opening and closing of the front door and the footsteps. Smiling as Ava appeared he leaned forward, folding his hands together on his desk.

A check in her hand, Ava crossed his office without a word and laid it in front of the lawyer and took a step back. "I need you to get that to Eddy, please."

Billy frowned as he held up the check in one of his plump hands, peering at it through the thin reading glasses propped at the end of his nose. "Ava, sweetie, this is . . ."

She didn't let him finish, bothered by his need to call her pet names. "It's half of the money, after taxes, if the bank calculated it right. I don't know the best way to send a check that large, but I thought you might. Can I trust you to get it to him?"

"You don't need to do this."

"Yes, I do. It's our mother's money. He should have half of it."

"But . . ." Billy chose his words carefully. For a man who talked for a living, he was stumped as to how to say what he wanted to say. "This money was left to you."

"And only me. I know." Ava's face was set. "But what I don't know is why. Do you?"

Speechless. He was speechless. Ava waited for the truth for an entire minute, but no words came out of the man's mouth.

"Thank you." Ava left. Reaching into the pocket of her blue jeans, she pulled out a remote and pushed a button, unlocking the shiny black SUV parked in front of the courthouse as she exited the building without looking back.

Hoisting the bags of groceries onto her hip, Ava used her free hand to turn the knob on the door to her father's house. Forcing the door open as far as it would go, she squeezed herself and the plastic bags into the mostly blocked front entranceway and the narrowed hall. She could hear Wheel of Fortune blasting through the buzzing speakers of the 13-inch television on her father's dresser. Entering the room, she found him sitting in his chair in sweatpants and a t-shirt, a line of empty beer cans on the table beside him. Ed's eyes followed his daughter as she crossed in front of his view and sat the bags of groceries down on the end of his unmade bed. Ava stood beside the bags and faced her father, who was looking at his television, again.

"Dad?" She wanted to be sure she had his attention, not that it would matter. The show went to a commercial. Ed flipped open the cooler beside his chair, grunting as he reached for the last can in the back corner. He popped the top and took a big swig. She continued. "I'm moving away. Tomorrow. Or this weekend. As soon as I have everything packed."

"Where you going?" His words were slurred.

"New York. I already have an apartment. And I have money saved from Mom's estate." Ava didn't know why she made the last comment. Ed had never paid for anything, never offered her a cent. How she could afford to live in the expensive city wouldn't be a concern for him.

Ed looked at his feet.

"If you need anything, you'll have to call Eddy. He's a ways away, but he'll be a lot closer than I will. Do you still have his number?" He didn't answer. Ava leaned over on the bed and picked up a pen from the nightstand. She wrote the digits of Eddy's number boldly on a can-sweat-stained napkin, underlining her brother's name above it.

"Here it is, again. If you ever need it."

Ava grew silent, watching her father. They had done a good job with the burns, in healing them, but there was scaring on his neck above the seam of his shirt. The charges were pending, but the county jail had run out of room, so they released him on probationary terms and no doubt a good recommendation from Sherriff's Deputy Ellis. A trial would happen sometime later and Ed would most likely be convicted and go to jail for a few days in lieu of paying a fine. At least if he were in jail, Ava would know he was eating regularly.

Even as the worry entered her mind, she had a simultaneous feeling of relief knowing her father's wellbeing was not her concern anymore. She had done everything she could for him. She had done everything she could for her mother. She had done everything she could for her brother, but she had still lost all three of them. She lost them at different times, in different ways, but each was a loss she would continue to mourn the rest of her life. It had taken 24 years, but Ava finally understood that she controlled her own actions, and she accepted that their actions were beyond her control. Like the feeling of standing on the roof, she was letting go. Letting go of the things she could not control. Of the things weighing on her. For the first time in her life, she was going to live for herself. She was going to do whatever the hell she wanted, despite what the world dictated. For her own wellbeing, she was going to be selfish and wasteful and unavailable. It was self-preservation. It was freedom. It was, finally, living.

Ava considered her father from the three feet between them a moment more, took two steps, and bent over and hugged him. Ava felt his arm across her back, briefly. "Bye, Dad. Love you."

Ed nodded his head. It was more than she expected. She left him as someone on the television across the room bought the letter "I."

Shannon and Audie and Ava made themselves at home, kicking back on an ancient tractor tire leaning against a couple of stacks of treadless truck tires. The Mustang sat in front of them at the edge of a deep ravine where people had dumped old furniture and appliances and pieces of vehicles for decades. It wasn't good for the land. The chemicals in the refrigerators and car engines had leaked, the metal rusted. So much so that the creek running through the pasture and in a culvert under the dirt road behind the farm house had a reddish tint with areas of pooling shiny blues and greens. Dora May had stopped renting the section of land for pasture years before, fearful of what the contamination would do to the cattle's drinking water.

Shannon sucked in a long drag of the Pall Mall in her mouth and chugged from the bottle of Jack Daniels in her hand. She held the bottle out to Ava. Audie reached across Ava and took the whiskey as Ava narrowed her eyes and aimed the pistol in her hand at the rearview mirror. Pulling the trigger, her arm jerked to the side with the kickback. The bullet pierced the plastic rim of the mirror and shattered the glass and lodged itself in the driver's side front panel of the Mustang.

"Goddammit!" Shannon yelled, her voice raspy from the four cigarettes she had chain smoked in rapid succession, though she claimed not to have had one for years. She stood up and dug a wad of cash out of the pocket of her tight jeans. Finding a five, she threw it on the pile of bills already on the ground by Ava's feet.

"Thank you, ma'am." Ava grinned. She opened the chamber on the gun to confirm it was empty, then traded it for the whiskey with Audie, so it could be reloaded.

"You know you can't do this sort of thing in a city." Shannon lit her fifth cigarette off the end of her fourth.

Ava drained the bottle of whiskey. "I don't know if that's a good thing or a bad thing."

Shannon laughed. "It'll be a different world. What if you hate it?"

"I'll come back?"

Audie handed the gun back to Ava. "And we will welcome you back with open arms. I don't know why you would ever want to come back, though. It's going to be so awesome, Ava. I'm so excited for you. I think this is exactly what you need. Get away from everything. Start over somewhere. Meet an amazing rich guy who sweeps you off your feet. Travel the world selling your art. It's like a movie. It's very Sex and the City. Shan's just jealous."

"Yep. Of the noise and the crime and the smog and the traffic and the hordes of people and the astronomical rent . . ." Shannon paused. She was jealous of Ava and angry at her and happy for her and it all came out in an instant wave of drunken tears.

Wrapping her arm around Shannon, Ava patted her massive hair and handed her the gun. "Here, shoot something. You'll feel better."

The women giggled, Shannon through tears and smoke. Though not without its rough spots, it had lasted longer than it had a right to. Through 20 years of men and babies and life, of school and marriage and jobs, the three girls stayed friends. The kind of friends who could see each other every day for a week or not see each other for weeks at a time and fall right back into the place they had left off at.

"I'll give you all of your money back if you hit the lock by the door handle." Ava felt the need to bring the situation back to positive.

She demanded they come over so she could break the news of the move. Audie supplied the gun, which she kept in the glove compartment of her convertible, Shannon the liquor, which she hid in the jack compartment of her minivan, and Ava the cigarettes, which she'd bought on her way through town. They came up with the idea to shoot the car when they found out Ava planned to send it over the bluff to its death. It was brilliant. Ava felt like with each shot she was actually killing something, something like the stress, the hatred, the carry-over emotion that had been inside of her since her mother's death. She hated the car, but as she unloaded bullets into it, she realized she loathed it much more for the fact that it was her mother's than for the multitude of inconvenient mechanical issues.

Shannon held the gun like she had been born with it in her hand. She stood in front of the backdrop of dirty tires in a field of dead grass. Her cigarette hung off her lip. Her hair frizzed out in the wind. She looked like a white trash princess. If her husband and her daughters and coworkers at the hospital could see her, they wouldn't believe it. She took the shot and missed the car completely. The bullet whizzed into the trees on the other side of the chasm.

"Goddammit!" Shannon yelled. Then she emptied the chamber, missing the car five more times.

"You ever head that saying about the broadside of a barn?" Ava asked her friend through laughter. Audie was laughing so hard she was snorting.

"Glare." Shannon shook her head. "Fucking sun in my eyes." She bent and laid the gun on the ground with a side step and a drunken stumble.

"Alright, we've all too much to drink." Ava climbed to her feet as she lit a cigarette for herself. "Tell her goodbye, ladies."

The land led downhill, but not enough for the car to get going by itself. Ava leaned across the seat and pulled the parking break and shifted the car into neutral. With her hand on the frame of the open driver's door, she used all of her strength to rock the car back and forth until the hunk of metal began to crawl forward. Walking with it as it rolled, the tires picked up speed and Ava pushed the steering wheel to the right to direct the car to the closest part of the rim. A few feet from the edge, Ava jumped back and watched the red hunk of metal go over. The front tires spun and the undercarriage smashed down, the tilting front high centering the vehicle, but not for long before the weight of the engine pulled it the rest of the way over. Landing on its roof, the frame bent and the window that hadn't been shot out smashed into a million shards of glass. Ava cringed at the sound, finding herself standing between Shannon and Audie who had joined her to watch the carnage.

The worn belly of the relic and the slowly rotating tires made Ava think of a beetle, kicking its legs around, frantically fighting to flip back over, fighting for its life. It didn't take long for the tires to stop moving, though. Any life it had left was gone and it blended into the pile of other broken metal objects below. Ava smiled, thinking of how horrified her mother would be. She would have chastised her daughter for the wastefulness. She would have kept the awful thing forever. She would have been convinced it would be worth something to someone someday. Dora May would have sold it for far too much money to some poor soul passing through.

Ava flipped her cigarette into the pile of junk below and together the three women walked away side by side.

His squad car was in the driveway, so chances were good Ellis was home. Ava parked on the road. She didn't pull in to the driveway, hoping to sneak the sweatshirt onto his porch. She had contemplated putting it in a box and mailing it to him, but she knew she'd forget. It would end up lost in her things and moved to New York and months later she would find it and the guilt from accidentally keeping it would intermingle with the guilt of never properly ending things and she would be haunted by the piece of fabric forever.

She crossed the yard, climbed up the front porch steps. Holding the freshly washed and folded sweatshirt out in front of her as if it were contaminated, she took a deep breath and reached for the door. She pulled her hand back, gathered herself, took another breath and reached again, again chickening out before her fist made contact. Ava paced across the porch, looked around at the deserted space. There was no chair or obvious other place to put the garment and run away. Gathering herself one last time, Ava stopped in front of the door and raised her hand, but before she knocked on it, it opened.

"Ava?" Ellis wore a ripped pair of jeans and a t-shirt with wet paint on the front of it. The smell of freshly sawed and stained wood hit her. He was working on the kitchen, finishing it up on his day off. There was no doubt in Ava's mind that it looked beautiful and part of her wished she could see it when it was done.

"Hey," she responded. "I, uh, I wanted to return this."

"Thanks," Ellis took the sweatshirt from her. He looked different to her, but in a way she couldn't quite pinpoint. It was like she was looking at him through someone else's eyes. He was no longer the man she was falling for, but just a random guy from town. He was attractive, tall, but the something extra, the draw she had felt for him was gone.

"I'm moving."

"Oh, yeah." The distrust he felt for her came through in his voice. "New York?"

"Yeah."

"That's great." He was saying the things he was supposed to say.

Ava shook her head. "I'm sorry." Ellis didn't respond. He looked at the sweatshirt. "I really am sorry."

"Me too." Ellis's words were quiet. She left him standing in the doorway. Almost to her car, Ellis yelled after her, "Good luck, Ava!"

His eternal politeness may have been his only flaw. Ava thought he should allow himself to be angry. She waved in his direction and climbed into her car.

The SUV was stuffed as tightly as she could possibly pack it. The doors to her workshop were wide open and inside supplies were neatly sorted and lined up on the workbench on the front wall. A couple of the smaller finished pieces she was most proud of were tucked under boxes of photo albums and suitcases of clothes, but otherwise the rest of her work would be left behind. She would create more. She would work in her apartment until she found studio space. She would be renowned. Famous. Ava Schaffer. The artist. People would pay her huge sums of money for her work in galleries and for commissions for their homes and offices. She would do installations in Central Park and in other cities. Atlanta. Seattle. Boston. And other countries. France. Japan. South Africa.

The world was slightly warmer than it had been the

previous few days. And humid. It was supposed to rain and maybe sleet as the night cooled. Ava felt a drop on her face where she stood on the landing and looked in from the outside. Drained from the frantic packing and the excitement of leaving town in the morning, she exhaled deeply. It was late. She knew she should go to bed, but the worn leather couch in the corner called to her and she crossed the concrete and sunk into it. This was her place of solace, a happy place, like Martha's and the riverbank and Pode's truck.

Ava heard an engine in the distance. Headlights cut the dark as they popped up over a hill and into her view. Lighting struck the middle of an empty field behind the approaching vehicle and Ava counted two Mississippis before she heard the requisite boom of the thunder following the white streak. Fall and winter thunderstorms were rare but not impossible. No weather condition could be counted out of any day any time of year in Kansas. A cold rain instantly began to fall, hitting the walls of the machine shed and echoing. Pode's truck turned at the end of the driveway and he parked and got out, his shirt completely soaked in the time it took him to walk the 20 feet to the shed. The dim light from above shined off the wet on his face.

"Nice car." Pode pointed over his shoulder at the big dark vehicle.

"I'm leaving town, Pode." Ava rose from her spot on the couch and stood face to face with him.

Ava and Pode examined each other for a long time. Ava opened her mouth like she might speak, but didn't. She had spent three entire days trying to figure out what to say to him, how to tell him. She hadn't answered her phone when he called. She hadn't eaten lunch at Martha's for fear she would run into him. She was terrified if she told him, she wouldn't be able to do it. Not because he would talk her out of it, but because in his amorous presence she would lose all courage, change her mind, and spend the rest of her life with him in Flynn.

Pode rubbed the rain off the back of his neck. "I heard."

The flannel shirt he wore over his white undershirt only had one button buttoned and the single button was buttoned wrong. He was growing his beard out again. Pode's jeans were wrinkled, his appearance as a whole disheveled. The image of Ava was not much better, her hair messily braided to the side, an oversized t-shirt stained with paint hanging off her shoulder, exposing a black bra strap and covering tight jeans tucked unevenly into her black boots.

Pode didn't have any idea what to say to her, either. He had never been more frustrated with her, or more in love with her, than in this moment.

"New York," Pode muttered, the words punctuated by well-timed thunder.

Ava nodded her head.

"You scared?"

She nodded her head again.

"You shouldn't be." Pode took a few steps closer to her, until he was standing within arm's reach. "You're going to own that city. They're not going to know what hit them. They got gangs and rock stars and billionaires, but they ain't seen tough 'til they've meet Ava Schaffer from Flynn-fucking-Kansas."

A smile spread across Ava's lips and Pode returned it. It was the exact thing she needed to hear. He raised his hand to her face, a movement so natural, and kissed her gently. Ava kissed him back. Her eyes closed. She shut off her mind and let her body sense every bit of surging feeling. Her arms wrapped around his neck, his around her waist and up her back under her shirt. Then he pulled away. His large, rough hands on either side of her face Pode touched his forehead to Ava's, whispering against the sound of the rain on the tin roof. "I don't suppose if I told you I love you that would make you stay?"

Ava drew him into another kiss so she could avoid answering the question. Pode lifted her effortlessly, her legs around his waist, and carried her out of the shed and through the downpour to his truck.

"Where are we going?"

"I can't tell you," Pode yelled over the sound of the storm. He quickly joined her in the shelter of the cab. Reaching under the seat, he produced a thick knitted afghan he usually kept on his bed.

"Is this the part where you kidnap me and take me into the wilderness so I can't leave you?" Ava joked, but genuinely appreciated his thoughtfulness in the physical gesture of warmth.

Pode spread the blanket out over her, playfully covering her head like he might try to smother her with it. "Yep."

He drove across the countryside south. Ava kicked her boots off and pulled her feet under her and bundled herself in the seat beside him. She watched impressively vivid lightning strike all around them. Forking out into jagged white lines that illuminated the shapes of the clouds, the storm was stunning and immense and frightening. Dirt kicked up onto the side panels of the truck from the tires as Pode pulled off of a shortcut dirt road he had taken to reach the highway west of Flynn. Not on the blacktop long before darting off on another county road, they cruised over rough gravel and new mud.

"Railroad bridge?" Ava asked, trying to guess where he was taking her.

Pode nodded confirmation. The road grew narrower. A strip of grass poked up down center of it.

"While back, Baker told me about being in a deer stand he had out here by the bridge. Said it started storming and so he hung around watching the lightning from his truck as the storm passed through and then it struck the bridge. He said it was one of the most amazing things he'd ever seen. Sparked and lit up the whole clearing. I've been driving out here during thunderstorms ever since, but I haven't seen it happen, yet."

Ava was enthralled. She didn't know Pode spent stormy nights in the clearing. And she felt honored that he would share the experience with her. That she would be in on Pode and Baker's secret. The boards across the narrow bridge groaned with the weight of the Ford. Pode parked in the center and shut off the lights and the engine and slid across the bench seat. Ava shared the afghan with him. Silent as they watched the weather rage, lightning struck high, an exchange between two clouds almost directly above them. The surface of the river water and the thick overgrown trees on either side of the entrance to the bridge lit up like they were in middle of the day sunshine. The flash disappeared as quickly as it appeared and again the world was plunged into darkness.

The severe part of the storm seemed to be letting up, giving way to torrential showers. Thumping the roof and the hood of the truck with metallic plunks, heavy drops splattered and dripped down the windshield. They wove back and forth on the glass, meeting other raindrops and joining them. They moved faster and faster down until they came to rest in the indention that held the nonmoving wiper blades. Pode took a deep breath and Ava could tell he was disappointed. The lightning was so far and few between now it was unlikely Baker's phenomenon would take place this night.

Ava nuzzled into Pode's chest. "It's still wonderful," she whispered. It absolutely was.

"Yeah, I just thought maybe . . ."

And it happened. Before Pode finished his lament. The second to last of the biggest joints near the end of the support beams that wove back and forth above and around took the full force of a stray bolt. Connecting and sparking, it was gorgeous and petrifying. The iron bridge seemed to come alive with the force of the electricity surging through it and both Ava's and Pode's hearts stopped. They would swear every time they recounted the story for the rest of their lives that they could internally feel the rush of power from the instantaneously created magnetic field they were suddenly in the center of.

"Hell yeah!" Pode hit the dash with a flattened hand. "Baker was right! That was fucking amazing!"

Ava couldn't form words. The incredible picture etched in her mind of the electrified bridge hindered her ability to speak. Pode looked at Ava with a wide smile as he studied her blank face.

"Ohh. Oh." They were sounds. Ava could only eke out sounds.

Pode's lips were on hers as she frantically searched for the single done button on his flannel shirt. Lying together across the length of the seat, shirts and boots and jeans landed under the seat with the blanket that had also sunk to the floor. Ava felt the warmth of Pode's skin against her bare stomach and the prickliness of the whiskers on his face against her neck and chest. He kissed her breasts and his hands grasped her hips as she traced the outline of his broad collar bone with her fingers. Ava sealed the shape of his thick muscular shoulders in her mind, an impression she would take with her always.

"Ava."

She was already half awake. Her left foot was frozen, hanging out of the side of the blanket. They curled perfectly together. Ava's head on Pode's chest, Pode's arm serving as a pillow for both of them, his other securing their bodies together. They were in a cocoon of content. Daylight was shining through the heavy tree cover and though unlikely, they would be an embarrassing discovery for someone who decided to take the deserted road. Ava and Pode fast asleep and completely undressed and blocking the bridge so that no other vehicle could pass.

"Ava," Pode said her name a little louder the second time. He kissed her forehead.

"No," Ava moaned and closed her eyes tighter to block out the rays of sun.

Pode disturbed the comfort, pulling his arm out from under their heads and shaking the tingling deadness out of it. "You have to go." Pode hovered over Ava, his face close to hers as she shifted onto her back. There was a dark blue oil paint stain on the inside of her forearm, like a birthmark.

"Come with me." She kissed him as she ran her fingers through his hair.

"Huh," Pode laughed, kissing her back. "Yeah. That would be funny. Me in that city? My life's here. I belong here, Av. Out on the farm. Cows in my yard. Mud on my boots."

Ava laughed, too. She wrapped her arms around his back and squeezed and knew he was right.

"Ava."

"Hmm."

"I love you."

Her voice was barely audible. "I love you, too, Pode.

\* \* \*

269

The breeze was cool, for June. The kind of cool breeze that makes everyone hopeful the impending summer will not be as hot as the previous ones. It is false hope. The following day always turns back to unbearable hot. The kind of hot summers should be in Kansas. City pool parking lot asphalt melting, black vinyl car seat burning, homegrown tomato ripening hot. The enjoyment of the one rare cool day in the summer is nothing more than a tease.

It was before the drought, the 10-year drought that seemed would never lift, and so the river was wide and deep under the railroad bridge. The duplicitous cool breeze moved the cattails and the tall grass on the banks in soothing ripples. Ava sat on the cooler of bait, holding a fishing pole out over the water, awaiting a bite. Pode sat beside her on the overturned five gallon bucket they brought along to hold all of the millions of fish they planned to catch. His face was set. He leaned forward and glared at his fishing line, as if, if he concentrated hard enough, he would will the fish to bite.

Ava giggled, thinking her friend looked silly. He refused to acknowledge her, pretending to be annoyed by the little girl's squeaky laughter. All of the other kids at school their age only traveled in same-sex groups, but Ava and Pode had grown up a mile down the road from each other. They had known each other before school. Found something in the other that was not the same, but instead to complement a difference, a shortcoming, or a gift. Ava was a thinker, artistic, quiet, while Pode was a doer, practical, a talker. They were simply meant to be together.

"Stop laughing," Pode frowned at Ava. "You're going to distract me and make me miss my fish."

"You look dumb. You can't stare a fish down." Ava playfully shoved Pode's shoulder.

"Hey, stop it."

She stood. "What if I don't?"

Pode dropped his pole and rose to his feet. They were the same height, but it would only be for another year before Pode started to shoot up.

"Then I'll throw you in the river." Pode crossed his arms across his chest with the threat.

Ava squinted at him. She didn't believe he would really do it. Taking a step forward in her threadbare tennis shoes, she reached out only a finger and poked him lightly on the arm.

"Alright, that's it!" Pode yelled as he went after her. Ava tried to escape, the quicker of the two, but only made it a few steps before she felt his arms around her waist. They may have been the same size, but he was already stronger. Lifting her up off her feet, he took a step and tossed her like a bale of hay off the bank and into the river below. As she fell, she caught his ankle and pulled him over with her, both of them splashing into the sandy river bottom.

Laughing so hard he began to cough, Pode pushed a wave Ava's direction and she jumped him, trying to dunk his head under the water. After a short struggle, she managed to pull him over and submerge them both. Breaking from each other, out of breath, Ava and Pode stood up in the water that barely reached their chests. Their eyes met and they each had the same identical thought. They were just kids, but they saw the beauty in the innocence of the moment and both silently wished it would never end.

# 11

Ava sped down the highway, slowing only as she reached the end of the blacktop and the beginning of the red brick. She considered avoiding Flynn completely, certain she would pass several curious people she would have to politely wave to. Everyone would learn the story of her leaving soon enough, though, no matter which way she traveled out of town.

The original intent was to start earlier in the day, but Pode's arms around her felt too good. He made it as easy as he possibly could, dropped her off with a final kiss and a final smile that showcased the single dimple. He didn't feel like smiling. Ava knew he was pretending to be happy for her sake. She hated that they knew each other so well.

Squinting into a sun that was high in a clear, after the rain sky, Ava recognized Pode's truck parked in front of the feed and seed. Something moved on the top of the building. Ava hit her breaks hard, shifting a couple of boxes forward into the back of her headrest. She tumbled out of the SUV and stepped back so she could see over it. On the roof, Pode's silhouette stood out against the bright sunlight. His hands were in his pockets, body aimed east, toward the wide open fields and the river bridge and the road about to take her away from him.

He turned to the street and looked down. They were too far away from each other to see facial expressions. Pode wore the same shirt from the night before and a baseball cap. Ava wrapped a string of wildly blowing hair around trembling fingers, barely able to grasp it.

She was the first to break their exchange by withdrawing to the driver's seat of her new car and slamming the door shut. She pressed on the gas pedal, tears in her eyes, and adjusted the rearview mirror to reflect the tops of the buildings behind her. Ava found Pode, shrinking as the distance grew between them, until he disappeared.

## ABOUT THE AUTHOR

Lindsay Bergstrom grew up on a farm outside of Clyde, Kansas. She now divides her time between hanging out with her amazing family and friends in Kansas, Tennessee, and Colorado. She loves sunshine, potatoes, animals, whiskey, and sarcasm and hopes to someday travel to space.

Also by Lindsay Bergstrom

*Sailtoads & Fireworks: A Short Story Collection*